ALSO BY GREGORY BLAKE SMITH

THE DEVIL IN THE DOORYARD

POSEIDON PRESS

NEW YORK

LONDON

TORONTO

SYDNEY

TOKYO

SINGAPORE

•••

THE
DIVINE COMEDY
OF
JOHN VENNER

GREGORY BLAKE SMITH

POSEIDON PRESS
Simon & Schuster Building
Rockefeller Center
1230 Avenue of the Americas
New York, New York 10020

POSEIDON PRESS is a registered trademark
of Simon & Schuster Inc.

POSEIDON PRESS colophon is a trademark
of Simon & Schuster Inc.

Designed by Liney Li
Manufactured in the United States of America

10 9 8 7 6 5 4 3 2 1

Library of Congress Cataloging-in-Publication Data

Smith, Gregory Blake.
    The divine comedy of John Venner / Gregory Blake Smith.
        p.   cm.
    I. Title.
PS3569.M5356D58   1992
813'.54—dc20   92-11021
                                                            CIP

ISBN: 0-671-78854-X

ACKNOWLEDGMENTS

FOR THEIR SUPPORT

IN THE WRITING OF THIS BOOK,

THE AUTHOR WISHES TO THANK

THE NATIONAL ENDOWMENT FOR THE ARTS,

THE BUSH FOUNDATION,

CARLETON COLLEGE,

THE MACDOWELL COLONY

AND JANET HOLMES.

•••

CONTENTS

CHAPTER ONE: VENNER'S INFERNO 13

CHAPTER TWO: ON THE LONGEVITY OF VIRGIN
CELIBATES 28

CHAPTER THREE: ORDERS CONCERNING INTERCOURSE
BETWEEN THE SEXES 34

CHAPTER FOUR: SNOW WHITE AND THE INCUBUS 44

CHAPTER FIVE: STEALING SISTER SABBATHDAY'S
SPIRITUAL SELF 59

CHAPTER SIX: SELF-TORTURE AS AN APHRODISIAC 74

CHAPTER SEVEN: ON THE METAPHYSICS OF WHITE
PICKET FENCES 88

CONTENTS

CHAPTER EIGHT: A GARDEN ENCLOSED IS MY SISTER, MY SPOUSE 108

CHAPTER NINE: VENNER'S PURGATORIO 121

CHAPTER TEN: IN WHICH EVE TRIES TO SORT THE GOOD FROM THE BAD 123

CHAPTER ELEVEN: CHERUBIM POSTED AT THE EASTERN GATE 138

CHAPTER TWELVE: DOING WHAT THEY DO OUTSIDE THE GARDEN 148

CHAPTER THIRTEEN: THE PERSISTENCE OF HUMAN VISION 175

CHAPTER FOURTEEN: THE MONSTROUS MYSTERIUM OF THE LOINS 201

CHAPTER FIFTEEN: CONFESSIONS OF A ONCE AND FUTURE VIRGIN 225

CHAPTER SIXTEEN: VENNER'S PARADISO, SUCH AS IT IS 247

THE

DIVINE COMEDY

OF

JOHN VENNER

CHAPTER ONE

VENNER'S INFERNO

Mother Ann:
I am a member of the world's people. I've got the fury and the mire running in my veins and the sickness thing in my soul. The moral mud of America sticks to me like nobody's business—ditto the dust of destruction—and if that's not enough, I'm in love with your final virgin.

For a year now I've been spying on her, mapping her movements, her routine. At dusk I lock the chapel office, get on my bicycle and pedal along Undermountain Road until I get to the New Eden community. I hide in a tangle of scrubby bushes across the road from the white clapboard buildings. I set up my tripod on the dead leaves, screw on my spotting scope and take out a 300mm lens. If I get there before six o'clock I can watch her at work in the Sisters' Weaving Shop, see her through the Shaker-paned windows, in the soft Shaker light: the angle of her elbow in one pane, the flannel knuckle of her shoulder in another, the incurve of her waist, a vagrant scrap of hair falling from under her bonnet, and in one antique pane—in the distorting glass of another century—her inexplicable face.

• • •

Her name is Sabbathday Wells. Sister Sabbathday Wells. She's the last Shakeress.

My name is John Venner. I'm a doctor of divinity in love with a woman sworn to chastity.

• • •

In the winter it's not so easy. It's cold and it gets dark early. I take my ex-wife's car out, and under the cover of darkness, vault the white picket fence that encloses the grounds. Sometimes I see her footprints in the snow, the chevron grid of running shoes (my modern sweetheart!) going from the Weaving Shop to the Goods Shop, the barn to the Dwelling House. I stand in the lee of one of the outbuildings and wait for her bedroom light to go on. There are no curtains and no shade on her window. At the sight of her nineteenth-century underwear, I bite my mittens in tumescent torment and hurry back into town.

"If you're going to lay me," my ex-wife says, "lay *me*, not her."

"Okay," I say, trying to get her undressed.

"And don't call me Sabbathday this time."

"Okay."

"And don't sing 'Simple Gifts' for Christ's sake!"

"Okay, okay! Jesus!"

"And not so fast. Give me a minute. Kiss me."

I kiss her.

"Kiss me again."

I kiss her again.

"Okay, now. Easy. No!" she says. "You'll have to do something."

I reach for the Vaseline.

"Something better than that!"

I do something better than that.

"All right," she says finally. "All right."

I try to hold back. One minute. Two minutes. Three minutes. But I've got visions of white picket fences in my head. Clean clapboards. I can see her ankles in the summer dust, the cloddy look of her Nikes kicking out under her hem, the sizzle of snow. And then there's her neck, the mystery of her hair always hidden under that cap, the white bloomers, the white bodice, the white skin. There's the aphrodisiac of virginity, of simplicity, of plumbness, of six-paneled doors and tiny-paned windows, of stone walls marking the world into neat acres. There's the tease of her virgin hands working her loom, reaching behind her to untie her virgin underwear, her virgin bloomers falling in a puddle around her virgin ankles. I try my best not to, try to force the urge down inside me, stifle it, but the thought of her hair tumbling out from under her cap does me in and I start bellowing "Simple Gifts" into the pillow. I sing it right in rhythm. Right in rhythm with the squeak and roll of the bed. I sing it strained and hoarse and shivering.

"You bastard!" my ex-wife is cursing under me. "You bastard!"

" 'Tis the gift . . .' "

"You godly bastard!"

" '. . . to be simple . . .' "

"You saintly son of a bitch!"

• • •

Mother Ann:

My name is John Venner. I'm a doctor of divinity with sores on my soul. I teach religion at the local college and live up in the chapel steeple. I'm a man without land, love or light, but I've got this idea. I've got this idea about joining the Shakers before it's too late. I'm going to join the Shakers and in a few years when Eldress Rachel, Sister Antoinette and Sister Chastity (octogenarians all) snuff it, I'll be left with nineteen Shaker-clean buildings, one hundred sixty-eight acres of God's green earth, a museumful of Shaker furniture, and the purest atmosphere in America—all tax-free and all mine.

I've studied it out, prepared a plan of action, a campaign. It's not that I'm greedy, but a pure soul is a rare thing in this, our postmodern America, and Venner wants one of his own. I can tell already that the problem is going to be Eldress Rachel, Eldress Rachel who's a wily dame if there ever was one. She's eighty-nine years old with a face so wrinkled you have to look twice to see the two dots of suspicion where her eyes ought to be. She rules the New Eden community like it's a kind of New England Vatican. But I'm going to get her. I'm going to get her desiccated soul and water it with the effluvium of my love. I'm going to get the house she lives in, the Weaving Shop, the Brothers' Workshop, the stone barn where the ghosts of Shaker cattle low in the New England twilight. I'm going to get those one hundred and sixty-eight acres of God's fruitful earth. And I'm going to get it all for free. For giving up sex. For letting Christ establish an address inside me.

"Fat chance," my ex-wife says. Her name is Medusa. She's the lead singer for an all-female rock band called the Gorgons. When I want to make her angry, I call her by her real name, which is Sally. Otherwise she's Deusie.

"I've got the gift," I tell her.

"Fat chance."

"The gift," I repeat and let a Lordly light come on my face.

"You mean you're going to *pretend* to give sex up, don't you? You're just going to fool them into *thinking* you've given it up?"

"No fooling," I say. "These are three smart virgins."

"And all your cute coeds who think it's so great to do it with a Man of God?"

"Slander," I say with some dignity.

"And what about twenty-three-year-old Sister Sabbathday? Going to give her up too?"

I point out that I haven't *got* her to give up.

"But are you going to give up the *idea* of her? The idea of doing her in her white underwear? I mean isn't that the point? Don't you want to do her in her white underwear?"

"Not me," I say.

"Don't you want to do her while the gift is upon her?"

"Not me."

"While she's speaking with the voice of God or something?"

"Not me."

• • •

The truth is, Mother Ann, I want to do her in her white underwear so bad I get faint at the very thought of it. I want to pollute her with love. I want to wreck the springs of her bed, shake the walls so hard that the Bible on the shelf above tumbles down on top of us like the walls of Jericho.

O! to violate something that feels the violation! Is there anything more unsatisfying than modern sin? How do you sin against something that won't recognize degradation? Won't recognize an original state of grace from which to fall? O! we live in a lost America! I've seen it all. I've seen the drive-in churches and the Leaning Towers of Pizzas and the Wish 'n' Wash Laundromats. I've seen the imitation this and the imitation that, the two-by-fours that don't measure two by four, and O! you know, the moral thinness. I've seen the ghastly grin of Anti-America, and I tell you, Mother Ann, it's an impoverished world we live in. I have been reduced to mailing obscene literature to a trio of octogenarian Shakers. For two years running it was my only hope of providing my life with a moral dimension. I used to make a monthly run down to Boston, spend a night in the bars of the Combat Zone handing out Shaker bookmarks like party favors to all the rejects, and in the morning, drive a lazy circuit homeward, stopping at random post offices to mail off packets of filthy humanity: for Eldress Rachel pictures of women trussed up in leather, for Sister Antoinette photos of men with impressive plumbing and for Sister Chastity a potpourri of the unspeakable engines of love.

But for Sabbathday Wells I am reserving my own obscene and sacred self.

• • •

"Are you serious?" my wife Sally says; "Are you serious?" says my ex-wife, Medusa; "Are you serious?" says Deusie. "You've been mailing pornography to them?"

It's 2 A.M. and we're up in the steeple of the college chapel, where I've been living ever since the judge threw me out of my house three months ago. It's open to the air by virtue of four arched unglazed windows high up where the bells are. I've got my cat with me, got a monkish mattress and a table and chair, and I've got Shaker photos and prints on the walls, on shelves all my Shaker books and pamphlets and Xeroxes and newspaper articles, and on the wall facing my bed, hundreds of candid glossies taken of Sabbathday Wells.

"You mail them dirty pictures?"

"Not anymore," I say. "I've found other ways of purifying myself."

"But you were," she says and shakes her head. She's just come from her job at The Missionary Position and she's dressed in her stage costume still: black heels; fishnet stockings, garters, black corset with a push-up bra, her hair braided into thirteen shoulder-length snakes. Under the stage lights she looks like a bona fide Gorgon, fit to turn you to stone.

"And you were doing all this while we were still married?"

"Yes."

"And I didn't even know it?"

I shrug.

She makes a face and snaps a garter. "You're lucky you didn't get caught."

She comes to visit me like this, at all times of the day or night, after a job when it's gone well or gone badly, for lunch in the Student Union; comes and sits in the back of the lecture hall in the middle of the afternoon, making faces at me, coughing now and then when I talk of Augustinian versus Thomastic sin, snorting outright when I turn to the physics of the spirit and the metaphysics of the flesh. Sometimes she raises her hand with questions; sometimes I call on her. She addresses me as Professor Venner, Professor Venial, Doctor Venereal, Saint Venner: the students laugh. We're a topic of conversation around campus. I'm up for tenure this coming year.

"Did you send some to her, too?"

"Her?"

"Yes, *her*. Who do you think, *her?*"

I consider a moment, uncertain I want to be letting her in on all this. "No."

"Why not?"

"Because," I say, and then: "I meant them as mere mementos of the flesh."

"Mementos? And—What's-her-name—she doesn't need a memento?"

I, of course, won't answer that.

"Or is it that you think she needs *you* for a memento?"

Ditto, that.

"And one last question," she says like it's a corker, "why does Venner have to be such a prick?"

Because, Gentle Reader, if the truth were to be known, Venner has on and off loved his sweet Sally to desperation. In college, after Mariology and the Cult of the Virgin, I'd time getting my things together so I'd leave the classroom just behind her, watching the slice of her hips in the hall, the maddening nubs of her shoulder blades under her sweaters. Whenever we had a paper due, I'd hang around the BT 600s until she showed up, and then creep apace of her, one stack over, peering through the gaps and the gunholes at her green eyes, at the opals in her ears, at the notebook that hid her blessed bosom. She was nineteen, a philosophy major, and I was an incubating theologian, dazzled by her dating the

Kappa Delta Phi guys on Saturday nights and on Sunday mornings singing a Bach cantata in the Collegium Aureum. I finally wrote her a letter full of love and obscenity, which she keeps to this day, though she won't tell me where. (I've been on search-and-destroy missions, Zippo lighter in hand, through her bureau drawers, her books, the plastic file box in the closet where there are folders for Insurance, Mortgage, Income Tax, Divorce, but none for Love and Obscenity.) It is, of course, possible that she has long since burned the letter herself and just won't tell me. There are many mysteries in matters of the heart.

"Not," I say to Medusa's question whether I am going to lay her tonight or not.

"Then I'm going home."

"Okay," I say, but instead of leaving she tugs on one of her snakes. Hard, so I think it must hurt.

"Oh, come on!" she says. "Help me out, for Pete's sake."

"You know the rules."

"Lay me or tomorrow my lawyer asks your lawyer for more child support."

"No."

She crosses to the corner where the BB gun I use to shoot at the Body-Rite Fitness Club out my window is leaning against the wall. "Lay me, V," she says picking the gun up and pointing it at me.

Up high through the arched openings in the steeple I can see the Man in the Moon eying Virgo the Virgin on the blue horizon.

"No."

"You don't think I'll use this?" she demands.

"Yes, I do," I answer.

"You don't think I will?"

"Yes, I do."

And she does. My wife, my ex-wife, my former date to the college cotillion shoots me with my boyhood BB gun. I feel the sting of the BB smack over my heart.

"Jesus!" I say. And I think, So that's what those fitness freaks feel when I shoot them.

"Now come on," she says. "I could have had a half dozen college boys at The Missionary Position. But it's you I want. Do it like that night in Gloucester. That night you—" and she pauses, searching for the right word—"that night you violated me."

I rub my chest and gently inquire what does she mean, that night I violated her?

"Don't give me that."

"What?"

"That."

"What 'that'?"

"That 'what,' that's what."

We glare at one another. She's still got the gun leveled at me.

"My memory of Gloucester," I say finally, "is that you were drunk—"

"We were *both* drunk."

"—that we were *both* drunk and that the knotted scarves were *your* idea."

"I'm not talking about the knotted scarves."

"And the hose clamp."

"I'm not talking about the hose clamp."

I peer up at the four enormous bells hanging over our heads. "Gloucester," I repeat. I remember various degrees of reality, but no violation. From their insides the bells drop tuned circles of darkness down on us. My cat, Sometimes-Why, comes and rubs along my shin, and I pick him up, hold him to where my skin is still stinging. When we were first married Sally and I had six cats, an entire litter we'd acquired from humanitarian impulses. We'd named them A, E, I, O, U and Sometimes-Why. Now, Sometimes-Why is the last left. Curiously, the others ran away and/or died in alphabetical order.

"Sorry," I say, giving up. "I don't remember any violation."

She lets out an enormous sigh and drops the gun. "Oh, baby!" she says, and she trudges over to my mattress and falls down face first. "I'm in despair."

"Me too," I say.

"It's just not going to go."

"The Gorgons?"

"Our drummer can't drum, our bassist can't bass and our singer can't sing."

"The singer *can* sing," I say. And she can: Medusa has got a whopper of a rock voice. "But you're right about the drummer."

"We hired her because of her breasts. We thought we'd get booked easier. She's got beautiful breasts."

To which fact Venner would attest, but says instead, "Get rid of her."

"Should we?"

"Get someone who can drum."

"But her breasts—"

"Don't worry about her breasts. Nobody's looking at her breasts. Everyone's looking at you." And then in that old voice of mine, "It's *you*, baby, they're looking at."

"Oh, Venner!" she says, and she turns over and holds her arms up to me. I lie down beside her and we kiss.

"I'm in despair, baby," she says. "Thirty-one years old and playing music for mall rats with purple hair. I'm never going to make it from existence into essence." From down on the floor Sometimes-Why jumps onto the mattress and climbs on top of us. I kiss each of Medusa's thirteen snakes. Sometimes-Why lies down and begins kneading her stomach. It's just like old times, I think.

"It's just like old times," I say.

"Yes," she answers; then, her face darkening with the reality of Reality: "No."

I look at the hundreds of photos of Sabbathday Wells. Sabbathday Wells in snow, in summer, in spring; Sabbathday Wells capped, encaped, bebooted; Sabbathday Wells through the blurry window of the Weaving Shop; in telephotoed compression, zoomed geometry; Sabbathday Wells at dusk walking through the fields with an ancient Shakeress on each arm; Sabbathday Wells turning from a rude tourist, hiding her face from a photographer; Sabbathday Wells all glossed up by Kodak, distant and undoable.

"Baby," Deusie says beside me, "I need you to talk to me tonight."

I say I will. Because—think what you like, Mother Ann—when push comes to shove, Venner's got sympathy for the human heart.

"Talk to me," she says again.

I ask her who's got Eve. Is there a baby-sitter waiting?

"She's with my sister," she says; and then nuzzling her face into my neck, speaking with tragic dimension, "Tell me about *her*."

So I do, though to spare her feelings, I go with the historical stuff, the stuff I've gleaned from back issues of *Time* and the *Boston Globe*, how a squad of counterculture types showed up at New Eden in the late sixties, drawn by the simplicity thing and the vow of chastity, and applied for membership. How, at Meeting, the gentle voices of Christ and Holy Mother Wisdom began speaking through the new members more than they had ever spoken through the Elders, displaying newly acquired vocabularies, denouncing gender inequality, the politico-repressive symbolism of the missionary position. Then how, as the sixties turned into the seventies, the neo-Shakeresses drifted off, leaving behind a bewildered sextet of septuagenarian virgins as well as a three-year-old Sabbathday whose mother "did not accept the concept of motherhood outside of a communal definition." There was an attempt by the state to gain custody of her but oh, you know—etcetera and etcetera—in the end she stayed.

"So she was brought up by six grandmothers?" Sally asks.

"More or less. Less, mostly."

"And there's how many left now?"

"Three and counting."

She sticks an elbow into the mattress and lifts her head up onto her hand. "So how are you going to do it?"

"It?"

"Are you just going to present yourself and say God has moved you to become a Shaker?"

"I don't know."

"Or are you going to try to insinuate yourself gradually?"

"I don't know."

"Or maybe woo one of them?"

I don't know. The fact is, except for Sabbathday Wells there hasn't been anyone accepted into the New Eden community since 1932. And judging from the way Eldress Rachel looks at me when I visit the archives at the village, my chances are not good. But Eldress Rachel is pushing ninety and God in His-or-Her wisdom has a way of dealing with folks who overstay their welcome on this, His-or-Her green earth. And Sister Chastity is next in line to be Eldress, and she's senile and told me once I had pretty hair.

Which is true, I *do* have pretty hair.

"So the old broads," Deusie asks beside me, "what are their names again?"

I tell her: Rachel, Antoinette and Chastity.

"And the home-wrecker," she says. "What's her name?"

I don't answer that.

"Hello?"

"You know her name."

"But what was it originally? Back when she was three years old. She wasn't born Sabbathday, was she? What was it?"

"Never mind."

"What? What was it?"

I still don't answer. She gives my shoulder a shove.

"Just how much do you know about her anyway?" she says. "I mean, have you ever discussed things with her? I mean like life? Have you ever discussed life with her?"

"Knock it off."

"Have you ever even spoken to her?"

I jab her in the thigh. "Your snakes are getting hungry, Sally."

"Have you? Have you ever even heard her voice?"

I turn over on the mattress, away from her.

"Maybe she talks funny. Ever think of that?"

"Knock it off."

"Or maybe she's physically deformed under her clothes. Under her underwear."

"Go home now."

"Maybe she's so innocent she doesn't even have a vagina. I've heard of that happening."

"Go home."

"Really. It's a medical fact that Doris Day did not have a vagina."

"*Sally!*"

"She had to have a special operation in the sixties. In Sweden. It was in all the papers."

I get up and cross to the corner where my BB gun is and climb up the step stool until I can see out the window. It's 3 A.M. and there's no one across the street at the Body-Rite Fitness Club so I have to wait for a pedestrian to shoot. But there aren't any pedestrians either: it's 3 A.M. I hoist myself up onto the window opening and sit there.

"Don't jump," Deusie says from back on the mattress.

I can see her car—*my* car; the car the judge stole from me—parked at the curb below. I take aim at one of its headlights.

"I see your car," I say.

"Good. Put it out of its misery."

I turn back inside and shoot the bells instead. In Westminster order: *Ping*-ping-PING-PING.

"Come down here and lose yourself in the flesh," Deusie says.

"No."

"Come on. Be a sport."

"No."

She stands up on the mattress and starts singing one of the Gorgons' songs—"The Flesh and the Spirit," lyrics by Anne Bradstreet—and I start shooting the bells again. Random, this time. She rhymes "meditation" with "fornication," which is not how Anne Bradstreet has it, I'm pretty sure. Somewhere in the second verse she starts taking her clothes off—"A Puritan striptease!" she shouts—and I have to concentrate on my shooting.

"Come on!" she says. "You're missing all the good stuff." And off goes a stocking on "Take thy fill."

"Come on!" Another stocking on "of what you will." Then her push-up bra; her garter belt.

"Here I am, sweetheart!" she shouts. I can see her naked out of the corner of my eye. "In the flesh!" But I am ringing out a hymn on the bells, *pinging* and PINGING myself into chastity, into celibacy, into Shakerhood, into a denial of the flesh, of Deusie, of Medusa, of my sweet Sally.

"Sweetheart!" she yells.

Ping-*ping*.

"Baby!"

PING-PING.

"Baby, don't make me feel bad!"

PING.

"Don't *humiliate* me!"

There are BBs ricocheting all over the place. I feel the sting of one on my arm. Sometimes-Why runs for cover. But I keep shooting, pumping the air gun and shooting, shooting the bells for waking me up every day at eight o'-goddamn-clock in the morning, for reminding me of the mutability thing, shooting everything I can think of, my lawyer, Judge Sapperstein, the entire twentieth century, the whole notion of America, of Anti-America, Mother Ann Lee, God Him-or-Herself for coming up with the idea of love in the first place, shooting until I hear Sally yell out, "Ow!" and then again, "Ow! You bastard!"

And at that I stop and look down at her. She's got the bed sheet wrapped around her like a caftan, and she's peering up at me with a look of hurt and rage and despair and like she's going to burst out crying.

"Come home, baby," she says. "Give all this up, and come home."

"Can't," I say. "Sorry."

"Come home."

I muster all the control and determination and spite I can and tell her that the world is out to pollute me, that the flesh is the flesh and the spirit is the spirit, and that somehow you have to make a stand.

"A stand?" she cries. "Against what?"

"Against—" and for a moment I am stumped—"against *this!*" I say finally with a gesture that somehow includes the world inside and out, the Body-Rite Fitness Club down below and New Eden in the dark distance, and inside the steeple my miserable mattress and my photos of Sabbathday Wells, Medusa's underwear on the floor, the chimes of Western Civilization hanging over our heads, love in the BT 600s, the sacred and the profane. . . .

"I'm a desperate man," I tell her. "You ought to know that."

"I do," she says. "Oh, baby, I do."

CHAPTER TWO

On the Longevity
of Virgin
Celibates

Why they live so long, your professor doesn't know. Perhaps the conjoining of loins is as destructive to the flesh as it is to the spirit; or perhaps the Lord graces them with the iron heart of Methuselah for not having followed the century's suit in thumbtacking His carcass to the cosmic Lost and Found; or perhaps it is merely the mud-beloved body hanging on as long as it can just to spite the skyward-gazing soul. Whatever the explanation, the disproportionate number of octo- and nonagenarians amongst the United Society of Believers in Christ's Second Appearing is a phenomenon that was remarked upon even in the last century. I direct you to articles M and N on reserve in the library.

As of this lecture, there are seven legit Shakers left: three here at New Eden, two over in Canterbury and two at Chosen Land in Maine. And there are five neo-Shakers, the one here, a young woman you may have seen around town—and if you haven't, here are a couple of photographs, let's say half a dozen, to pass around—and four up at Chosen Land, all men. The Canterbury Shakers don't recognize the newly admitted members at Chosen Land, and the Chosen Land Shakers don't recognize the Canterbury Shakers' right not to recognize them. New Eden keeps mostly mum about the whole business. The controversy revolves around whether the Society has been closed to new membership. Canterbury says yes, Chosen Land no, and New Eden, in its last communication on the matter (1973, Item P), seems to say it's been closed for the parent ministry at Canterbury but not for New Eden, witness its own four-year-old member. But even then, they're not very clear. No community, at any rate, is being besieged with acolytes.

The Shakers were founded in America by Ann Lee, an illiterate tailor's daughter from the dreary moors northeast of Manchester [LIGHTS OFF; PROJECTOR ON], who in her early twenties fell in with a radical batch of Quakers who had themselves fallen under the spell of the Camisards and other straight-faced insisters on indwelling divinity see Chapter Eight in your textbooks. For now, picture if you will an eighteenth-century northern England, all moor and mist, the sound of history and mechanical looms on the soundtrack, poverty and industrialism on the rise, the old Protestant schisms on the wane, and somewhere on the bleak moor, in a stony cellar, in a rough-framed hovel, a group of Believers meeting semi-illegally, trance-eyed and quivering as if they have been hypnotized by the Hand of God. At their center is a woman of thirty or so, fair-complected and blue-eyed, according to the hand-colored lithograph in my office. She has about her the halo of belief, the witchcraft of divinity, the intent readiness of the moral high-jumper standing poised for flight. Let us leave her a moment on the precipice of her ecstasy.

Did she ever Do It? the mud-footed amongst you wish to ask. Indeed, she did. She was married in 1762 at the age of twenty-six to Abraham Standerin, a blacksmith whose soul the Lord would not have touched with a ten-foot pole. There followed three children, each of whom died in infancy, and then a fourth, Thomas, after whose death she fell into a near-psychotic state of morbid awareness, convinced that the death of her children was a judgment upon the concupiscence of the marital state. Fearing to arouse her husband's fleshly passions, she began to go sleepless, walking the darkened house from room to room, listening for the voice of God, for some sign of His will, in the hallway, in the kitchen, in the moonpallid parlor. She began to fast, to deny herself her carnal existence; her gums bled, her hair fell out; she inflicted sores and stigmata on herself until, in the fertile meadows of the hallucinogenic state, she heard the first tender whispers of her Lord. In the ecstasy of purity she wasted away until she was too weak to move, until the last rags of depravity slipped from her body and she felt herself reborn in a Christly state, part human and part divine.

There followed some years of evangelical zeal (you may refocus the picture of her on the threshold of ecstasy), years in which she brooded upon the cohabitation of the sexes as being Satan's reward for his work in the Garden. At Meeting she went into trances, spoke in tongues, whirled about the floor singing and chanting, warning her fellows off lust and depravity. She was accused by the outside world of heresy and witchcraft, stoned by one mob, bound hand and foot and carried to a second-story window by another. Thrown in jail for breaking the Sabbath, she had a vision of Adam and Eve in an unappled Garden, Eve the equal of Adam, and not a reptile in sight. In another trance she felt herself ravished by Christ, and ever afterward maintained that she was His wife, and He her husband. Released, she was treated as saint and martyr by the other shaking Quakers. Within a year—after the revelation of a Chosen People awaiting her in New England (that's you, my moral toddlers)—the tiny sect emigrated.

And what of her husband, Abraham? How did he feel about having Christ kick him out of bed? Curiously, though never a member of the sect, he followed his wife to New York, whether out of love or loyalty, spite or spleen, or thoughts of economic advancement who can say? Once in the New World he led a life of delicious debauchery, even bringing home a woman of easy virtue one night and threatening to stick her in Ann's stead if she didn't that instant I mean it drop her celibate drawers. When the Society's first commune was settled in upstate New York—Sisters downstairs, Brethren upstairs—Ann went, and blacksmith Abraham disappears in the misty history of federated America.

Now, some statistics: At its height, in the decade prior to the Civil War, the United Society of Believers in Christ's Second Appearing numbered six thousand adherents in fifty-eight families in nineteen communes in eight states: New York, New Hampshire, Maine, Massachusetts, Connecticut, Ohio, Kentucky and Indiana. Income was gained from various manufactories: brooms, shoes, chairs, leather goods, clocks, barrels, hats, oval boxes, blankets, garden seeds, medicinal herbs. Their handiwork was prized above the ordinary. They invented the circular saw, the common clothespin, the flat broom, an apple-coring machine, the first permanent-press fabric, the screw propeller, machines for planing wood, for making tongue-and-groove boards, for filling seed bags, etcetera. "Hands to Work, Hearts to God" was their motto, and as such they regarded labor as a spiritual activity, a kind of worship of God through the hands. A Shaker chair was a conversation with the Lord made visible. That chill you feel running up your spine, boys and girls, is your disregarded spiritual self trying to tell you something.

Worshipwise, the early Shakers were famous for shaking; also: howling, scowling, frothing, writhing, rocking, rolling—in short, the usual atrocities of the rapt spirit. How their bodily agitations differed from those of the teenage girls in seventeenth-century Salem is a curious psychohistorical question. Contemporary descriptions of their respective gyrations are eerily similar. But one was ascribed to Satan and the other to God, and there you have it: the binary cleavage of the American mind, which we have been discussing since the beginning of September. At any rate if you attend Sunday Meeting out at New Eden—still open to the public in the best

Shaker tradition; your professor urges you to go—you will see none of that. With the decline of faith came a decline of visible manifestations of that faith, until in the second half of the nineteenth century the ecstasy of the founders had been replaced by choreographed dancing and singing. It's still a sight to see, but it is nonetheless just one more example of the degradation of etcetera and the detritus of etcetera etcetera.

Let's see, dum-di-dum: what else? They held property in common, which makes them communists. They ate communal meals. They slept three or four to a room. Dogs and cats were forbidden as useless animals. Gender equality was an honest-to-God reality, although there was still work that was women's and work that was men's. To be inspired of the Lord was to have a gift, although in case of conflict an Elder's gift could overrule a member's gift. There were stairways for men and stairways for women, and to go up the wrong stairway was to be contrary to order. It was also contrary to order for a Brother and a Sister to be in a room together without company, for the Brethren to go into a room while the Sisters were making the beds, for a Brother and Sister to milk together, for a Brother to touch a Sister and vice versa, for a Brother to shake hands with a world's woman without confessing it, to write or receive a letter from the world without the Elders' perusal of it, to converse with the world's people beyond the business at hand, to pick fruit on the Sabbath, to read worldly books on the Sabbath, to have right and left shoes, don't ask me why, and above all to allow the shining light inside to become sullied by the sumps and sewers of this world.

In short, my teenage debauchees, they lived by their beliefs. None of the ethical relativity that so bedevils your postmodern souls. They lived—live still, seven of them anyway—the dream of America [SOUNDTRACK: DRUM AND FIFE], the dream of redemption by picket fence, of marking off the virgin world by the dictates of fair play, the dream of a new Eden wherein hundreds of Adams and hundreds of Eves might live the essential ecstasy of the pure soul as long as said Adam didn't noodle said Eve. It was an experiment in creating heaven on earth, an attempt to minimize the body's hold on the spirit by making the physical a manifestation of the spiritual. Hence, the squareness of their stone walls, the rectilinear perfection of their furniture, the heaven-pointing gables of their houses, the square dealing, the simple clothes, the love. O! the love.

Any questions?

Any answers?

CHAPTER THREE

Orders
Concerning
Intercourse
Between the
Sexes

S he comes into town to shop every Thursday, and every Thursday Venner hides out in the mall waiting for her. She is a sight in her Shaker clothes: a calico dress in the summer, dull wool in the winter, but always a shawl-like yoke hiding her bosom (or the rumor of her bosom). I follow behind her and mark down for destruction children who taunt her, men who stare, women who glare and girls who giggle. Above us, the public-address system plays valium versions of the Top 40 of ten years ago, Mozart's Greatest Hits, what sounds like a ukulele-and-kazoo version of the "1812" Overture, and once—in the winter, like a special revelation—"Appalachian Spring," whose quotation of the Shaker hymn "Simple Gifts" made my precious virgin stare up at the ceiling as though someone were booby-trapping the world just for her benefit.

Amidst the fluorescent irreality of the mall she looks like a private hallucination—one hundred and twenty pounds of

Americana, a spirit borrowed from my dreams and plopped down into the germless shine of The-Mall-at-Maple-Brook. Sabbathday Wells! What overlap of centuries, what rift of moral physics is behind this gift? By the accident of the Longevity of Virgin Celibates, a soul exists that was formed in the womb of another America: this girl-woman arriving every Thursday in a taxi (it used to be Sister Antoinette's job, getting the week's supplies—but Sister Antoinette only gets around with a walker nowadays), shopping for groceries in the Safeway, purchasing some nuts and bolts, a pound of eightpenny nails at the TrueValue, pausing before the tank-topped mannequins in the window of Casual Corner, checking out the forty Wheels of forty Fortunes on the forty TV screens in Appliance City; this girl-woman buying a couple of yards of calico, of muslin, of interfacing at Needles n' Pins, and finally loading her purchases into the waiting taxi (without once recognizing me—*me*, Sister Sabbathday, this stained American male who's in love with you, who follows you around with his doggy loins, who has divorced his wife, lost his daughter, will soon lose his job—are you so blind to the flesh that you've never noticed me? Never noticed how I always just happen to be in the next aisle over? How I seem to need a bag of Gold Medal whenever you need a bag of Robin Hood? How my hands touch the twill, the thread, the linen yours have just touched?); this girl-woman being driven through town, past the college, past my steeple, past Sally's house, out Undermountain Road to the New Eden community where—while the taxi driver unloads the trunk and I drive coincidentally past—she deftly trades in the fluorescence of my world for the incandescence of hers.

Up in my steeple I have spent hours devising plans of action, daydreaming of casual encounters, of just happening along, of absentmindedly maneuvering my shopping cart into hers (Oh! I beg your pardon! Allow me!), of brandishing outrage at some group of teenage hoodlums taunting her in between the potato chips and the pretzels. When things get really bad I wrap myself in my Shaker blanket (woven by *her* hands) and sit in one of the steeple's windows, watching the fitness freaks come and go, trying to dream up ways of making the impossible merely implausible, then the implausible possible, the possible right around the corner. Could I phony up some scholarly project (college letterhead, JV:sw down below) that would require interviews with each living Shaker? Or a manuscript on Shaker domestic arts (Chapter One: Weaving)? Could I wangle an assignment from the *Globe?* Or try to get an NEH grant to live at the community for some cultural anthropological purpose? (There is, after all, the Hired Men's Quarters, where non-Shakers lived, unused all these years.) I long for some physical ability, consider the possibility of passing myself off as a spiritual-minded mason and offering to rebuild their stone fences. I try to smuggle Eve in as a kind of letter of reference but fear she is too much a memento of my coital past. Then there is Venner confessing to spiritual eruption, Venner whirling into conversion during Sunday Meeting, Venner falling on his knees before Eldress Rachel, blubbering with spiritual needs, Venner presenting himself to the Chosen Land Shakers (getting in by way of the back door, as it were), Venner doing this, Venner doing that, Venner sneaking into the Dwelling House at night and holding the four of them hostage until they admit the validity of his claim.

"What I really need," I say to a dozing Sometimes-Why, "is to confront her by some seeming coincidence and to do it when the moral props are at a minimum. And that means to confront her away from New Eden. And that means to confront her some Thursday in the mall."

Sometimes-Why agrees with this.

But how? All my dreamy inspirations revolve around banged shopping carts, dropped packages, directions asked: too short, too generic, too fallible. I need something—some ruse—listen carefully now: something that will put her in my presence for a period of time during which she will have no recourse to the outside world.

"Kidnap her," says Sometimes-Why, at which suggestion Venner pictures himself, Quasimodo-like, carrying a fainted Sabbathday Wells up the steeple stairs to the bell room, where, with the chimes of Westminster ringing the dimensions of civilization, she comes to love his hunchbacked soul.

• • •

The next Thursday, instead of tailing the shopping Shakeress I stake out the taxi driver. I've got an idea that involves sabotaging his taxi and then offering a ride to a stranded Sister Sabbathday. He leaves his cab unattended long enough for a quick bit of Luddism, but I go chickenhearted at the thought of it and drive away. That Sunday, along with a dozen other tourists and three of my religion majors, I sit on the planked seating along the perimeter of the Meeting House and watch while the four Shakeresses go through their neo-ecstatic routine. I feel so stuffed with envy and desire that I know something's got to give somewhere. Back in my steeple I make a list of alternatives.

Alternative A: Venner could write her a long letter filled with confession and remorse and maybe a blush of obscenity. (It worked with Sally, sort of.)

Alternative B: Venner could bank on her having the usual velvet imagination of the adolescent and request a midnight assignation. (Here he is, at quarter to one, alone on the courthouse steps, a police cruiser passing him for the third time.)

Alternative C: He could sneak into the Dwelling House at night and leave by her bedside missives of his love.

Alternative C¹: He could sneak into the Dwelling House at night and leave by her bedside missives *about* his love and sign them (a) Mother Ann or (b) Holy Mother Wisdom or (c) Christ or (d) go the whole hog and sign them God Him-or-Herself.

Alternative D: He could just tell her the truth about everything. (Q: What *is* the truth about everything?)

• • •

"What *is* the truth about everything?" asks Sometimes-Why. He's sitting on my teaching copy of the *Confessions* and is in a philosophical mood. "Consider, for instance, the matter of sex."

"Consider shutting up," answers Venner from up in one of his windows. He's drinking Wild Turkey and cradling his BB gun.

"Are we pro or are we con?"

"What do you mean *we?* You don't even know what gender you're interested in." Which is true: Venner once caught his occasionally consonant cat trying to hump a male Manx.

"Are we pro or are we con?" he repeats. "Vis-à-vis Sabbathday Wells, I mean."

"We're pro."

"Are we?" he asks, lifting a psychiatrist's eyebrow.

"We're con," I confess.

"Exactly."

"We're pro."

"*Exactly.*"

It's the duality of the body and the soul, you furry faggot, I want to say, but I keep it cool. "The truth," I intone carefully. "The truth about everything," I say precisely, "is that I want Sabbathday Wells because she's pure and I don't want Sabbathday Wells because she's pure. I mean, as soon as I have her she won't be pure anymore. Correct?" And I take a swig of Wild Turkey. "That's the dilemma of the American experience, correct?"

He looks at me with that superior look of his and doesn't answer. I consider shooting him just to show who's boss, but I haven't got it in me.

Out my window I can see, a mile distant, the pastures of the New Eden community. I can see the red roof of the barn, possibly the white sides of the Dwelling House, and behind, the radio towers atop Spirit Mountain. I'm holding on to my BB gun even though this side of the steeple doesn't look out on the Body-Rite Fitness Club. As Sometimes-Why is quick to point out, I have a conflicted personality.

• • •

The following Thursday, in a squall of misery and self-contempt, I head out to the mall and wait like a gangland hood behind the wheel of my car until I see the taxi arrive. I watch as Sister Sabbathday gets out and crosses the parking lot, then—just like the week before—as the cabbie goes into the Revco. With hardly a hesitation—and with a kind of dumb awe at the boldness attendant upon self-hatred—I get out and cross to the taxi, pop the hood and yank off a couple of spark-plug cables. Then I close the hood and, while a housewife watches in wonder, cross back to my car and throw the cables in the trunk. It takes barely a minute in all. I reach in through the passenger window, get one of Eve's Dairy Queen napkins out of the glove compartment and wipe the engine grime off my hands. On my way to the mall I pass the driver coming back with the *Manchester Union Leader* and a Snickers bar.

Inside, instead of following Sabbathday around, I place a half-dozen calls to the taxi dispatcher, sending the rest of the fleet on wild-goose chases to the outskirts of town, to New Lebanon, up Spirit Mountain and, because she'll still be asleep from last night's gig, to Sally's house. Then I wait in my car until Sabbathday is finished shopping, until everything is loaded into the taxi and the driver tries to start his car, wait until he gets out and opens the hood, until he pulls his head back out and looks around as if aware for the first time that there is evil in the world (O! not evil, love. Love!), until he sits back in the driver's seat and picks up his radio microphone, and only then—with a kind of seasickness inside—do I get out and stroll past. Without looking into the rear seat, I ask if there's a problem.

Oh, Mother Ann!

There's no problem; he'll radio in for relief. So I go on my way to the drugstore, hiding among the comic books and the *Playboy*s thinking I can still quit, I can just walk back to my car and go home, or kill an hour in the mall. But the despair of love is upon me. After purchasing a bogus package of something or other, I return to the parking lot. The hood is back in place now, but they're still sitting inside.

"I've got jumper cables," I offer.

"No, thanks."

"A push?"

"No."

I look past the cabbie's shoulder into the back seat. "Why, it's you, Sister Sabbathday," I say with kindly surprise and then turn back to the cabbie. "What happened? She just go dead?"

The cabbie is a man blessed with beauty of form and face. I mark him down for future destruction. "Someone stole my spark-plug cables," he says.

"They *stole* them?"

"That's right."

"A joke? A prank?"

"Some joke."

I mug a look of dismay and then gaze again into the back seat. "If you're heading back to the village, Sister, I'd be glad to give you a lift."

Neither of them says anything.

"It'd be no trouble."

She peers at me with something like resentment. Does she recognize me after all?

"No trouble," I manage to repeat; and then, with a weak smile, "Your dairy products will spoil."

If we get the archetypes in gear here what we've got is unfigged Sabbathday and scaly-skinned Venner, apple in hand, hiss in throat. I'm on the verge of saying forget it when she unpockets a crumpled pyramid of bills and, leaning forward, pays the cabbie. I stand back and, in the late summer sun, meditate upon the doctrine of free will.

So we load her packages from the trunk of the cab into the back of my car. I feel giddy with success and/or damnation. When I open the passenger door for her she climbs instead

into the back seat along with the groceries. I stand there looking in at her, or rather, down at where the hem of her dress
drapes over her knees, and then, feeling left-footed, close the
door and cross around to the driver's seat. Inside, I start the
engine and then sit there thinking a moment. I can see her in
the rearview mirror, sitting back there surrounded by her
things like an immigrant.

"Sister," I say finally, turning around, "it's customary in
a private car to sit in the front seat along with the driver."

She eyes me and doesn't answer.

"I'm sure you've observed that."

Still no answer.

"I mean I know about the Orders Concerning Intercourse
Between the Sexes and everything, but ..." And I smile—
winsome Venner—but she just sits back there stiff and silent
and ungiving.

For the first couple of blocks I try small talk, tell her my
name, tell her I teach at the college, religion, I say, as if that
will win me some points. But I get no response. I try asking
her if she's seen me around, out at Meeting or in the archives,
tell her I'm doing research for an article. "On the Metaphysics
of White Picket Fences," I say and try to smile into the rearview mirror, but at the sight of her sitting back there, hands
on her lap, eyes straight ahead, voiceless, my wits scatter.

We pass the college and head out Undermountain Road. I
consider just giving her a ride and not pushing it, letting the
contact, the fact of our sitting in an automobile together become our first acquaintance. Wouldn't she have to acknowl-
edge me the next time she saw me out at the village? The
occasional hello might lead to a conversation which might
lead to a friendship which might lead to which might lead to.
But I feel a kind of panic as the car eats up the highway. It's
only a five-minute ride.

"I live in a steeple," I say suddenly. "I live in a steeple and
I have a daughter named Eve."

In the rearview mirror I see her turn away, peer out the
window at the telephone poles drifting past.

"I live in a steeple and I have a daughter named Eve, and the Christmas after she was born I threw Jesus out of his crib and laid her down in the hay in his place."

Reader!

"This was at the Saint Mary's crèche," I say, trying to return to reason, but my head is spinning. Ahead, I can see the level ridgepoles of New Eden, and the silos square to both earth and heaven. "Can't you talk to a man who would do that?"

"Pull over," she says.

"What?"

"Pull over."

She sounds angry and like she'd bust me one given half a chance. "I'm sorry," I start to say, but she says it again—"Pull over"—and in the mirror she's got such a look on her face that I wheel the car to the side of the road, then let the tires run on the shoulder until we roll to a stop in front of the Dwelling House.

"Now listen to me," she says, and she leans forward over the passenger seat.

"Okay," I squeak.

"I don't know how you fixed this," she says. Her voice is shaking but she keeps her eyes on me. "I don't know whether you paid the cabdriver or what. But don't ever do it again. Ever! Understand? As for following me around every time I come into town—" and for a second she seems lost for a threat—"do it again and I'll get a court injunction against you."

She throws the door open and gets out of the car. I sit frozen for one witless moment and then scramble after her.

"I'm sorry!" I say. "I know it's a horrible violation of your—your— Here, let me!" She's leaning forward to take up her packages. "I'm a wreck," I say. I muscle past her and grab a grocery bag. "I'm lost. I really am. I don't believe in God or anything, but I still feel this need to be saved. I really *do* live in a steeple but it's not helping any. And I've got an ex-wife with three different names. She used to be a Mariologist but now she's a Gorgon and goes around with her hair braided in snakes. And you! You!" I shout. She turns and starts down the path to the Dwelling House. I follow, a grocery bag in each arm. "You and your picket fences and everything. I'd give anything to have been brought up a Shaker. Instead I'm stuck in a fallen world. The Adam thing, etcetera. I just got divorced and I lost my little girl. I've sworn off sex, but it's not the same thing. Oh, I shouldn't be saying this to you, I know. But I'm a desperate man. I'm a man at the end of his rope. If the world doesn't shape up soon, I don't know what I'll do." She tries to open the door into the house, but I hurry ahead and stand in the way. "You in your clean room," I say, "weaving at your loom, eating dinner in silence, feeling Christ inside you while you sweep the walk. I mean Jesus!" She bangs the screen door into my knee. "You've got the last chance in America for salvation. Do you know that?" She takes the bags out of my arms and places them on the floor inside the door. "I thought my ex-wife could do it for me," I say. "When she was a Mariologist, I mean. Then I thought my little girl could do it. But I don't know. I need to be saved," I say. "I need to be healed. I need to be—"

"If you're not off the property in one minute," she says, "I'm calling the police." The screen door slams shut.

"No!" I cry and press my face against the screen. "Sister Sabbathday!" But she's walking down the wide hall, grocery bag in each arm, her hips moving under her dress. "You don't understand! Sister Sabbathday!" I sob and sink to my knees as she disappears around a corner. "Oh, Sister!" And in misery I lie flat on the ground—heaven and the pinnacle of a Shaker gable spinning overhead—and then crying "Oh shit shit shit shit shit!" roll over onto my side like a dog.

And there, fifty feet away, watching me from the stoop of the Goods Shop, is Eldress Rachel.

Back at my steeple, the fitness freaks pay dearly.

CHAPTER FOUR

SNOW WHITE AND THE INCUBUS

" ' Simple Gifts'!" I shout for the tenth time from the back of The Missionary Position. "Play 'Simple Gifts'!" The tables around me hiss. Up on the stage, Medusa ignores me.

Mother Ann, I am contrary to order. I have taken into my person Ardent Spirits. I have drunk stimulating beverages of man's compounding. I have watered my fleshly Appetites and Passions. I have stupefied my body in violation of the Covenant of 1841. In short, Mother Ann, I'm potted.

Up under the stage lights the Gorgons launch into "Essential Ecstasy."

> *I want to move, move, move,*
> *From existence into essence;*
> *And to groove, groove, groove,*
> *Till you're crazy with tumescence.*
> *And to see my face*

In the vacuum waste
Of the sanctifying, obscene,
Purifying TV screen.

I get up and ask the woman at the table next to me to dance. Then the woman at the table next to her. Then each of the three women at the table along the wall. But it's the same old story: no one wants to dance with a man bent on destruction.

So I dance by myself, up on the rinky-dink hardwood floor the management has laid in front of the stage. I practice my Shaker gyrating, whirl and spin with the gift, practice the tranced-out expression I'll need someday out at Meeting (Will I? after this afternoon's fiasco?). I am worshiping God. I am under the control of supernatural powers. I am following the Biblical precedents of Miriam the prophetess, the virgins of Shiloh, David the Giant-Slayer (who danced for deliverance from captivity: Holy Mother Wisdom, deliver *me!*). I shuffle, I skip, I do a step-song, then the "forth and back." My head is spinning with alcohol, or maybe Divine Light. Difficult to tell which. When the band breaks, Medusa pretends she doesn't know me and sits at the Gorgons' table.

"You idiot!" she whispers when I collapse all sweaty beside her. "You're embarrassing me."

"Impossible," I say and tap myself on the chest, on the heart. "Nothing to you."

"You're my ex-husband. And everybody knows it."

"Reflects credit on you then. The ex- part, I mean. Give me a kiss."

"Forget it."

"Just one," I say. "Then I'm off to do the self-slaughter thing."

"No. Now listen. There's supposed to be a New York agent here tonight."

"Jump out of my steeple."

"He's down from the White Mountains. He's heard about us. About *me*."

"Land on well-built volleyball player."

"Venner!"

"Make them sorry. Contrite. Baby, let's get married again." And I start to put my arm around her. She gets up and fishes around in some clothes piled on a chair in the corner.

"Here," she says, coming back with some keys. "There's a mattress in the back of the van."

"Oh, baby," I say, grateful; and then, leaning over and whispering, "But plumbing in doubtful working condition."

"Go lie down," she says.

"Without you?" I say/realize, and I am overtaken with sadness.

"One more set," Deusie says, "and I'll be out."

I lift up an arm and smell under it. "Corruption," I say; and then: "Oh, Sally! I've lost my chance. Salvation, redemption, purification. Poof! Gone." And I bite the tablecloth with my teeth.

"Don't chew the scenery, V."

"Only given wonsh to every man," I say between clenched teeth, pulling the tablecloth so the empty beer bottles, the ashtrays, come sliding toward me. "Mish it and poof! All existence, no esshence." Medusa yanks the tablecloth out of my mouth.

"Behave!" she says. "Now, tell me, what happened?"

"Too awful to speak of."

"What?"

"Jumper cables."

"Venner," she says and tries to give me the keys.

"Jumper cables!" I roar, sitting bolt upright. "Live in steeple! Have ex-wife named Sally!"

"Are you all right? V?"

I look at her snakes, her cleavage, the vaccination daisy on her skinny bicep. "Perfect," I say and delicately touch fingertip to fingertip. Coordination proven, I lay my head on the table.

"You can't pass out here."

"Just resting."

"Come on."

"No," I say and lift my head. "Oh, baby, it was awful."

"What happened? Something happened. What?"

The recollection is so painful I slap myself across the face.

"What?" Deusie says, grabbing my hands. "What happened?"

"I had my first intercourse with Sister Sabbathday today."

"Intercourse?" she says. The drummer—the one with the beautiful breasts—comes over and gets her cigarettes, smiles at me and then moves away.

"Whatever whiff of essence I had about me . . ." I start to say but I can't go on. "She knows who I am. She said she'd call the police."

Her face registers surprise, or maybe delight.

"She said she'd get a court injunction against me."

"Sister Sabbathday did?"

Definitely delight.

"What happened? What did you do?"

But I wave her off. A flush of nausea starts down in my ankles and ends up in my throat, and I have the sudden idea that I must go see Sabbathday. That if I can only explain. Stand below her window throwing pebbles. The moonlight, Juliet, etcetera.

"I have to go," I say, getting up.

"You're too drunk," Deusie says and grabs hold of my arm. "Did you ride your bike out?"

"Walked," I say. Someone is trying to pull the floor out from under me.

"Here," Deusie says.

First they pull it right, then they pull it left.

"Honey, take my arm . . ."

So I put my right foot where my left ought to be and my left foot—

• • •

In the van I dream of Sister Sabbathday sitting astride a black swan flying over a grounded Venner who, in spite of the killing suck of gravity, nonetheless tries to see up her dress.

Then there are nuns' habits floating down on me like feathers.

And then snowflakes.

• • •

And then the next thing I know I'm trudging out Undermountain Road toward the New Eden village. I've got my socks and shoes off and the soles of my feet are tormented with sand. I have a dim memory of sliding down an embankment on my fanny, and then walking along a riverbed, going from rock to rock, pool to pool, so that no one could follow me (*cf.* various Hollywood Westerns). I feel ill. Drunk still, but a sick kind of drunk. I am walking while nightmares flash through my head like vaudeville acts: octogenarian barbarians, picket fences marching in lockstep, a sneaking suspicion that one of the women I asked to dance back at The Missionary Position is on the Tenure Advisory Board. I have half an idea that the plan is *Alternative E:* get out to the village and start work on the stone pasture fences that need rebuilding, and be at work at sunrise when Sister Sabbathday wends her way to the Weaving Shop. I am drunk-certain that if I can rebuild the walls square and true, I will have banished from the garden of her grace this afternoon's serpent.

There are beer cans along the side of the road; fast-food Styrofoam thingies; a boot; a mitten.

"Sister Sabbathday," I say to the glinting pavement, and I try to think of something about the detritus of a lost America, but I am impotent of mind and probably mettle, not to mention etcetera. I step over a piece of dead nature. A raccoon, I think.

"Sister Sabbathday."

A true stone fence should have its first course laid below

the frost line. That's how they do it in England. But here in New England the frost line is down around three feet, and what a mess of stones it would take to start from that far down. So we build them above the ground and the winter lifts and tosses them. Venner actually knows something about stone walls, having spent two college summers getting his ten thumbs crushed as a mason's helper.

Up on Spirit Mountain there are headlights along Lovers' Lookout. The radio antennas blink on and off.

"Sister Sabbathday," I say, addressing the road, the night, the summer stars overhead, the lovers loving. "We live in a Junkyard of the Flesh. Even you, out in your clapboard *sanctum sanctorum*. We live in an atmosphere where radio waves cluttered with pop music, sex talk shows, call-in housewives, salacious advertisements lance our most intimate organs, and we don't even know it. We are riven with VHF and UHF on whose wavy wavelengths hangs the electronic gibberish of Anti-America, the Pillsbury Doughboy, for instance, also: talk-show hosts, Nazi-underweared veejays, discount saviors beamed down from satellites cruising the underside of heaven."

I stub my unshoed and unsocked toe on a lump of tar. There's a car approaching from behind.

"It comes in through the windows, through the walls, through the roof, down the chimneys. And there is no virginity of the mind, no palisade of chastity that can keep it out."

The car has pulled alongside me. I am distantly aware that it's Medusa, Medusa with a wifely intuition as to where the drunk in the back of the band's van has disappeared to. She waits until I run out of words and then tells me to get in.

"No."

"Yes," she says. "Get in."

"Barbarian," I say. She keeps the car apace.

"Where's your shoes?" she asks.

"Stolen," I answer.

"Stolen? And your socks?"

"Lost."

THE DIVINE COMEDY OF JOHN VENNER

She revs the engine. "Get in."

"I'm on a crusade," I say. "I'm going to save the New England Jerusalem from the infidels. Keep out of my way."

"Get in. I'll give you a ride."

"You'll kidnap me."

"Don't flatter yourself. I just don't want to see my child support stop when you get hit by a truck."

I gaze suspiciously at her. "Your New York agent. What happened to him?"

"Who knows? Get in."

I get in. The soles of my feet are sore. Medusa is still snake-haired but she's changed into her Sally clothes, jeans and a baggy sweater out at the elbows. Gazing at her in the green haze of the dashlights, I see like a palimpsest behind her snakes the pixie cut she wore when she was nineteen, the pageboy of twenty-three, the sweaty ribbons pasted to her face four years ago in the delivery room.

"This crusade," she says, "it isn't going to land you in jail, is it?"

I start picking grains of sand out of my feet.

"I mean you're not going to be loud and violent, are you?"

She's driving slowly, on the shoulder: the village is only a quarter-mile away. I put my mortified feet up on top of the glove compartment.

"Think," I say, "of the radio waves even this instant barbecuing your body."

"Honey?"

"Infidel."

A car zooms past us.

"Let's go to Dunkin' Donuts," she says. "Coffee and a chocolate eclair. My treat."

"Tattooing your body with . . . with . . ."

"Detritus," she offers with a sigh.

"Yes," I say; and I think there is hope for my ex-wife yet. "Pull up there," I say, pointing to a blind of laurel bushes.

"What are you going to do?" she asks, braking the car.

"Never mind."

• 50 •

"What?"

There it is: Jerusalem by starlight, Augustinian symbol of the believing soul. Even in the geometry of drunkenness it right-angles me. I get out and lean on the hood of the car and gaze from building to building, from gable to gable, from stone wall to picket fence to pasture. I feel the old amour, the old heartsickness. In the windows of the Dwelling House the moon flashes like white fire. "Oh, Sally," I blurt out and start across the road.

"What are you doing?"

"I'm going to kiss it."

"What? You're going to kiss what?"

"Everything," I say. "The wood, the brick, the windows, the flowers, the barn door, the paths where her feet walk. You kiss it too."

"Venner."

We go through the gate onto the grounds. I can feel the sudden sting of morality under my bare feet. Sally takes hold of my hand and tries to tug me away.

"The police patrol here. Remember?"

She says this because I've been caught trespassing more than once. I get down on my hands and knees and kiss the granite stoop of the Goods Shop.

"Oh, Christ."

I kiss the paneled door, scoot across the lane and kiss the bootjacks outside the Brothers' Workshop, then crawl on my hands and knees along the sacred earth. At the Weaving Shop I can feel the sun's heat still in the brick foundation; I run my fingers along the pointing, caress the clapboards as though they're the skin of God. I put my ear to the door latch and hear in the pitted iron the hundred ghost hands of a hundred Shakeresses who worked the looms before my Sabbathday. I sit on the stoop drunk-dizzy with religion and lust. Sally comes over and stands in front of me.

"Let's go home and make a big sandwich," she says.

"She's here," I say and peer up to the second floor of the Dwelling House. "This is the air she breathes."

"With ham and salami and fresh lettuce."

"This is the ground she walks on," I say and point to the flowers that seem to have sprung up under her step.

"Let's go home and have a sandwich and a couple of Eve's root beers and lie on the bed and watch a late movie. What do you say?"

I can see her window, second from the southeastern corner. In it, by some vitreous trick, the moon has a reddish hue. I move my head to the right, to the left, trying to get rid of it. The antique glass wrinkles and winks, but the reddish tint stays.

"I wonder what she looks like when she's asleep," I say. Sally does the female hand-on-hip thing and gazes away. "We could get in. I know how."

"Get in?" she says. "You mean break in? No way."

I have a vision of the two of us tiptoeing through a wide corridor of sleeping Shakers. "We could see what it looks like. The upper floors of the Dwelling House, I mean. They're the one place where the world's people are not allowed. Come on, I'll show you." And I get up and start walking.

"Please, V."

"We could check out a trio of octogenarian virgins in bed. That's a once-in-a-lifetime opportunity, wouldn't you say?"

"Let's go home," she says, following me.

"We could leave mysterious notes at their bedsides, disapproving notes about the decimation of the order, and sign them Mother Ann."

"Doesn't a ham sandwich and *The Glenn Miller Story* sound better?"

"I'm going in. Give me a hand."

"What?"

"Give me a hand." And I bend over and grip an iron manhole cover that sits down a couple of inches below the sod.

"What's that?" Sally asks.

It's *Alternative F:* an underground sluice that runs from the Machine Shop to the laundry in the basement of the Dwelling House. Venner explored it one criminal night after he discovered the foundry bill for the manhole cover in the archives. It's brick, flat on the floor, the walls arching in a half-circle to a height of about twenty inches. It's something like thirty yards in length, a downward slope that ends in a kind of well or holding tank in the cellar of the Dwelling House. The first time I made the trip I crawled uphill first to the Machine Shop and then downhill to the Dwelling House, crouching in the well there long enough to rest and then turning back without going into the house itself. I had thought to save it, to save the theatrical extravagance of the tunnel for some crisis when rising Lucifer-like out of the earth might be put to good use. But after this afternoon, Venner is surrounded by crises.

"Spiders," Sally is saying, kneeling and peering down into the dark. "Snakes, creepy cocoons."

"I've been through before."

"Albino bats."

"With a flashlight," I say, and nudge my way past her. "Come on."

It's damp and dark and close, and yes, there are daddy longlegs and mummified cocoons, but the only snakes I know of are the thirteen on Deusie's head hanging through the manhole. I call back to her to come on, but she won't, says, "Bad idea, V," says she's going home, good night, good-bye. I crawl five yards infantry-style, take a rest; another five, another rest. I listen for her, but there's nothing but the roar of claustrophobia. The bricks are murder on the elbows and knees, I can tell you, also my bare toes. I know from my spying that next to the laundry room is the kitchen, and as I crawl I have thoughts of being heard by an octogenarian insomniac raiding the midnight fridge, also of meeting the police when I emerge. (We are, after all, in addition to the usual transgressions, guilty of breaking and entering.) I'm on the way to having severe second thoughts when I see the hazy zero of the well opening a few yards ahead. I make it in a burst of energy and bruised elbows.

And there, Class, ascending into the antique atmosphere

of white pine and plaster, your drunken professor feels the creep of Holy Mother Wisdom along his spine. It's the laundry room he's in, just off the big kitchen, site of two centuries of white linen and unblemished underwear. O! Let us enumerate the gifts: there's the weave of moonlight on the slate floor, the walls paneled and drawered and cubby-holed with the wood of the wilderness, the fir rafters, the cedar beams, a ladder-back chair ($2,000 easy at a Boston antiques shop Venner knows), the ancient air still reverberating with the fanatical voices of nineteenth-century America. I can smell the ghost of tallow in the air, feel under my bare feet the sole-worn stone, hear the right angles, the euphony of well-joined wood, the sleeping souls two floors above, and I imagine how it will be—never mind what happened this afternoon—I imagine this same moonlight a year from now, two years from now, the rustle of Sister Sabbathday's dress, the hush of her underthings as she climbs, say, the Sisters' stairway to the second floor; and Brother Venner, Shaker-garbed and devout, keeping order in the presence of the first-floor ghosts by taking the Brethren's stairway. Until, alone on the second floor, we meet for an illicit kiss, our thighs just grazing, the thrill of damnation in our pulses. Picture it [TREMOLO ON THE VIOLINS]: Eldress Rachel dead and buried, perhaps sick Sister Antoinette too, and senile Chastity happy in her room at the Spirit Mountain Convalescent Center (paid for by the Shaker Trust Fund) and just Sister Sabbathday and Brother Venner with this museum of the utopian soul for their theater, this sanctuary of quiet air and moonlight. Oh, sure, there will be letters from the communities at Canterbury and Chosen Land inquiring after us, hinting at the impropriety of our cohabitation and urging that we take up residence with them. There will be newspaper reporters, perhaps court challenges. But in the blooming garden, by the dusky hearth, in the snow squalls of spring and the Indian heat of autumn, we will invent ourselves, Sabbathday and I, authors of gusty emotions and the lamentations of love, menders of stone walls, repairers of picket fences, island dwellers in the land of Anti-America, regenerate and redeemed, unpolluted by—

There's a television.

I see it through the kitchen doorway, a squat thirteen-inch Sony eyeing me with a certain smugness. It's sitting on the counter, right next to a bowl of fruit, and I wonder what the story is, does Rachel watch the six o'clock news while making dinner? Or Sabbathday? Or is it MTV? (On whose heaven-reflected waves, by the way, Medusa yearns to fly—*cf.* "And to see my face/In the vacuum waste/Of the sanctifying, obscene,/Purifying TV screen," not to mention numerous pre- and postdivorce discussions concerning the possibility of Essence in the Postmodern World—but more of that anon.) I cross into the kitchen, walk beside one of the ten-foot-long countertops, past an old cast-iron cookstove, over to the counter where the television sits, front man for a shiny toaster, a blender for Christ's sake. Whether it's the dim light or the antics of the mind, they seem to wink at me, as if they recognize in me a secret brother. Gingerly I push the on/off button, zip the volume down and sure enough there's Jimmy Stewart as Glenn Miller, glasses and trombone pixeled for eternity. The kitchen glows with that irradiated blueness which—oh, you know what television looks like, unregenerate Reader, damn your soul! I punch the on/off button again and head for the stairs.

Up on the first floor I try to soothe my soul with the ordered rows of benches in the Meeting Room, with the rustle of angels' wings in the corners, or the ghost of the rustle of angels' wings, and failing that, then the godly patina of the floorboards. But it's no soap. I'm feeling the pollution thing. I'm feeling the vanity of vanities thing. I think of Sabbathday sleeping above me, Sabbathday in her white nightgown trimmed with red (or her red nightgown trimmed with white: which?), and I consider for the moment the possibility of *Alternative G:* Venner creeping into her room and impersonating the incubus. It'd be better than pornography through the mail, though nowhere near what we've imagined in our better moments, *e.g.* doing it in piles of clean linen down in the laundry room, seraphim singing "Simple Gifts" the whole while, and etcetera, you get the picture.

Or *Alternative H:* We could take an ax and split her head open, which is probably what the poor dear expects of Venner the Shaker-stalker, I mean, you know, murdering virgins the way some men murder prostitutes.

Reader, I'm not a well man.

When I get near the top of the stairway I can see her door. This is it, the moment of truth. Is drunken Venner willing to risk jail time for a glimpse of paradise or not? Heart aflutter, I tiptoe up the remaining stairs, cross the hallway and look inside her room. And what I see is the metallic glint of a walker standing at the foot of a bed, and then the bed itself, and finally, the sheeted form of a Shakeress, not Sabbathday, but Sister Antoinette, Z-shaped, the fetal position at the age of eighty-seven. I mentally count exterior windows and realize I'm one off, that Sabbathday (white nightgown with red trim or red nightgown with white trim?) is in the next room down. I start to back up, but change my mind and take a few steps into the room, another few, and then, with a kind of horror, bend down onto my knee and look into her face.

It's a weird feeling, being kissing-close to such decay. Even in the dark I can see the lines in her forehead, the ravaged eye sockets, the unmuscled lips. And I can smell her innards on her breath, the aroma of cancer or cirrhosis or God knows what. I try to imagine her a young woman in the nineteen-twenties, the decade of the flappers, Shakers and Shakeresses deserting by the dozen, but Sister Antoinette tending her virginity, taking care of the village's herb garden as the years go by, breathing the impossible air while Hiroshima melted and Buchenwald burned, weeding while the Apollo astronauts played golf on the moon. And now because of the longevity of virgin celibates her skin is putrefying even before her heartbeat has ceased. Metaphysical Venner reacts to all this by wondering whether he's to take it as the defeat of the flesh at the hands of the living spirit, or the victory of the flesh, turning itself into compost just to prove its power. Physical Venner, on the other hand, wants to hold his nose and run screaming from the room.

Which he does, more or less, though the scream is silent, and the running checked by having to do a volte-face once he's in the hall, and then tiptoeing down to the next doorway. . . .

And sweet Jesus, there she is, white walls and white sheets, moonlight and everything. I can see her under the covers, the lift of her hips, the twist of her back, her long hair on the moonlit pillow, a trapezoid of skin where the sheet has betrayed her, and God damn/bless my soul if I don't feel all the spite and the hate and the dregs of drunkenness vacuumed out of my veins. I take a step in, get the honey color of the floorboards on my feet and feel the first shiver of redemption. The room itself is Shaker-clean, the floor free of furniture except for the bed, a bureau, a small table and a chair. But along one wall there's a load of books, I mean a load: novels, histories, art books, books about weaving and tapestries, Isaac Asimov explaining the universe, *Natural Wonders of the American West*, model railroads, a Chilton's repair manual for a 1968 Corvette for Christ's sake. On one shelf there's a long row of look-alike books, those dime-store jobs with marbleized covers that you can write in yourself. For a second or so I don't get it. And then I'm lifting one up, seeing in the dim moonlight what I think must be her handwriting. Even then it takes a couple of heartbeats for Professor Venner to realize what he's stumbled onto here is a multivolume diary of Sister Sabbathday's spiritual self (not uncommon among nineteenth-century converts: the progress of the soul, etcetera). I go weak-kneed at the thought of the intimacies recorded inside, not to mention the potential orgy of voyeurism. I get so worked up I have to break away, cross to the bureau and—still holding on to one of the diaries—open the top drawer, where I find Sister Sabbathday's handmade underwear, neatly ironed and folded. I hold a pair to my face, sniff the Platonic freshness, kiss the crotch, tug at the drawstring with my teeth, and then with ideas of converting my briefcase into a reliquary back at the steeple, stuff them into my pocket. I stick the diary inside my waistband and then, feeling heartsick with love and desire, turn to where she lies sleeping.

The desiderata are many. There's the head-hollow on her pillow from some previous toss or turn, the shading of her legs under the sheets, the tracery of shadow, the witchery of light, the silver shimmer of down on her neck, the this and the that of the female form. Suppose Venner were to kiss her? (*Alternative I*). Suppose he were to lean over and brush her flesh with his lips? We wonder whether she's a deep sleeper or whether she's even now wandering on the fringe of consciousness, soon to spring up and scream bloody murder (*Alternative J*). I squat beside the bed, squat so my face is not twelve inches from hers. I can feel the stumble of my heart against my ribs. The truth is, Sister Sabbathday Wells is beautiful. Not Hollywood-beautiful or Madison Avenue–beautiful, not the beauty of housewifey harlots hawking dish detergent or panty-hose posers, but Shaker-beautiful, a kind of austerity in the upslope of her cheekbones, an economy of eyelash, a cleanswept complexion with no trace of the rougey warpaint of the average Americaness. It's as if the Lord carpentered her in His own Shaker Workshop: plumb, true, simple of line and graceful of limb. I feel bitten with despair.

And for the first time I think I get it, I mean *truly* get it: the exquisite self-torture behind celibacy. It was the Marquis de Sade who said that the libertine's paradox was to love that which was pure and never to be able to possess it because to possess it was to defile it. Is that why you took Jesus as your lover, Mother Ann? Because you knew you could only keep love alive for someone who never left the waste of heaven? Are we doomed then to impossible purity, you to your Jesus, America to its western horizon, the Marquis to his maids and Venner to his virgin?

CHAPTER FIVE

STEALING SISTER
SABBATHDAY'S
SPIRITUAL SELF

"Pass one another like angels," said Mother Ann Lee. By
which she meant, I suppose, that her devotees should be
tender of one another's spiritual selves. What I did was steal
Sister Sabbathday's twelve-year-old spiritual self and Xerox it
at 3 A.M. in the department secretary's office, then sneak it back
into her room by dawn. I was tender of it the whole time.

And for the entire afternoon and into the evening I pore
over the squiggle and kick of her handwriting like a Talmudic
Peeping Tom: vicarious Venner watching Sabbathday Wells
on the precipice of puberty, peering in at the window of her
soul hoping to catch her in some state of moral undress. What
I do is catch her being teased by the kids at school, teased for
her name, her clothes, the boys saying dirty words to her, the
girls uppity in a way only the newly fertile can be. She has
one friend, it seems, someone named Valerie, with whom she
gets intimate about things like boys and bras, and who calls
her Lara when they're alone. It's that last that gives Venner a

thrill and/or chill, the first bit of evidence he has that Sabbathday has longed for ordinariness, that there is some fantasy of Larahood in her (her original name, if you must know, Sally), some twelve-year-old's picture of life with His-and-Her towels and pink flamingos and a Revlon face looking back at her from the morning mirror.

Out at New Eden, Sister Antoinette is teaching her to weave. She likes the smell of the wool, and the colors, and the sound of the loom. She doesn't like the patterns. They're boring, she says. And she doesn't like the tourists who come to buy the blankets and shawls the Sisters weave. She hates taking money in the store, making change, answering questions. What she really can't stand is when they ask if she takes plastic. Other things she can't stand are perfumed forty-year-old women and high school boys who use the straightaway out in front of New Eden for a drag strip.

But let Professor Venner recede into the role of editor.

SATURDAY, NOV. 5
They look at me like I'm part of a museum exhibit or something, or sometimes like I'm a toy, a scale model version of a shaker. I hate them. I hate them when they tell me I'm cute. I hate them when they ask me about being a shaker and I hate them when they're quiet and reverential like they think I'm contemplating god all the time or something. [Twelve-year-old Sabbathday's handwriting is a sight to see. She writes like her pen's an engine chugging from left to right. She tries to get schoolgirl-feminine from time to time, tries to dot her i's with a circle or sometimes (Val's influence?) a tiny heart, but once she's got a head of steam, she reverts to a crabby dot. Ed.] *I hate—all right, I'll put what I hate in order, least to worst. I hate the ones who ask me if I've got long or short hair up under my cap. I hate the ones who come to meeting, sitting on their benches like it's a play they're watching. I hate their cars and their cameras and I hate their stupid questions. Do I enjoy dancing? Do I enjoy singing? Do I really hear the voice of Christ? Do I really think I can spend my whole life away*

from people? (Like with you as a specimen it's going to be hard?) I hate the ones who're surprised that we use electricity. And the ones who argue that if we use electricity why not a telephone. (Because it would connect us to you, clown.) Then there's the ones who want to know where my parents are. And there's the men who look at me.

That's what I hate. Now this is what I like.

[A blank page follows. Sabbathday Wells, the twelve-year-old comedienne. *Ed.*]

TUESDAY, NOV. 8

In arithmetic class today it was so boring I couldn't believe it. I spent practically the whole class—we were doing three figure division which is just like two figure division which is just like one figure division so what's the problem? I spent the whole class trying out signatures in my notebook. Sincerely yours, Lara Wells. Lara Sabbathday Wells. Lara S. Wells. Miss Sabbathday Wells. [These are repeated down the page with variations of form and flourish. *Ed.*] *Terry Moses kept leaning over my desk to see what I was doing but I wouldn't let him see and anyway I was just waiting for him to try to put his hand on my back because everybody knows he tries to feel you there to see if you're wearing a bra.*

At lunch they did it again but I don't care.

FRIDAY, NOV. 11

It started snowing today in second period and by fourth period it was so bad they let us out. I was going to go home but Val said no come over to her house and I knew that nobody except maybe Rachel would know that school had been canceled so I went. We went up to her room and she showed me her new albums and her panty hose and the makeup kit she says her mother bought her and then while we were trying on some of her clothes told me about Eric again and the bleachers like I didn't know already only this time she said he actually put his hand up there. At least that's what she says this time.

SATURDAY, NOV. 12

It happened again, first the wiggling lights and then the pain. It scares me so much. I was in the Sisters Shop dressing the loom for Antoinette when it started. They're like wiggling worms in the air, like those whitish bugs you see burrowing in garbage, only it's like they're electric, flashing and squirming and you can't see because of them. When the pain started I started crying. I couldn't help it. I thought of going back to the house but I didn't want Rachel to see me like this again so I ended up climbing into the yarn dolly and curling up like a baby. I held hanks of yarn to my temples and repeated Mother's words over and over again. IF YOU SEE LITTLE BRIGHT LIGHTS IN THE AIR AROUND YOU, BE THANKFUL TO GOD, FOR THEY ARE SPECKS OF ANGELS WINGS. *I tried to keep my eyes open to see them, because if they really are angels wings then I want to see them, only they don't look like angels wings to me. They feel like some punishment but for what I don't know. They stayed about half an hour and then the air cleaned. And then there was just the pain.*

Now I'm up in my room with the door closed and the shutters pulled and I can hear the disapproval in Rachel's footsteps when she goes by in the hall. And Sister Antoinette doesn't understand why I didn't finish dressing the loom.

What I want to know is did Mother Ann Lee really see the same things I see? And did she feel the same pain afterwards? And how could she think they were angels wings? Or are they really angels wings and I'm just not right to see them and so it hurts because I'm not right?

[It's a migraine headache, isn't it, that Sabbathday's describing here? And the aura that goes with it? *Ed.*]

WED. NOV. 16

Eldress Sarah is sick again, worse this time I think. She's going to die. I know it. If not now then someday soon. Rachel will be made Eldress and then look out Sabbathday.

[Eldress Sarah Stanford died in December 1981, a month after Sabbathday's entry. *Et in Arcadia ego. Ed.*]

THURSDAY, NOV. 17
They did it again and this time I couldn't help it I told on them. Mrs. Marshall scolded them and then stood with me in line so I could get a free hot lunch. But afterwards Ben pushed me when no one was looking and Alicia called me a virgin. In reading class I lied and said I had to go to the girls room and when I got there I just sat on the toilet and tried to think of a new hiding place. Later Mrs. Marshall said I could leave my lunchbag in her desk drawer each morning but I said no.

FRIDAY, NOV. 18
When I got home from school today my bed was made and lying on the coverlet was a piece of paper with the paragraph about intercourse with the world's people from the Millenial Laws copied out on it. It was in Sister Rachel's handwriting.
At dinner I sat and didn't say anything. What does she know?

THURS. NOV. 24
I took Eldress's Thanksgiving plate up to her and then stayed and talked. She asked me about school and stuff and then talked about when she was a girl going to school out here in the village. I felt that strange feeling I feel sometimes, like there are ghosts around me, all those kids who lived here and went to school here and now all of them gone. It got kind of creepy because Eldress started talking about how they were all going to die, they were all going to die by the time I was twenty and then what?
I read an article in a magazine about the Mennonites and it said that some of them go to college and learn to be doctors and teachers and stuff and then afterwards go back to the community. But Rachel says the only reason I go to school is because it's the law. That they could teach me at the village

themselves except the state says they can't. And when I'm sixteen then I can quit school. I told Eldress Sarah about the article and she just sort of looked out the window and said something I couldn't hear. I asked her what and she said it again. "Who would you be a doctor or a teacher for?" she said.

THURSDAY, DEC. 16
Today I couldn't believe it! There was a television cameraman and a reporter following me around school. I couldn't believe it. They were right there in the classroom with us and with this incredibly bright light on the camera and the camera pointed at me and everyone trying to act like it was normal or something. They even came into gym class. The reporter asked me questions about school and about home and about my cap and I was so scared and stupid I answered them. They got pictures of me shooting a basketball. When I got home I told Eldress Sarah but she just shook her head. But Rachel found out somehow and she was so mad she was walking around the dwelling house kicking chairs. But it wasn't me she was mad at. She was mad at the television station and at the school. She wants to know who gave permission. Did I say it was okay? No I told her. Nobody asked me anything about it. She says she's going to school with me tomorrow.

SUNDAY, DEC. 19
In meeting I could feel it. I could feel it!

[What? What? *Ed.*]

MONDAY, DEC. 20
I got called down to the principal's office today. At first I thought I was in trouble but when I got there he smiled a lot and said he apologized for not asking me if it was okay for them to take pictures of me. I didn't say anything until he asked me if I accepted his apology and then I said it was okay.

But I guess I was on television this weekend. At least that's what everybody says.

[Your editor had been unaware of the existence of this videotape of twelve-year-old Sabbathday. Phone calls to WEEB, KKAT and WNET are in order, it seems.]

FRIDAY, DEC. 24, CHRISTMAS EVE
I've been thinking about it. What WILL it be like when Sarah and Rachel and Chastity and Antoinette are gone? I really will be alone. I mean ALONE. Already it's kind of weird to eat in the dining room, just the four of us, with places for thirty. And the kitchen, with just the modern stove and refrigerator next to the old ovens. Can you imagine me here alone? Walking the halls by myself? Going out to the barn to milk? Can you imagine it in the winter when it gets dark early? It'd be like a ghost town only I'd still be here.
And then there's the Lara me who is just waiting for them to die so that she can leave.
Sometimes I daydream about a New Eden that's got shakers all over it again. I mean like the photographs in the books in the Goods Shop. Only we're wearing regular clothes and not old clothes. But we all live together, Val and some of the people from downtown and I don't know, but people. We're like a big family, just like Mother Ann Lee wanted. I know we get letters from people wanting to join. A couple every year. Eldress told me once. So did Chastity. I don't see why we can't let them. Why can't we let them? Wouldn't Mother Ann have wanted them? What would be wrong with being shakers who drive cars and sell things to the tourists as long as we were still shakers? I mean as long as we worshipped and sang and danced and didn't get married? Why can't that happen again?
When the angels come and I think I hear Mother Ann's voice, I think I can tell that she's angry. I think she's angry that we aren't shakers the way we used to be. I think she's angry at Eldress and Antoinette and Rachel and even Chas-

tity, and maybe at me too because I don't do anything about it.

And I know about Chosen Land where they actually have new shakers even though Eldress Sarah and Rachel say they aren't really. Antoinette said once that when they were all dead I would move there and they would take care of me. But I don't want to move there. I want to stay here. This is my home and I'm going to stay here.

MONDAY, JAN. 3
Alicia and Ben and the others are ignoring me. It's like I'm cool because I've been on television, but I'm not cool because I'm me and so they don't know how to add that up. Let me clue you it's not the only thing they don't know how to add up.

Your editor doesn't know what it is, Reader. Whether it's the girly normalcy of S.W.'s writing. Or the unsavory after-taste of voyeurism. Or just the hopelessness of breathing. But somewhere in the deep evening of perusing Sister Sabbath-day's spiritual self, he finds himself alternating between wanting more, between sneaking back into the Dwelling House for episodes two through twenty, and wishing he'd never met twelve-year-old Lara S. Wells, *et al.* The question seems to be this: Is Sabbathday Sabbathday? Is she the maiden of my id or is she, you know, etcetera? I lift her soaking underwear (which I am using as a cold compress) off my eyes and peer at her hundred selves on the steeple walls. Over on his windowsill Sometimes-Why cautions against taking too bleak a view of things.

"Just because she threatened to call the police on you," he says. "Just because she threatened to get a court injunction against you."

I'm lying on my mattress, headache in full bloom, although I have yet to see any angels' wings.

"Just because she banged the door into your shin the first chance she got."

"Go away."

"Tut-tut," he says, holding his paw up to me like the Pope. "Let us consider the alternatives. *Alternative A . . .*"

"Don't."

"*Alternative A:* Sabbathday *is* Sabbathday and you are being misled by the vagaries of adolescent identity formation. Volumes two through twenty would help clear this up. *Alternative B:* She's masquerading as Sabbathday and really she's Lara, ducking out of the compound after hours and hitting the town bars, doing it with college boys out behind the stadium and getting back on the reservation before sunup."

"Ha-ha."

"Or *Alternative C:* She's both A and B. In short, there's no difference between the two of you except that she's got the inside track on outlasting the octogenarian trio and getting all that beautiful land for free."

Above my head the Westminster chimes begin ringing the quarter hour. The motor whirs into life and the triphammers rear back. I stuff Sabbathday's wet underwear into my ears as Western Civ leapfrogs down the major scale: *bong*-bong-BONG-BONG. A hundred Sabbathdays vibrate on my walls.

"This love stuff is tricky," says Venner.

So sometime after midnight it's a couple of stiff drinks at The Missionary Position, a pep talk and then back to New Eden, back through the underground sluice, up through the kitchen and into Sabbathday's room. With none of the moony lingering of the night before, I take her most recent diary off the shelf and carry it down to the kitchen where I sit on the floor and read by the light of an open refrigerator door. And, dear Lord, it's even worse than I thought. For one thing she knows about me out in the bushes. (*Does he think I can't see him out there with that telescope thing of his?*) For another, I was right the other night, she *does* think I'm the serial-killer type, or at least she entertains the notion. (Worse, she doesn't seem to be particularly frightened by it.) At any rate, Venner appears not to have been quite the subtle serpent he thought he was being. Listen:

He had the little girl with him this time. She has thick hair like her mother. [Like her mother? How does she know what her mother looks like?] *She kept trying to tug him into the next aisle, but he made a show about this and that thing, some baking soda they needed. I have this urge sometimes just to turn to him and ask him what he wants. But I don't. Why, I don't know. I'm not afraid of him, at least I don't have the fear of him I ought to have. But I can't do it. The truth is there's something about having him watch me that gives me, I don't know, a feeling. Not a good feeling, but not exactly bad either. I remember that time he followed me into Sears and I found myself walking with just the faintest exaggeration of my hips. Today, in the supermarket, I made as if my cap were bothering me, took it off and let my hair out. We went for two aisles before I put it back up. (Rachel, if you are reading this behind my back, as we both know you are, what will you do about that?)*

I fool around sometimes thinking of things to do to him. Not just making a point of buying tampons when he's following me in the supermarket. But maybe some night getting into town the way I used to do and finding out where he lives and hiding in HIS bushes, watching HIM. Or if that's too crazy, then sneaking a note into whatever document he's been reading in the archives. Or maybe ripping out a page of one of those magazines and slipping it in for him to see. What would he do?

Or perhaps I don't think of doing any of those things. Perhaps I only write them for you to read, Rachel.

There are other entries, entries in which I make the occasional cameo appearance, but mostly given over to Sabbathday's daily life, the same worries about money as ten years ago, a business meeting in which the question of charging for tours is raised for what sounds to be the umpteenth time, Sabbathday being of the opinion that Rachel will eventually drop the democracy and make a dictatorial decision herself. There seems to be as well a professional cabinetmaker, a reproducer of period furniture who wants to use the New Eden name for his Shaker chairs, to sell them in the Goods Shop for a percentage, etc. Sabbathday has asked for his name and address and evidently plans on writing to him, asking whether he would agree to abide by Shaker order if his wares were sold at New Eden. (*And when he writes back and tells me how he already wears simple clothing but do I mean ALL of Shaker order, I'll ask him does he ever make a chair with only three legs?*) And there's talk of whether New Eden should apply to Canterbury for funds to hire an outside handyman, ending with the question of whether Sister Sabbathday is being overworked and whether the Sisters can expect etcetera. The next time I'm mentioned, it's because (hold on to your hat, Reader) she's called up Medusa, or rather she's tried to call *me* (she's got my name from the visitors book at the archives, my old number from the telephone book), and gotten Medusa instead, who of course tells her that no, Professor Venner doesn't live here anymore, but yes, she does know where he lives.

I'd been thinking about it the last couple of days and what I decided was I decided to fight back. So tonight I waited until I saw him out there with that telescope thing of his and then changed into my town clothes and went out the side door. I had to keep close to the pasture wall until I reached the far field and then climb over a fence onto the road. It took me twenty minutes or so to walk into town. I had to keep turning around to make sure he wasn't catching up to me on his bicycle.

In the old days—before we had it out, Rachel—I used to feel like a spy going into town like that, hanging out in the library reading Vogue, *or the YMCA or even, that once, slipping into the lounge side of The Adam's Apple. At the college, I'd sit at a table in the Student Union with some french fries and pretend to be studying, the whole time watching the world out of the corner of my eye, the fraternity guys playing cards at the table next to me, the jukebox going while a guy* and a girl made out in a corner booth. And the whole time I expected to be caught, as if there were something fluorescent about being who I was, never mind my blue jeans and college windbreaker, something that marked me, my face, my eyes, the way I walked, as different.

I kept it up for a year, all the time with ideas of leaving the village, at least with ideas of thinking about leaving, and then, after New York, quit.

[New York?]

And now he's got me doing it again. Though not with any idea of trying the world on for size. Now I only go with specific objectives in mind. Tonight the objective was to turn the tables and spy on him for once.

And, well, you can call the police after all, Rachel. Because he's got photos of me, hundreds of them, taped up all over the steeple walls. And he's got everything ever written about us, books and articles and you name it. I couldn't believe my eyes at first. It made me feel so queer. Was this man crazy? The kind you read about after they've murdered seven nurses or something?

I rifled through his papers, thinking there might be some sort of diary about me or something, but there was nothing except sane-looking lecture notes, his daughter's kindergarten drawings, some scholarly-looking article he must be writing. I went through his clothes, checked his coat pockets, even pawed through his laundry. But he seems to live like a monk, nothing but the essentials. There was a jar of peanut butter next to the mattress, and some saltines. And a cat, watching me from up on one of the windowsills.

I sat on the edge of the mattress and tried to think. Was he in love with me? Was that it? Or did he want to murder me?

Back outside, instead of heading home, I wandered around the campus, across the dark quad, out behind the gym where there was a nighttime basketball game going on, then into the library where I zigzagged through the stacks. Suppose he was in love with me? What did that mean? And suppose he wanted to kill me. What did that mean? Though if you

*think about it killing me makes more sense. Because he would
be killing the idea of me. The Shaker idea. That's what those
mass murderers do, don't they?*

*On the other hand, maybe he just thinks I'm beautiful and
wants to take photographs of me.*

*When I crossed the quad again, I noticed his bike was in
the bike rack and the light was on up in the steeple. I thought
I could see him sitting in one of the windows. I went into the
building across the way, the art building, and climbed up to
the second floor. I found a classroom that looked out onto the
quad and went and stood at the window. He was in there, in
the steeple window, just sitting.*

[Good thing Venner didn't have his gun in hand.]

Well.

*I have at different moments imagined him violently at-
tacking me or shyly approaching me in the pasture or appearing in my room in the middle of the night, but I had not
imagined him sabotaging my taxi and then pretending to
have just happened along.*

*At first I thought he wasn't going to come this week. He
wasn't in the mall when I was doing my shopping. I looked for
him, though perhaps he was finally being discreet, keeping an
aisle away from me in the supermarket maybe or maybe
watching me from the top of the escalator. But he wasn't
there. I had a fleeting thought that he somehow knew that I'd
been up in his steeple. And instead of him scaring me away,
I'd scared him. But back outside when the taxi wouldn't start
and he came by, offering to help without even once glancing
back at me, I knew this was it, this was the day I was going to
find out.*

*But I didn't find out. Or I found out, but what I found out
is that all he wants is to make fun of me. And that doesn't
make sense. Not that someone would want to make fun of
me—that happens all the time—but how do you reconcile
that with the photos and all the time he spends out here at the*

archives, not to mention in the bushes? All that, just to make fun of me? I felt angry, and strangely, betrayed. As if I'd trusted him in some queer way. I was so angry I deliberately banged the door into his knee. I feel a little silly for all the thought I've given him, and the stupid dreaming. I'm embarrassed at myself.

Anyway, is that it? Was he just trying to provoke me? Make me say something or come out of my Shakerness somehow? Did he feel like the only way he could reach me was to rile me? Or was he just nervous, having me at last, and it came out that way? Or maybe he thinks it's just a big game, like I don't take my life seriously and he's in on the joke, and everything today was supposed to be a giant wink of collusion between us. Like I'm aware of the ludicrousness of being a Shaker on the verge of the twenty-first century and am just keeping it up out of a sense of drama or perversity. Like my Shakerness is a camouflage from behind which I can watch the world with impunity. Like he was saying: I know that you know that I know—

But if that's true, if it was all an elaborate attempt to strike some sort of secret joke between us, why did he get so panicky at the end? I mean he really did. He got like he was crazy with—with I don't know what. If I hadn't been so angry, I would have been scared of him. Him and his photos of me. And yet he seemed, I don't know, tender of me. Calling me by my name, calling me Sister as if he were used to talking to me in his head. I'd never heard a man call me Sister before. Not that way.

Boy, I don't know.

The choices seem to be these:

1. He's in love with me.
2. He wants to kill me.
3. Both.

And that's the end.

Reader, is that what I look like to her? (Reader, is that what I look like to you?) I shut the refrigerator door and climb the two flights up to her room. I'm going to put the volume back but I'm also fighting the urge to wake her and tell her I'm not a rapist, I'm not a mass murderer, I'm not trying to make fun of her, I'm not just another Ben or Terry Moses trying to see if she's wearing a bra. But by the time I get up there I realize how impossible it all is, how impossible the dream of my bruised soul taking the balm of her inviolate spirit. (Not to mention that from a certain moral angle Venner can be viewed as *precisely* another Terry Moses trying to see if she's wearing a bra.) In the end I just place the diary back on its shelf, spend a Quasimodo-ish moment gazing at her sleeping beauty, and then crawl back through the sluice on my belly (*cf.* an earlier polluter of an earlier Eden). I start pedaling townward, but whether it's a lack of oxygen due to sleep deprivation or simply the crushed state of my spirit, I only make it as far as Medusa's. But Medusa is with the Gorgons up at Lake George for the week. And Eve is with Sally's sister. I use my key and go inside the house anyway, go inside and gaze at the treasonous artifacts of my former life. I take a shower but that doesn't help. Neither does David Letterman, searching for love letters in Sally's drawers, self-abuse. I end up draining a bottle of bourbon and falling asleep on the couch. On the couch, Gentle Reader, because I can't bear the thought of Sally's bed.

CHAPTER SIX

SELF-TORTURE AS AN APHRODISIAC

And for the next several days I live in the ghost of my former marriage, moping from room to room during the bad moments, playing slapjack with Eve on her bedroom floor during the good. Toward the middle of the week I get a phone call from Medusa up at Lake George, and then on Sunday another, only this time it's from New York, where she's talking with some agent. In the morning she's meeting with a couple of record producers, she says, can I handle Eve until the middle of the week? And could I call Rick at The Missionary Position and cancel for Tuesday night? I can tell by the control in her voice that someone's with her. I ask if she's got a new drummer yet and she says she's way past that now. I don't ask what she means.

Instead I bundle Eve into the baby seat on the back of my bike and take her out for a spin. She tries to keep a conversation going, shouting into my back that Marilyn Monroe has died, Miss America too, though Helen of Troy is still moving a little.

"People can die too," she says. "Not just hamsters."

"Right," I answer, realizing it's the pets at daycare she's talking about.

"When you're dead you can't do anything."

"You want an ice cream?" I ask, in spite of it's being late September and chilly.

"You live . . ." she says.

"A milk shake?"

". . . and then you die."

I buy her a lime sherbet, hoping the color of life will rub off on her.

This is my daughter Eve whom I've been hiding from you, Reader. I used to adore her right down to her tiny toes, but these days she gives me the creeps. She's been morbid her whole short life, even as an infant, it seems to me now, always dazzled by darkness, going for midnight walks in her mother's Snuggly, eyes wide-open, always a fan of somber-hued books, music in the minor key. Dinosaurs, dodo birds, the worms go in/the worms go out, you name it: if it's dead or dying, my daughter's enamored of it. What this means I don't know, but I like to think it's a way she has of relishing life, a kind of self-torture that lets her feel first the abstract play-act of her own death and then the exquisite reality of living. I remember once during a January thaw finding a lizard with its head half out of its hole and trying to explain hi-bernation to her, and how she kept saying the lizard was dead and didn't know it. I gave up and just watched her peering at the half-frozen thing, watched her tuck away the cold horror of it, until finally with the strangest smile she turned her face to the sun: a three-year-old feeling the deep egotism of the alive.

From the ice cream parlor we go to the college library, where for no particular reason we spend an hour hanging around the BT 600s. She goes up and down the stacks, pulling out the occasional leatherbound book, whether because her instinctual fingers are drawn to the dead animal hide or the dead knowledge inside I don't know. I sit on the carpet under the buzzing lights and take down books my sweet Sally has read, books on Mariology grading into Mariolatry, looking for her handwriting in the margins, find the ten-year-old due dates stamped in the back, the May 5 dates I know are hers. It's a sad thing, dead love, isn't it? I can almost feel a twenty-year-old Sally Shannon in the antique library air, in the hush of the air conditioner, Sally with her pixie cut, her carrel heaped high with books, Sally who doesn't even know who John Venner is yet, though she gives him weird looks now and then, who has neglected to check out the books she's using for her term paper (a fact Venner ascertains one spring afternoon when she goes to the bathroom and he just happens to be loitering in the stacks), Sally who finds out when she comes back from the bathroom that someone has stolen all those unchecked-out books.

Reader, it was an act of desperation. I checked them out myself, making sure to write my name legibly, even including my campus extension so she could get in touch with me easily. It took her two days to figure things out. When finally she called me she told me she knew who I was, that I was the kind of person who'd steal someone's class notes just before an exam, who'd steal library reserve material, the kind of person who'd dump an alkali into someone's lab experiment just to screw it up, and that she was going to file a complaint with the College Judiciary Committee. In the meantime, no she wasn't going to give me a chance to explain, in the meantime she wanted her books back. Did I understand? A couple of days later I received a letter from the dean of students instructing me to write a report about the incident. Instead I wrote a letter full of love and obscenity and sent it to Sally via campus mail.

Some days I believe it was the love that won her; others I know it was the obscenity. She came to my dorm room white with nerves or embarrassment or anger or her own profanity

(I never really realized which, if any, or maybe all), came and sat on the corner of my bed while I told her I loved her, I loved the way she looked and the way she talked; I loved the way she wrote her name on her notebooks; I loved the thick glasses she wore when she didn't have her contacts in and the iron-red nail polish she put on on weekends (and the way she let it rust out during the week); I loved the questions she asked in class, the sound of her voice quizzing and unsatisfied, the way she pronounced Spinoza's *amor dei intellectualis;* loved the whiff of her soul glimpsed in the marginalia she left in her library books; loved the way her rear end sliced from side to side when she walked, the way the curve of her shoulders reiterated the curve of her etcetera; loved the way she was flushing and blushing even now while I talked; loved in short, every frigging thing about her and what was she going to do about it? For a moment she looked like she was going to haul off and slug me that's what she was going to do about it, then for a moment like she was simply going to get up and walk out, then like she was going to control herself and tell me a thing or two, buster. But O! dear Reader! Paint putti in the margins of this page! Whatever the previous urgings I had been proprietor of—oh, you know, the monstrous myste-rium of the loins—they were naught as compared to the bliss of Sally's soul (*cum* body, I admit). There followed a couple of months of essential ecstasy, the incomparable pleasure of sleeping two to a twin bed, watching a supple Sally on the tennis courts, a various Venner quoting Aquinas, Boethius, Julian the Apostate, reading and writing together in the library, meeting in the cul-de-sac of the BT 600s, mak-ing out with Sally's back against the ribbed spines of centu-ries of Mariolatry (Venner pressing into her a bit too hard and almost causing the stacks to topple). When summer arrived she got a job with a produce distributor and I hired on with my stonemason again, and every day at noontime she would come to me wherever I was, come to me in her plucky Toyota laden like Persephone with grapes and plums and nectarines, and while my partners sat scummy with the dirt of this earth, we would feast upon our fruits and talk of Isis and Goethe's *Ewig-Weibliche* and the Doctrine of Perpetual Virginity.

Now I'd call that essence, wouldn't you?

But alas! the truth is it wasn't all Persephone and persimmons. Even then there was in Sally a leaning toward a different sort of essence, a kind of essence of the ersatz. Coming across *amplexus reservatus* in some out-of-the-way article on Catholic sexual practice in the sixteenth century (*amplexus reservatus:* the conjoining of the married male and female in the sexual state but without the movement usually accompanying said state, a static activity sanctioned by the Church to allow an expression of sexual love without the attendant risk of a new soul getting started), she insisted we give it a try. So we did, and though Venner felt sort of stupid the whole time (try it, Reader, and see for yourself), his twenty-year-old fiancée seemed to find something in the static intensity, in the contact without effect, in the love without loving, that held some sort of meaning for her. And then—I blush to relate it—there was her Elvis collection: on her dorm walls photos of the King taped side by side with the Blessed Virgin, his records, his movies, an Elvis ashtray brought home from her pilgrimage to Graceland spring vacation junior year, a statue of Jesus with Elvis's head, condoms with his face printed on them, a scrapbook of articles on his Resurrection in Des Moines, Denver, Bozeman, a news story of his appearing like the Virgin of Guadalupe to a trio of teenagers in a Houston laundromat. The kicks she got out of this were various and (to Venner) unfathomable (here she is at a Kappa Delta Phi keg party, lip-synching "Jailhouse Rock" while dancing an entire dictionary of dance steps, both period (*i.e.* fifties-ish) and anachronistic (*i.e.* moonwalking), a cellarful of anti-Vennerites urging her on), but it all had something to do with a kind of pop syncretism, the welding of icon to icon ("Hail Elvis," she used to say in postcoital lethargy, "full of shit, blessed be the fruit of thy tomb"), a love of idolatry that should have warned Venner of coming destruction, not to mention heartbreak and lawyers' fees.

Oh, Mother Ann! You don't know how it was that first year of marriage, before Little Debbie Snack Cakes and Monica the Madonna (students with whom I ventured a passionate celibacy, *vide infra*). The truth is, I loved my wife. I loved the sound of her voice, the vaccination scar on her bicep; I loved the sight of her tiny shoes unfooted and forlorn in the corner; I loved the various Marys Scotch-taped to the walls of her study, the duplicate Sallys in the morning mirror, the tubes and jars in the shower, the cinnamon smell of her underwear. I loved talking with her about her dissertation ("On the Physicality of the Virgin Mary"), listening to her differentiate *dulia* from *hyperdulia* worship, reading aloud an anonymous Ethiopic text on the sensuous beauty of the Blessed Virgin, discussing Aquinas's concupiscible appetite, Venner's ditto, nineteenth-century Catholic pornography, and at night comparing the consubstantiation of Mary's breasts with my sweet Sally's. For a couple of years there I was a happy man. I participated in the common weal, sat on college committees concerned with community relations and academic honesty, rescued A, E, I, O, U and Sometimes-Why from certain death, and at the end of each day came home to a house with forty-two prints of the Blessed Virgin (and only a half-dozen of Elvis) and love between the sheets. I had the sacred and profane all in one shot and damn my soul didn't realize it.

And damn your soul too, Sally. Because it was you who wandered first. It was you who left the consolations of philosophy and grew your hair into snakes and started parading your black underwear—*my* black underwear, the black underwear I bought you—in front of the world. What made her do it—what serpent in what garden—Venner didn't understand then and he still doesn't. To hear Medusa tell it now, some private dialectic had started her thinking that the only way for her to move from Existence into Essence in this our postmodern America was to get her body on MTV, to drop the Virgin Mary like a hot potato and shoot for an electronic Assumption, to get her immaculate self assumed body and soul into the glitzy heaven of Hollywood: Medusa become immortal along with Lucy and Colonel Klink and the June Taylor Dancers.

At first it was just a weekend bar band while she was finishing up her dissertation. They were called the Orchids and they played Top 40 here in town at The Adam's Apple, then got a few gigs at the ski resorts over in Vermont, then better money up in Conway and the White Mountains. She used to pack a bag every weekend and go, and I didn't mind. I kind of liked having a sexual intellectual for a wife. She'd play North Conway or Portsmouth and on the way home stop in at the UNH library for some article on whether Mary had a vagina or not or an ILL book imprinted with the Vatican's *Nihil Obstat* and then back at the house sit reading with her thick glasses slipping down her nose while I hummed a happy hymn in the kitchen. After each draft of each chapter we'd go for a ride to talk about it, driving through New England like we used to do in graduate school, sneaking into Catholic churches to check out the stained-glass windows, peering into confessionals, talking about the this and the that of Catholic sexuality and the theological implications of orgasm. (*E.g.,* was orgasm a physical type of spiritual ecstasy? And if it was, did that make the sexual act a form of worship? Or more: of union with God?) We batted saints about—mostly Aquinas and Alphonsus—batted about the ethics of different marital positions, the hell of *coitus interruptus*, the purgatory of *amplexus reservatus*, the heaven of *delectationem veneream*, until we got so worked up we had to find a sheltered parking spot and climb into the back seat.

But sometime in the second year things began to go wrong. Whether it had anything to do with a marked increase of Elvis sightings in the late eighties or, more reasonably, with her getting pregnant I don't know (though I *do* know it was Venner pricking holes in his condoms—Venner afraid of losing his wonderful wife—that allowed the Holy Ghost of his sperm into Sally's penetralia in the first place), but she started getting depressed, tired of her dissertation, of me, of things as they were. It was a feeling of . . . of . . . *evaporation*, she said, not a good kind of evaporation (What does she mean by that? wondered pre-Medusa Venner; answers post-Medusa Venner: The evaporation of the media star, of the Visual Image, the transubstantiation of the self into 211,000 pixels and the zapping of the ionosphere with an image that is at once us and not us, a kind of *amplexus reservatus* of Being), but a bad kind of evaporation, like she wasn't there anymore but wasn't anywhere else either. I smiled a husbandly smile and quoted some *Cosmo* quack on the doldrums of the second year of marriage, related my own experience of sophomore slump when writing my dissertation. I could see her trying to keep herself going, keep at it with the Virgin Mary, keep up her friendships, keep loving me. (Or maybe it wasn't *loving* me that was the problem, maybe it was never a question of love, but rather of isolation, of Sally exfoliating into Medusa and realizing along the way that the kind of teflon essence she imagined coated the souls who inhabited the video universe disallowed a loving and beloved husband, and that to get herself assumed into that particular heaven meant the shedding of all bodily attachments, does that ring a bell, Mother Ann?) At any rate, she got irritable and sullen and silent.

One day standing in the checkout line she saw an *Enquirer* headline about the Virgin Mary appearing to a cashier in a California convenience store. She bought the paper and read the story over and over again. I thought it was just a lark, but when the phone bill came that month there were all these charges for California numbers. I asked her about them, but she evaded me, said something about tracking down an unpublished dissertation. So, secretly I called the numbers. They were all for Jack-B-Nimble stores in and around Salinas, except one that was the home phone for someone named Diego who said yeah, some chick called him a few weeks ago about the Virgin Mary, who sure he saw all the time, but not in the Jack-B-Nimble and no he wasn't the guy in the *National Enquirer*, although yes his co-workers knew about his intimacy with the Blessed Virgin, but the fact was that whenever he saw her it was always on TV, on the VHF channels he meant, because on UHF you get Jimi Hendrix. . . .

After that she began reading the tabloids, sitting in bed or on the couch in a kind of quiet hysteria, looking for some sign in the words, in the stories about misborn babies and resurrected movie stars and a virgin birth in Galveston. Just what signal she was expecting, what star in what sky, I don't know. But I would catch sight of her sitting at her desk, pages of manuscript spread out before her, a rapt emptiness on her face. Or I would come home from class and find her lying on the bed, remote control in hand, watching Tower of Power and MTV in quick succession. The forty-two prints of the Virgin Mary began to decrease in number, one here, one there. (Even more scary was the fact that the Elvis prints didn't increase.) I tried to talk to her about it, but either she wouldn't respond or she'd pull out some article from *Redbook* on *pre*partum depression and tell me to never mind, after the baby had come she would be all right. She'd learn some new songs with the Orchids, finish her thesis, love me.

And then one night, in bed, in her seventh month, with "Miami Vice" in the background, she experienced her *voluptatem* so hard I thought she was going to turn herself inside out. Why it happened I don't know. She was turned so that she could see the TV, and although I can't swear she was watching it the whole time, who knows but what Sonny's tan or the cut of Tubb's clothes or the slick guitar licks of the musical score or the immaculate sexuality of the airwave universe or the advertisement that came on in the middle of it all had something to do with it. Afterward there was this euphoric look on her face and I heard her say under her breath, "So *that's* it."

"What's it?" I asked, but she didn't answer and I didn't press her.

In the hospital for Eve's birth, she spent the three days of her convalescence watching TV: monster-truck shows, costumed wrestlers, "Soul Train," anything that was shallow, glossy, glitzy. Home, in a single half hour on the phone, she fired every member of the Orchids and then spent the first month of Eve's life auditioning backup musicians from all over New England, changing the name of the band to the Gorgons, practicing her makeup in the bathroom mirror, slowly creating Medusa out of Max Factor and Victoria's Secret. When I tried to call her Sally she wouldn't answer. When I tried to get her to tell me why Medusa, she laughed. Didn't I see that it was perfect? No, I didn't, what did it mean? It didn't mean anything. It was just a name, a persona, a visual image. It was perfect.

"In that case, why not Circe?" I wanted to know.

"Why not?" she agreed.

"Why not Medea or the Sibyl or Tiresias in his female phase?"

"Why not indeed?"

"I don't get it."

She smiled a secret sort of smile. "Do you remember the cha-cha theory of love?"

"Yes," I said. The cha-cha theory of love was an undergraduate idea of ours which held that the only way love can survive the long term is for one lover to always be pursuing and the other receding, though as in the cha-cha, the partner doing the pursuing and the partner doing the receding have to alternate. "Yes," I said. "What about it?"

"That's what I'm after."

"The cha-cha?" I asked. "With me?"

"No."

"With whom then?"

She blushed, whether with pleasure or embarrassment I couldn't tell. "With the world," she said.

I closed my eyes.

"It's like with the Blessed Virgin. She's doing an eternal cha-cha, only the difference is she's always the one in recession. The world pursues. Same thing with Elvis. Same thing, really, with any rock or movie star. The world loves them because they're always there, vulnerable, losing in love, or *appearing* to lose in love, and telling the world all about it, and yet the world can't get to them, they're locked away in vinyl or celluloid or nowadays in binary numbers. They're there but they're not there. It's the way to win at love."

My head was spinning. "You're dumping me for this?" I said.

"I'm not dumping you."

"You're dumping me for a binary cha-cha with the world?"

"Nobody's dumping anybody."

She talked me into signing for a second mortgage on the house and used the money to buy new sound equipment and to rent a farmhouse over on the backside of Spirit Mountain where she and the Gorgons went into a six-month rehearsal and songwriting hibernation. For his part, Venner took to staying the occasional night in the chapel steeple. He took to buying cups of coffee for pretty coeds. He took to wondering about the twenty-year-old Shakeress out at New Eden.

(Listen to this: on the night of the Gorgons' debut at The Missionary Position I saw Medusa have an orgasm on stage. It was during the guitar bridge to "Essential Ecstasy," just after she'd finished singing. The room was really going (the Gorgons were good, I have to admit) and Medusa was just standing there, in the middle of the stage, legs pressed together, eyes closed, letting her snakes dangle onto her shoulder, moving her head this way and that so the tips of her hair brushed along her skin. She had a push-up bra on, and her garters and stockings. From my table along the wall I could see the strain come on her face, then the fainting smile, then the tremors. It was as if she were feeling herself touched by every person in the room, but from a distance, anonymous, unconnected. She had to lean on the amp behind her to keep from falling over. When the last verse came around she was hoarse and off-key and ecstatic.)

Is it any wonder that I sought solace in Little Debbie Snack Cakes and Monica the Madonna? (Also Kyrie Alison, but she was eager to go all the way which was more than

Venner had in mind.) I'll refrain from detailing the horrors of intramural pursuit, the little lies and flatteries, the ruse of congruent souls, the embarrassed this and the mock-shameful that. Little Debbie Snack Cakes was nineteen, a willow of a girl, skinny-thighed and limp-haired, and a virgin, I thought, until on our last day together I learned of Eddie MacSomething. And Monica the Madonna was a Catholic with a miraculous medal hanging around her neck who had to be talked into every step of every sin. Gentle Reader, it was a lot of work. I searched the groves of their souls for shade, for balm, for the seabreeze of innocence. Sometimes I took them on my rides through New England, threading my Peugeot into Boston, down to the Combat Zone, where I exposed them to the carriers of carnal disease as an antidote to the common weal. There was lots to see, dirty streets, lit-up marquees, homoerotic posters, whores, junkies, all-night pizza stands, winos in the doorways, sun-bleached photos of starlets Now Appearing. From time to time I'd hear the Gorgons' music blasting out of a club on Boylston or down in Kenmore Square. We'd pay the cover and sit at the back and listen (in one, with closed-circuit TVs four to every wall: Medusa in her first electronic avatar), Debbie or Monica saying, "That's your wife? Really? *Really?* Wow!"

It was in just such a depressed state that I started mailing off pornography to Eldress Rachel and the Sisters. Oh, just a puny perversion at first—I was sick for Sally; I was sick for love in the BT 600s—but it came to acquire the patina of a pathology. In the archives I searched for photos of teenage Shakeresses—Shakeresses on the verge of maturity, college-age Shakeresses, Shakeresses unable to conceal the weaponry of their breasts under their maidenly mantles—and licking a postage stamp in the Leominster or Nashua post office, kept the icon of this or that bosom, the image of Eldress Rachel as a twenty-something-year-old alive like a centerfold in my mind. It was the beginnings of self-torture as an aphrodisiac, of an awareness of the vitality of dispossession. I was invigorated with desire for the dead: two centuries of envirgined

Shakeresses pure and unpokable. It seemed a way to keep desire alive.

Back home I sat alone nights with a one-year-old Eve, a two-year-old Eve, a three-year-old Eve, while a twenty-eight-year-old Sally, a twenty-nine-year-old Medusa, a thirty-year-old Deusie band-vanned it all over New England. I remember the slamming of car doors out front at 3 A.M., the muddy counterpoint of voices—Sally's soprano and some dance floor Don Juan's bass—then the sound of a car pulling away and her high heels hurrying up the walk. I got used to hearing about New York agents, about demo tapes making the rounds of recording companies, and seeing every six months or so on the kitchen table a new batch of photographers' proofs of my wife in various states of dramatic undress. She joined the Body-Rite Fitness Club so she could work out on the Nautilus machines, toning her arms, her legs, her chest. She read *Rolling Stone* and *Variety* and *People*. She made it herself a couple of times into the local papers, once a feature in the Boston *Phoenix*. Two winters ago one of the New York agents said she had the voice and the face and the body but not the band, and out of the blue offered her a contract as a lady wrestler. Same name, same hair, same underwear. After a week of studying wrestling on cable, searching for metaphysical essence in the sham and showmanship, she turned it down.

It was during those three years that A, E, I, O and U died their alphabetical deaths. Somewhere between O and U we got divorced.

And now because I don't live with her anymore, Eve wants to know whether I'm really her father or whether, get this, the Holy Ghost is. I ask her who's been telling her about the Holy Ghost and she says Auntie Dante (her daycare duenna and one of the founding mothers of the local Pentecostal church). She says if I was really her father I'd be living with her like everybody else's father she knows so it must be the Holy Ghost who's her father. I try to point out the logical lacuna in her hypothesis, *i.e.* okay, Daddy doesn't live with you but the Holy Ghost doesn't live with you either, does he, and of course with Auntie Dante holding up cue cards she tells me that yes, he does, he lives with everybody. Venner gets out the Wild Turkey.

And dreams of the antiseptic air of New Eden. The simple truth is I can't accept a world where essence is a Visual Image. I need the intestines of belief, the self-torture of the Shaker, the deep circuitry behind the 211,000 pixels. Living in a steeple is not enough. Surrounding myself with photos of the last virgin in America is not enough. Judge, I say (we're cutting to the courtroom scene where Sister Sabbathday is seeking her court injunction), Judge, let me tell you about self-torture as an aphrodisiac, about the longevity of virgin celibates, about the monstrous mysterium of the loins, about a certain pronunciation of Spinoza's *amor dei intellectualis*, and then, if you must, condemn me to the delirium of impossible love, but don't forbid me the pursuit of my particular purity.

"I'm a desperate man," I tell Medusa when she gets back from New York. She drops something that looks like a contract on the kitchen table in front of me.

"I'm dumping you after all," she says, smiling.

CHAPTER SEVEN

ON THE METAPHYSICS OF WHITE PICKET FENCES

Class, the stone walls demarcating the earthly paradise of New Eden are a mess. Built sometime in the first quarter of the nineteenth century when the land was cleared, and for a hundred years maintained by the hands of celibate men, they've grown ragged and dissolute. What ought to be the ordered demarcation of heaven on earth has become the icon of a fallen world. It is your professor's task, as he sees it, to replumb Paradise.

So a couple of days after Medusa returns from New York, I dig out of the garage my mason's twine, my work gloves, a five-pound sledge, a spirit level, a couple of plumb bobs, load everything into my toolbox and drive out to New Eden. There's the usual Shaker softness about the place, morning mist, etcetera. In a mood less urgent I might take the time to rhapsodize—say, about the picket fences of New Eden, how they run across the land like the keyboard of the Lord, the sharps and flats of positive and negative space, and about how I mean to become the maestro of that keyboard, the basso of the white wood, the descant of the airy in-between, my fingers playing upon the soul (not to mention the body) of Sister Sabbathday, tra-la-la—but no, it's strictly business this morning. I haul my tools over the wet grass, past the moody eyes of a pair of cows, out to a stone wall that marks the boundary of the front pasture and the herb garden. Sabbathday's window happens to give on the pasture, but there's no sign of her, just the red eye of the morning sun reflected in the glass.

The wall is so tumbledown there's no point in trying to refit the stones. Nothing will do but to dismantle the ones that are left and start over. It takes a solid hour to push and kick and heave the first thirty feet clear. The ground is covered with hysterical centipedes. What the Sisters up at the Dwelling House think of all this I don't know. There's nothing stirring on the hill, at least nothing that I can see. I run a mason's line, hang a few plumb bobs, a line level, and with something like hope in me, begin the slow mysticism of building a stone wall.

At first I keep expecting a call from the house, or a police car, or a delegation of virgins wending their way through the tall grass, but stone follows stone and nothing happens. There's the occasional slamming of a car door, a tourist glimpsed now and then, but no sign that anyone is aware of the trespasser in the front pasture. Toward midmorning I take a break. My arms are sore, my hands too, and I think of the fitness freaks at the Body-Rite Fitness Club with some envy. Too, I'm hungry and thirsty and I haven't even a thermos of water with me, but some instinct tells me I can't leave now. I've got a purchase on salvation and I'm not moving unless I meet an irresistible force. Besides, the work feels good. Even the hunger and the thirst feel good, as if a touch of self-torture is indeed good for the soul. When I get up to work again, in spite of its being late September, I strip my shirt off.

And I'm at it for I don't know how long when suddenly someone asks what I think I'm doing. I turn and peer uphill. It's Sister Sabbathday.

"What?" I manage to say. She's standing on a little rise, just this side of the herb garden. She's dressed in her usual: nineteenth-century gown, twentieth-century sneakers, cap like an advertisement. The breeze blows her skirts against her thighs. Like Adam, I am abruptly aware of dirt and sweat and bare skin.

"What do you think you're doing?" she says again.

"I didn't see you coming."

She wades through the grass until she reaches the first of the spilled rocks. "Eldress has requested that you stop."

"Eldress?"

"We want you to go."

"We?"

She makes an exaggerated show of patience. "I'm asking you to go. Leave us alone."

I turn away from her, gaze down the pasture to the pond, across to the foot of Spirit Mountain in the distance. There are dozens of stone walls, all in disrepair. I gesture at them with a gloved hand and then turn back to the destruction around me. "It's a shame," I say.

"Everything's a shame," she answers. "And you're not helping any. Please go."

"No," I say and pick up a stone.

"I told you I'd call the police if you didn't quit hanging around here."

"So call them."

"Don't think I won't."

I drop the stone in place but it doesn't fit. I turn it this way and that and then roll it back onto the ground. "What do you think?" I say. "You think you can hog all the salvation to yourself?"

"Don't start."

"You think you can live on the last sanctified ground in America and keep everyone else off of it?"

She looks for a moment like she's going to laugh. "So what is it with you?" she says. "Are you just nuts or what?"

This takes Venner aback. Not only the colloquial vocabulary, but the sting of the thing. "What I am," I say with some dignity, "is a desperate man. And neither you nor your Eldress nor the police are going to keep me from saving my soul."

"If it's capable of salvation," she says.

I stop work and gaze at her. For someone who suspects me of being a serial killer, she doesn't have the proper awe.

"At any rate," she says, "you'll have to save it someplace else. We don't want or need you here. We want you to stop. We want you to go."

"It's not a question of what *you* want or need, Sister. It's what *I* need."

She takes a deep breath, as if she's dealing with a child or an imbecile or a lunatic, and then says with exaggerated precision: "Eldress has requested that you stop doing what you're—"

"I'm replumbing Paradise."

"—that you stop replumbing Paradise and get off the property."

"If she wants me off, let her come tell me herself."

"*I'm* telling you."

"No dice, Lara."

And I turn back to my stones. After a minute—and oh! it's difficult not to look up and see the expression on her face—I hear the sound of her dress moving through the high grass away from me.

For the next hour the stones fit with a kind of Zen affinity. I'm feeling a little faint from hunger, a little faint from the manner in which I have just raised the stakes, but I keep going. A couple of wandering tourists ask me what I'm doing, but I don't answer, *vide* the Orders Concerning Intercourse with the World's People. Sometime in the deep afternoon, I am aware of a couple of female bodies making their way through the high grass. It's Eldress Rachel with Sister Sabbathday backing her up, but I don't give them the satisfaction of seeing me look up at them. They come and plant themselves along my mason's line.

"Mr. Venner," Eldress Rachel says—whether she knows my name from Sabbathday or the archives I don't know—"Mr. Venner, do you see that wire there?"

"What?"

"That wire," she says and points to a line leading out of the Dwelling House to the road and, by implication, to the world's people. "You don't want your name printed in the Police Blotter, do you?"

I gaze at Sister Sabbathday. She is mute and expressionless and beautiful. I throw down the rock I've been trying to fit and hoist another one. "You should be ashamed of yourself," I say.

"What?" Eldress says. I don't answer so she turns to Sister Sabbathday. "What did he say?"

"He says you should be ashamed of yourself," Sabbathday answers. There's just the faintest tone of mockery in her voice, whether of me or her Eldress I can't tell.

"Ashamed?" Rachel says as if it's a thought that's never occurred to her. She turns back to me. "Why ashamed?"

"The Lord gave you Paradise to caretake and you've let it fall to ruin." I reject another stone. "I expect to see a serpent or two before I'm through."

They exchange looks as if the question of my sanity has been a subject between them. "We'll take care of *our* shame, Mr. Venner," Rachel says. "You take care of yours."

"I am," I answer, and I fit a stone that doesn't quite fit, just for punctuation. "These fences are the right angles of the Lord. They are the literal representatives of a moral belief and you have let them degenerate into disorder and ... and ..."

"Turpitude," Sabbathday supplies. We exchange looks.

"If you can't fix them, I can," I say to Rachel.

"They are ours to fix, not yours."

"You don't have a patent on purity, Eldress. You're the

caretaker of an idea, that's all. And if you can't properly do the caretaking, you should let those who can."

"Insulting me is not going to help," Rachel says.

"I don't mean to insult you. I'm sorry."

"Being polite isn't going to help either."

And for a moment we simply face one another off. "I'm busy," I say finally and bend down for another stone.

"I'm ordering you to stop," says Rachel, and in her voice there's something of the woman who kicked chairs over Sabbathday's TV interview.

"No," I answer and there's something in Venner's voice too. In the distance, Sister Chastity is trying to find her way through the herb garden.

"I'm ordering you," Rachel says. "I'm the Eldress. I'm ordering you."

"No."

"I'm ordering you. I'm Eldress. In New Eden, what I say goes."

"I've got the gift," I tell her. "I woke up this morning with the gift and the gift's telling me to build stone walls."

"I've got the gift too," she says. "And my gift overrules yours. Now leave."

I lift a boulder that ought to be beyond my strength and with a roar of masculinity drop it in place. I feel flushed and dizzily triumphant. If Venner is going to go down, he's going to go down swinging. Sister Chastity is making her way through the long grass toward us. She is fat and senile and smiling.

"Sister," Rachel says quietly to Sabbathday and with her forehead indicates Chastity coming down the hill. It's an imperative gesture, but curiously Sabbathday doesn't do whatever it is she's supposed to do.

"Lunch!" Sister Chastity calls out. Rachel turns with what sounds like an oath.

"Sister, you should be back at the house."

"I've made you lunch, Brother Michael!"

"Sister!"

She comes down onto the matted grass where I've been working. She's got an honest-to-God Shaker basket on her arm ($800) and she's smiling at me like we're old friends.

"Oh, thank you, Sister," I say and take the basket from her. "Is this for me?" She nods, beaming. "For me?" I repeat and open the basket. There's a box of baking powder inside, also a freshly laundered dish towel, a spark plug and an unopened jar of jelly. "Oh, it looks delicious," I say.

"Delicious," Chastity answers. She reaches up and touches my hair. "Delicious."

"Sister," Rachel says, "you have chores in the laundry."

"Delicious," she repeats and, spreading her skirts prettily around her, she sits on one of the rocks. Rachel glares at her. I lift the spark plug out of the picnic basket.

"Want to share?" I ask Sabbathday. She turns on the ice-maiden expression usually reserved for tourists. Rachel about-faces and starts uphill.

"I've been preparing myself," I call to her. "I've been searching my soul and what I've come to believe is that I need to be a Shaker. Notice I don't say 'want.' I *need* to be a Shaker. It's the only thing that can save me."

"Go to Chosen Land," Rachel calls back over her shoulder. "They might take you in."

"I need to be a Shaker *here*."

She stops for a moment. "Impossible."

"I need to be a Shaker here. I have a gift to be a Shaker here."

She starts back up the hill.

"I can help," I cry.

Sabbathday crosses to Chastity and takes her by the arm.

"Okay," I call after them. "You can get the police. Of course you can. And they'll haul me away. Okay, so you win. But that doesn't change things. Because from this instant onward I'm a Shaker. I'm a Shaker whether I'm here or in jail. I'm a Shaker and there's nothing you can do about it. I'm here. Me. Brother Venner. Get used to it!"

They go through the gate into the herb garden, Eldress

striding as best her eighty-nine-year-old legs will let her, and Sabbathday guiding Chastity by the arm. I kick a stone or two in triumph or defeat, who knows, unscrew the jelly jar and swab out a helping on my finger. I try to tie Chastity's dish towel around my head like a sweatband but it won't go. So I knot it around my neck like a bandanna instead. I watch them disappear around the corner of the Dwelling House and then get back to work.

When the police arrive, I'm a little sick from an overdose of jelly. They cross the field with that leather-creaking ease cops have when they're trying to show you they don't mean you any harm. They even spend a moment admiring the job I'm doing before they ask me to gather up my things. They lock my toolbox in the trunk of the squad car and drive me into town. At City Hall a sergeant asks me what I was doing and why I didn't stop when I was asked to. I try to answer as sane-sounding as I can, which is to say, I maximize the community-service angle and minimize the salvation stuff. Also I tell them I teach religion at the college, which seems to explain a lot. In the end they just take my name and address (I give them Medusa's), my phone number (ditto), and then drive me back out to Sally's car. They wait until I load my toolbox into the back seat and then, as if they mean to show they have confidence in me, drive away. No one asks about the dish towel around my neck.

The next morning I am up and out there by seven. I've brought a lunch with me. And a big cooler of ice water. This time it's a different pair of policemen who come to get me. They're not quite so polite. Or perhaps they've heard about me. They take my tools away and don't give them back. The desk sergeant charges me with trespassing and gives me a lecture. I try to tell him something about the boundaries of Paradise but he's not interested. I'm back on the street by eleven.

New levels cost close to forty dollars.

When they come the third time they tell me to assume the position. What position? I ask, and for an answer they spin me around and spread-eagle me just like on TV. Then they handcuff me to prove they mean business and drive me to the station. I'm charged with trespassing and destroying private property and a couple of other things I don't quite catch. They put me in a cell to await the assigning of a court date. I've never been in a cell before, but I'm comforted by thoughts of Mother Ann Lee spending weeks in prison for the dictates of her soul. I fall asleep on my cot and dream of Sabbathday handcuffed to her bed. Toward late afternoon, Sally shows up to retrieve me.

"Are you famous yet?" I ask her.

"What?"

"Are you on MTV yet?"

"V," she says. The police officer who's escorting us out of the building mugs a look but what's he know? We trot down to Sally's sister's car. "Is it true? Three times?" she asks, and when I don't answer: "Shoot, V. I thought this was an ideal love, not something to be put into practice."

I gaze out the windshield like your basic martyr.

"And what's building stone walls on other people's property got to do with it?"

"Not stone walls," I answer. "The right angles of the Lord."

"The Lord?" she says. "Which Lord is that?"

"Mine," I answer. "The one with the universal plumb bob."

She turns the car out Undermountain Road. "If I didn't know you . . ."

If she didn't know me, Reader, I wouldn't be in this mess.

We pick up Eve and Sally's sister Melanie, drive out to New Eden, where my old Peugeot is still parked at the side of the highway, and then head home. For the rest of the evening I play slapjack with Eve on the living-room floor, while out at the kitchen table Sally and Melanie talk of Medusa's new agent, black-and-white as a video statement, a Ron Woolf of Elektra Records, the possible dumping of the Gorgons, and when their voices drift to whispers, the sorry case of her former husband.

• • •

The following day I spend in the chapel. Sometimes-Why is pissed off from not having been fed in three days. Down in my office there's a stack of exams to be graded. I figure I'll act responsibly today, return my library books, look after my dependents, eat a balanced meal and in the meantime let the local virgins think they've won one.

But when the sun begins to go down I get antsy and a little crazy in my skin. I try to keep things even-keeled, to finish grading exams, sweep out my steeple, chant a mantra or two, but just after dark, yes, once again, Venner finds himself squatting in the weeds across the road from the Dwelling House. In the streetlight the picket fence that runs along the roadside shivers with the yes/no of white-painted wood and black in-between. Out a ways a stony serpent wriggles in right angles across the pasture. And in the deep distance, there are always the red radio eyes atop Spirit Mountain.

Sometime around ten o'clock the windows go dark. I wait another forty-five minutes for good measure and then cross the road, sneaky-Pete through the shadows over to the man-hole cover. In five minutes I'm through the sluice, into the kitchen and up the stairs. Reader, what this is about is I've got a note in my pocket, written out with a quill pen, a mysterious note to Eldress Rachel telling her in the voice of Mother Ann Lee to let me build the wall. It's desperate, I know, but I'm a desperate man, etcetera. I creep through the upstairs hall, past sleeping Antoinette's room, past a white-sheeted Sabbathday, to Rachel and Chastity's room. There I wait in the doorway until I'm sure they're asleep and then cross to a small table next to Rachel's bed. I'm about to put my note down and get out when I realize there's a pad already on the table. And a pen. I have a moment of indecision, and then pick up the pen and write on the pad: *Let him.* That's all,

none of the advice and scolding of my note, just *Let him,* off
the lines, shaky. I put the first note back in my pocket and
leave.

On the way out I can't make it past Sabbathday's room
without looking in. There's the same wallful of books, the
diaries, the shimmer of moonlit sheets, the virgin-white form
of the last Shakeress. She's lying on her side, head turned
toward me, one hand clasping the covers. It takes a moment
for me to realize her eyes are wide open.

"So go ahead."

I feel the scorch of adrenaline, and then an idiot's grin
trying to take over my face. I put my lips together to say
"What?" but nothing comes out. She lifts herself up onto her
elbow and whispers, "Whatever you've come to do—go ahead,
do it."

I can only stare at her, at the silhouette she makes against
the curtains, at the urgent incline of her shoulders.

"Please," I manage to whisper.

"I dare you."

Mother Ann, what kind of virgin is this?

"Go ahead."

I shake my head—denying what, I don't know—but I
shake my head and back out through the doorway. I almost
expect her to come after me, to follow me down the stairs into
the kitchen, infantry-style into the sluice. "Go ahead," I hear
her say, and I bang my elbows on the close brick trying to get
away from some phantom hand clutching at my ankle. Outside I kneel on the ground and whisper "Sabbathday" into
the black grass like a prayer. I say it over and over, but it's
"Lara" the grass answers back.

Up in my steeple I wait with the lights off for the police to
come. I've hidden my BB gun just in case they've had previous complaints and are in the mood to put two and two together. I climb up into the window that faces New Eden, Wild
Turkey in hand, and I wait and wait. I'm hoping when they
come they'll just think I'm drunk, and questions of sanity and
psychiatric evaluation will be forestalled. Nonetheless it's

breaking and entering we're talking about, and frankly, folks, Venner is up the creek and he knows it. Sometime around the criminal .10 blood level I get a little wobbly in the window, consider climbing down and going to bed, but I lean my head against the jamb and start counting stars instead . . . and the next thing I know Aurora is doing the rosy-fingered thing in the east and I'm cold and wet with dew. And still no police.

When I wake again I'm in bed, hung over, sheet-tortured, and Sometimes-Why is badgering me with questions, *e.g.* do I really think Eldress Rachel is going to wake up and think the spirit of Ann Lee has visited her? Or was the point of the shaky handwriting to make her think that she wrote the note herself in the middle of the night under the power of some gift? And don't I think, even if she had sufficient sympathy for the human heart not to call the police last night, Sister Sabbathday is going to spill the beans when she hears about the note? Isn't the jig, in short, up?

When the bells ring eight o'clock, I fumble my underwear on, my dirty clothes, and head over to the Faculty Club, where I down a quart of orange juice and try to figure just what cat-and-mouse game Sabbathday is playing. I run through a list of alternatives, A through D ending with Venner in jail, and when I can't stand it anymore head out Undermountain Road, whether to Sally's house or to New Eden I don't know. When I get near Sally's there's a black Porsche with New York plates parked in the driveway and since it's barely nine o'clock in the morning . . . oh, modern reader, you know what that means. I am left with Alternative E.

My tools are where I abandoned them two days ago. The plumb lines have sagged; there's a dusting of rust on my sledge. I try to stride out through the browning meadow but can only manage a trudge. I am on the lookout for snakes in the grass; also: police cars, sirens, the FBI up in Rachel's window, but the truth is I lift and lower rocks for a pure half hour without a sign of anything belligerent. The TV towers atop Spirit Mountain wink their usual winks; the quartet of sheep in the lower pasture ignores me; an autumn-stunned bumblebee buzzes by with no thought of stinging me. I feel like a defeated man, but isn't it just like the world not to accept me as such?

So I fit rock to rock waiting for destruction but get the gradual reality of a stone wall instead. The orange juice runs through me and sometime around midmorning I stop and pee in full view of the world, even take off my shirt for good measure—indecent exposure, lascivious carriage, etcetera—but no one's watching, it seems. I've left my gloves at the police station and my hands get bruised and sore but my hangover gradually dissolves and the truth is I'm not feeling too bad when, instead of a snaky Satan, it's Sister Sabbathday I see making her way toward me through the grass. I've got enough time to panic over what sort of face I should present to her—cool, cocky, collusive—but can only manage a kind of stupid impudence.

"Eldress would like to see you," she says in a toneless voice when she reaches the wall. "In the Elders' Room." Message delivered, she turns to go but as she does she calls out over her shoulder: "You're acquainted with the floor plan of the Dwelling House I take it?"

I have enough self-destruction left in me to want to call Slyboots Sabbathday on the carpet (we refer not only to last night's curious interview, but to the B & E of her visiting my steeple, to the question of her responsibility in reporting criminal activity, to you name it, Lara) but also enough self-preservation to admit she's overmatched me at present. I watch her head back through the pasture, wondering whether the slice of her rear end under her long dress isn't a tad exaggerated.

But for the moment there's the dirt of my hands, the sweat of my brow, the stink of my bodily being to worry about. This should not concern your true Shaker—work being the sincerest form of worship—but I am not feeling Shakerly and this dirt is more the mud of destruction than the dew of Paradise. I pick up my shirt and try to clean myself off, comb my fingers through my hair, then tuck and button and zip. Finally, unsure whether the jig is up or the game is afoot, I head up the hill toward the Dwelling House.

The Elders' Room is a small chamber just off the main hall. In the nineteenth century it was used for meetings and judgments of sin and salvation. When I enter, unescorted and deferent, Eldress Rachel is seated at a table with what looks like the village's bookkeeping before her. She has a brittle cleanliness about her, her cotton dress wrinkleless, her hair drawn tight across her scalp and held in by some invisible bun under her cap. She wears trifocals. When she speaks there's a quaver to her voice, the inroads of palsy. But for all that she has the self-assurance of a dictator.

"Please be seated, Mr. Venner."

I sit in a ladder-back chair. Mid-nineteenth-century. Four thousand dollars.

"Mr. Venner," she begins, "I'm told that you are a professor of religion at the college." She stops to scrutinize me. "That, plus the fact that you have spent weeks and weeks—" and here she taps the log from the library—"in our archives, suggests to me that you probably know more about Shaker history than we do ourselves." And she pauses for me to contradict her, but I don't. "So we wonder at your seeming ignorance of the fact that the United Society of Believers in Christ's Second Appearing voted in 1964 to no longer accept new members."

"Actually," I say, "the Society didn't vote. The Canterbury Eldresses decided for you. Eldress Sarah of New Eden was silent on the matter. As you no doubt know."

"As *you* no doubt know, Canterbury is considered the parent ministry of the Shakers."

"Chosen Land doesn't think so."

"Chosen Land," she says with a wave of her hand as if to dismiss the renegades there. "Chosen Land is of no consequence here. And even if they were, I can say that it is the opinion of *this* Eldress that the Society is closed to new members."

"Since 1964?" I ask.

"Since 1964."

"Then Sabbathday Wells, she isn't a member?"

She doesn't blink or blanch, as if she's foreseen this quibble. "Sister Sabbathday is a special case."

"Every human soul is a special case," I say. "*I'm* a special case."

"Not to us you aren't."

I look at the hairless scalp, the triplication of her eyes, the magnified moons of light just above her cheekbones, the fantastic web of wrinkles, the skull under the skin, and I can't help wondering what this virgin's life has been like for these eighty-nine years. Why did she stay? What does staying mean to her anyway, not so much now, but what did it mean when she was twenty and Model Ts were beginning to go by on the road out front or when she was thirty (Packards) or forty (Studebakers)? Just what sort of willpower or vision or belief kept her living in a moral museum when everyone else was turning out the lights and leaving?

"It's my belief," I say carefully, diplomatically, "that Mother Ann Lee, were she still alive, would disapprove of the closing of membership, that she would encourage new converts, and that she'd do everything—"

"Please," Rachel interrupts, waving me away like a bug. "These are old arguments. We get a dozen letters a month. Distraught housewives, homosexuals, true believers, insurance executives who want to make chairs for a living. During the Vietnam war we used to get letters from draft dodgers. The world goes by."

"The world is still alive," I answer. "The Shakers are dead."

"Not yet."

"Then dying."

She shrugs. "It only makes us more—" and she searches for the word—"more quaint. The world enjoys the pathos of an extinct species."

And she laughs, her face crumpling, a soundless gas escaping her lips. It creeps me out so much I absent myself by doing a quick count of the chairs in the room and multiplying by four thousand. Throw in the table and Venner has a black Porsche of his own.

"Extinction," she repeats and picks up a pen so I think she's going to write the word down. But she merely looks at the point as if trying to count the angels dancing there.

Is it cynicism? Or a vanity so vast it's difficult to recognize for what it is? Does Eldress Rachel want the world—her world, New Eden, Mother Ann Lee—to end when she ends? Is that it? Does she intend to take the utopia of the Shakers with her to the grave? And does my presence—*does Sabbathday Wells's presence*—threaten the egotism of that apocalypse? It would make her guilty of a kind of moral greed so great it makes Venner's own avarice seem puny indeed.

"Why did you send for me?" I say finally. I'm thinking of my stupid note. Am I just being toyed with? "Why not just the police again?"

She makes an equivocating gesture. "There's still time for the police."

"Oh."

And we sit for some time in silence. I listen for sounds in the house, the presence of Chastity or Antoinette, Sister Sabbathday eavesdropping in the hall. But the building is quiet. Across from me Eldress Rachel is consulting some notes in front of her, but I have the feeling it's just stage business.

"Sabbathday tells me you are recently divorced," she says finally.

"That's right."

"And you have a child. A little boy?"

"A girl."

She accepts the correction. "And you live in a steeple."

"Yes."

She seems to want to laugh at that, but coughs instead. I have an unpleasant sense of the room filling with the miasma of her breath.

"And your wife—"

"My ex-wife."

"—your ex-wife, she sings in a band."

This catches me by surprise. "That's right."

"In a rock-and-roll band."

"She used to be a Mariologist."

She blinks. "A what?"

"A Mariologist," I repeat, sans definition. Let her ask.

"And what is a Mariologist?"

"Someone who studies the Virgin Mary," I answer. But somewhere in the back of my mind I'm trying to remember whether that day in the car, in addition to my other indiscretions, I told Sabbathday that Sally was a rock-and-roll singer.

"The Virgin Mary," Eldress Rachel repeats, and she takes her glasses off as if there is something metaphysical in the room that needs to be looked at. "What is there about the Virgin Mary that needs studying?"

"A lot," I say.

"A lot," she repeats, musing. "Like what?"

"Like the female principle. The *Ewig-Weibliche*. The syncretism of early Mediterranean female deities."

She nods, absently, as if she's heard this all before and was just checking. "Tell me," she says finally, "why is it that you are so exercised by our stone walls?"

I am for a moment taken back by this directness. Also: why *am* I so exercised by their stone walls?

"Because they're a mess," I manage after a time.

"There are many things in this world that are a mess, Mr. Venner. Why our stone walls?"

"Because they ought to be the physical manifestation of spiritual order, and as it is—"

"You *are* a college professor."

"—as it is, they are the physical manifestation of Paradise gone to seed."

"*Are* they?"

"Yes, they are. And it's your fault."

"My fault?" she says, and again her face crumples with laughter. "You think these hands should be out there lifting stones?" And putting her glasses down, she holds her palsied hands out for inspection. "My, I can just see that!"

"If your hands are unable to lift stones themselves, they at least shouldn't prevent someone else from lifting them. Someone who has a gift to lift them."

"Oh, a gift," she says. "Well, as to that—" and she smiles a private smile—"that's why I asked you in here." She seems to consult her books again, but she doesn't have her glasses on. "What is the minimum wage nowadays, Mr. Venner?"

"What?"

"The minimum wage," she repeats.

"I don't know."

"I don't either."

We gaze at one another in a Mexican standoff. Is this more insult?

"I suppose I could find out," she murmurs after a moment.

"Are you suggesting I rebuild the walls after all? For minimum wage?"

"It's all we can afford."

"No, thanks."

She leaps on that like Socrates. "You require better pay then?"

"No pay at all. I told you, Eldress. I'm a Shaker. I consider myself a member of the United Society of Believers in Christ's Second Appearing."

"But you're not."

"Everything I have is yours."

She puts her glasses back on and peers across at me. "You are not a Shaker unless I say you are."

"I obey a higher authority."

"Whose?" she says and laughs. "Chosen Land's?"

"Mother Ann Lee's," I say, expecting more laughter, but her face blanches instead. I don't get it at first but then remember my note. Is it possible?

"We will pay you minimum wage," she says after a time.

Her voice is cold and businesslike. "We will do so in the tradition of the Shakers hiring outside help when needed. Otherwise it's the police."

"I'll just come back."

"You will *not* come back."

On the table between us is a vision of Venner hacksawing his way out of prison.

"Instead of pay," I say finally, "let me stay in the Gathering House."

"The Gathering House?"

"Yes."

She seems not as surprised by this as I would have supposed, as if she'd already thought of it herself. "The Gathering House would be better than a steeple, would it? Especially with winter coming on?"

And she squints at Venner, who squints back. Reader, FYI: the Gathering House is a small brick building that was used during the nineteenth century for housing novitiates who hadn't yet come into full covenant with the Shakers, and Rachel is sly enough to realize my staying there would mean I was not in family relation with her and the others, sly enough to realize that it would implicitly validate the possibility of new membership.

"The Hired Men's Quarters," she says finally. "If you would prefer to take your pay in housing, then you may live in the Hired Men's Quarters."

She *is* sly. The Hired Men's Quarters is a rough clapboard house at the very edge of the village. It's where seasonal laborers used to sleep, men who had no intention of coming into a gathering order. If I accept, I am tacitly acknowledging that I am not a Shaker. If I don't accept I lose the chance of at least getting a toehold in New Eden.

"All right," I say, "the Hired Men's Quarters."

She squares up the papers in front of her. "We will provide you with bedding, linen, towels, water. We'll clean once a week for you. There's no bathroom, you know. If the privy needs work, well, you are our handyman now. Where or how you take your meals is your business. But, as has always been the case when the world's people stay in the village, you will be expected to abide by Shaker order. If we find you contrary to order we will ask you to leave. Do you understand?"

"Yes."

"Do you?"

"Yes."

"Good," she says and stands up. I do the same, and then, stupidly, stick out my hand. She gazes at it a moment as though I'm offering her a dead fish and then turns her back to me.

"I remember the last man who lived there," she says to the window. The rear of the Hired Men's Quarters is just visible a couple of acres away. "It was after the war. His name was William, I think, or Williams, something Williams. He was very good with the animals as I remember. It was a pity we had to ask him to leave."

And with that she turns back to me. I don't dare say anything.

"At any rate the house hasn't been lived in since then," she says. "I'll have one of the Sisters open it up and clean. You'll give us a couple of days, please." She sits back down and busies herself with her papers and then abruptly stops and gazes up at me. "Mr. Venner," she says, "are you being truthful?"

"What?"

"Does the state of our stone walls truly disturb you?"

"Yes," I answer, and—goddamn it!—I mean it.

"Well," she says, and I don't know what it is, the ghost of some antique innocence in her or the vitality of my own yearning, but she seems suddenly to believe me. "Well, give us a few days."

CHAPTER EIGHT

A GARDEN ENCLOSED IS MY SISTER, MY SPOUSE

"Let me get this straight," says Medusa, home from New York, where Elektra Records says she's going to be the next Cher. "You left a note for Eldress Rachel saying 'Let him' and Snow White left a note for you saying *'Don't* let him'?"

"*Someone* left it. I don't know that it was Sabbathday."

"Who else?"

"Eldress Rachel."

"I doubt it."

"Or Mother Ann Lee."

"Venner."

"Or God Him-or-Herself."

"It was Snow White," she says, turning back to the mirror. We're in the bathroom, where she's trying on beauty marks. "And what the 'it' is she's not going to let you do is pretty obvious I'd say."

Not to Venner it isn't. Two days ago he crept upon all metaphorical fours to the Hired Men's Quarters and found there the cedar beams and the fir rafters of his dreams. He could hardly believe it. There were white curtains on the windows, white linens on the bed, the sting of ammonia in the air, the devil swept out of the corners, a ladder-back chair hung on the wall, a potpourri on the window seat, a Shaker-woven coverlet turned down in welcome. " 'I am come out of the wilderness like a pillar of smoke!' " I whispered over and over. I got so excited I had to use the chamberpot to pee. When finally I calmed down I spied a pad and pen on the night table ($2,500), and on the pad in a shaky hand: *Don't Let Him.*

"So what do you think?" Deusie says.

"I think it was God."

"I mean the beauty mark," she says and lifts her face to me. In addition to her snakes, Elektra Records has decided she needs a beauty mark.

"The grossness of the flesh," I answer.

She takes it off and tries it at the corner of her mouth, then high on her cheekbone, then at the wick of her eye. Then she unbuttons her blouse and sticks it down where her breasts rise out of her bra.

"How about that?" she asks and cups a hand under each of her breasts and lifts them. "It'd be a little more like this in one of my bustiers. What do you think?"

"Give me a break."

"Do you think it'd stay affixed during the act of love?"

During the act of love—should there ever be another act of love—Venner intends to run for the nearest fallout shelter.

"It's a little more subtle anyway," she says turning her breasts this way and that in the mirror.

I take a step back and quote some Song of Solomon to her, the stuff about the pillar of smoke, and for good measure the four score concubines and the virgins without number.

"Anyway, you'd only see it in a close-up."

" 'A garden enclosed is my sister.' "

"I mean a tight shot."

" 'My sister, my spouse.' "

She stops looking at herself and turns to me. "You know what Bigge's *Commentary* has to say about the pillar of smoke, don't you?"

"What?"

"God's phallus."

"Don't blaspheme."

"And the garden enclosed?"

"Don't blaspheme."

She turns back to the mirror, gives herself one of the sexy looks she's been practicing. *"Medusa,"* she coos and strokes her snakes.

· · ·

Reader, it may just be the stink of Venner's imported soul, but something is rotten in New Eden. I am stuck on two unpleasant possibilities: (1) that Rachel knows I wrote the note and is toying with me out of some quaint sadism; or (2) that she doesn't know I wrote the note, in which case Sabbathday Wells is keeping quiet about my midnight habit of breaking and entering, in which case why? If she *is* keeping quiet, then what on earth does Eldress make of the note? There's the midnight gift business, of course, also the spirit of Mother Ann creeping through the corridor. But I mean, really. It's more likely she thinks one of her Sisters wrote it, loony Chastity, Antoinette out of some old grudge, Sabbathday in a Lara avatar. It seems in her character to have confronted them with it, in which case Sabbathday either ratted on me or didn't rat on me, in which case she is either saving me or saving me up for her own enjoyment, all of which give rise to certain questions. On the other hand it's possible that Eldress has kept the existence of the note to herself, that Sabbathday does *not* know about it, and that *Don't Let Him* is a bluff on Rachel's part to smoke me out.

At Meeting I sit with the tourists along the short wall of the Meeting House and peer at the Sisters for clues, for the implicating gesture or the dead giveaway. But they are as ever, opening Meeting with a hymn, then praising God for all the usual, then singing and dancing in a degraded version of Ann Lee's shaking. They are adept at pretending we are not there, we members of the world's people. I see no glimmer of guilt, no hint of collusion or conspiracy or even suspicion. I keep my eye on Eldress Rachel, try to catch her out, though what catching her out would consist of—what revelation or subtle wink—I can't say. It's more than just the note: I don't really believe Rachel gives a goddamn about the metaphysics of stone walls, in which case why the heart-to-heart and the HMQ? What, after all—once we discount bargain-basement stone walls—what's in it for her? I watch her sing "Holy Fountain," watch her listen to Antoinette speak of the difficulties in understanding the Lord's will, but she is aloof, regal, the Eldress all the way, and I am left thinking it is Sabbathday and Sabbathday alone who has the requisite double consciousness to have written the note. And thinking that, I wonder if it's good or bad, I mean in the strategic sense, good or bad for the overall idea of becoming a Shaker and living with a solitary Sabbathday who is/is not the object of our physical affections (p. 1, *et passim*), good or bad that Sabbathday may be such a Lara at heart. I can't tell. But outside when one of the tourists lifts his Nikon to shoot her walking away, I tell him "No photos, please." When he shoots her anyway, I rip his camera out of his hands, unscrew the lens, smudge my fingerprints all over the mirror inside and hand it back to him. He chases after me asking for my name and address.

I tell him I'm a pillar of smoke, etcetera.

But the fingerprints give me an idea. At Mickey's Magic Shop I buy a detective kit, dust the pen from the nightstand with powder and lift the prints. I spend a surreptitious afternoon sneaking Eldress's prints from the Goods Shop, hardworking Sabbathday's from her loom, but back in the Hired Men's Quarters the prints on the pen don't match up to either. I take my own prints off my BB gun and sure enough, etcetera etcetera, although I don't remember ever handling the pen.

"It is, of course, possible," says Sometimes-Why from his new windowsill, "that you wrote the note to yourself. *Don't Let Him* being the expression of deep-seated hostility toward your own polluted person. Suicide, it seems to me, would be an appropriate course of action at this point in time."

On the sly I check the New Eden mailbox for handwriting samples, in the streetlight look the envelopes over for capital D's, L's, H's in the hope of spotting some fraternal likeness, but nothing strikes me. Mother Ann, if you please, provide Venner with a sample of your handwriting.

Also you, God.

In the meantime, this is the careful calendar of Venner's existence: Monday, Wednesday and Friday he creates light in the dank minds of doomed undergraduates; Tuesday, Thursday and Saturday he divides the earthly firmament with stone walls. On Sunday he rests. In lieu of the Body-Rite Fitness Club he's taken to shooting Sabbathday's sheep with his BB gun, but their wool is so thick they don't even twitch with the impact, such as it is. Perhaps in the spring when they're shorn and lamby-looking. He's still addicted to sniffing the fresh laundry on the line, putting his nostrils to the airy flutter of Sabbathday's skirts, to the gingham and gabardine of her aprons. And from time to time he still hides out in the midnight bushes, *cum* spotting scope, but some of that thrill is gone he's pleased/sorry to report. Also he's just plain weary by the time it gets dark, for Venner has come to recognize *inter alia* that once one is no longer attempting to antagonize virgins, building stone walls is hard work. All in all it seems the wise thing to do right now is not to push it—never mind the note, the duplicitous, the virginal double dare—the smart thing is to quietly consolidate the unimaginable gain of his new address. For he is laboring in the Vineyard, and the Devil and/or God only knows what sort of wine the vines will bring forth.

• • •

"I think you're crazy," Deusie says when she sees the Hired Men's Quarters. "I think you're crazy and I think they're crazy."

She's out here nominally to show me her new wig. Real human hair braided into thirteen snakes and paid for by Elektra Records. It beats her own hair, but makes me feel my ex-wife is becoming slightly ex-real.

"There's no bathroom, for one thing," she says, going from wall to wall, checking the locks on the windows, the draft around the mullions, the curtain linings. "No refrigerator. No stove."

"All part of the elevation of the spirit and the denial of the flesh," I say with a smile. "Allowed sufficient residence here, your ex-husband will no longer *need* a bathroom."

She sits on the bed, testing the mattress. In addition to her wig, she's got on cute shoes and costume jewelry and a snug sweater that laces up the front. I note the beauty mark has taken up residence at the corner of her left eye.

"I wouldn't mind a cup of tea," she says, nodding toward the hot water sitting atop the coal stove.

"There's a diner down the road," I tell her. "Here, you're against Shaker order."

"So what?"

"So no tea."

She makes a face. "What do I have to do to be *in* Shaker order?"

"Cease existing."

"Very funny."

"No joke," I say. "We can't be alone in a room together. If Eldress were to find out, I'd get canned. So say what you've come to say and leave."

"Oh, V," she says with kitty-kat dismay. She gazes at me with an old reproach and then pats the bed beside her, but I shake my head no. From the floor Sometimes-Why leaps onto the mattress, takes a few opportunistic steps and settles on her in my place.

"I wrote a new song," she says after a moment but I don't bite. Out the window I can see Eldress closing up the Goods Shop for the night. In half an hour or so, the evening bell will ring and it will be suppertime. "I'm leaving, V."

"I think it's best," I say and start for the door.

"I mean town. I'm leaving town. Elektra keeps an apartment in Manhattan. I'll be living there until we finish recording. I need you to take Eve."

"Excuse me?" I say.

"You have to. I can't keep asking Melanie to have her."

"Sorry. It's against Shaker order to live with one's own children. Too much appeal to natural affections."

"You can have the house," she continues. "I don't mean *have* it, but you can live in it, rent-free, for as long as I'm away."

"Thanks, but I already have a house." And I gesture at the pinch-hitting paradise around me.

"Oh, come on."

"Come on yourself."

"She's your daughter, for Christ's sake, V."

And she peers at me with genuine anger. Not the show anger of Sally scorned or Medusa minimized, but really angry this time, no existence/essence about it.

"Thing to do is for you to stay home and be her mother," I advise. "Forget about Elektra Records and Medusa and reducing yourself to a flickering construction of photons. Forget about achieving the American ideal of nonsubstance. Stay home and love, love, love. That's what I plan on doing."

"Come on," she says. "This is my chance. Why can't you help me out?"

"Your chance to do what?"

"To get famous!" she yells.

"Famous?" I yell back. "Who's going to get famous?"

"What do you mean who? *Me!* Who else?"

"Who's you?"

She peers at me like I'm a madman.

"Who's you?" I say again, and this time she seems to get it.

"Medusa," she says.

"Because, you know, I thought the whole point of this was to get *un*famous. I mean to get the you of you—Sally Shannon, the girl with the pageboy haircut, the one I fell in love with—to get the you of you unfamous, to get her so bogused up by this other you, this Medusa, that the Sally-you would become pure and inviolate, unknown even to her closest friends and/or husband. Just like you used to say about the Virgin Mary. How the invention of the 'Blessed Virgin' disguised her, warped her, and yet how by some magic that very violation kept her real self inviolate. Wasn't that your idea? When you first started writing those songs?"

"So what?"

"So 'a garden enclosed is my sister, my spouse.' "

"Screw the sister and screw the spouse," she says. "You're just jealous. You're jealous because I'm getting to essence faster than you are."

" 'A spring shut up, a fountain sealed.' "

"I'm going to be on TV getting saved for real while you're out here playing in the dirt. They're going to be listening to me in their cars, out on the highways, up in the mountains, across the desert, teenagers on a thousand Lovers' Lanes doing it for the first time to 'Essential Ecstasy' while you're out here getting conned by three old broads and an anatomically correct doll. They're using you to get their stone walls rebuilt and their doors rehung and their windows unstuck and then it's like Sorry, you thought you were saved but you're not. Have a nice time in hell. In the meantime, I—that's *me, I, Sally, Medusa*—I'll be alive forever, no matter what happens, changed into the magnetic particles of videotape, into radio waves, flying across America at the goddamn speed of light, going through trees, through rock, through heads, hearts, bedroom walls . . ."

"Good," I interrupt. "Get started by flying out of here."

She smiles a wicked smile. "In my own sweet time," she says and lies back on the bed. She adjusts her wig and then arranges the snakes around her. Sometimes-Why stretches out lengthwise between her legs.

"Don't," I say.

"Hot in here."

"Don't."

She unlaces her sweater. Underneath there's a T-shirt and, you know, the usual.

"Look," I say, "we are currently against Shaker order. So, if you don't mind . . ."

She kicks her heels off.

"So if you don't mind, go away."

"Feel it," she says.

"What?"

"The wig. Feel it. It's real."

I take a step forward and feel it. It's another woman's hair on the head of my ex-wife.

"Nice."

"Three thousand two hundred dollars," she says. "And you thought they weren't serious about me."

"I never said that."

"You implied it in your manner."

I pick Sometimes-Why up from between her legs and put him on a windowsill, then back off to the door. "That's my bed," I say.

"So what?"

"So don't lie on it."

She draws a snake across her lips, and then I'm damned if she doesn't look at me with one of her MTV looks, the ones she's been practicing in front of the mirror.

"Think it's ever been used? I mean by one of the hired men. You think they ever snuck a woman in here?"

I don't answer.

"You think we might introduce it to the frailty and sorrow of human love?"

"Give me a break."

"I mean wouldn't that be a kick? Doing it in here?"

She smiles and holds her arms out to me. When I don't move she lets a pouty look come over her and then turns herself over so she's lying on her stomach. At first I can't tell what's she's up to, but then I hear the snap of her skirt. She lifts her rear end ever so slightly in the air and you guessed it Mother Ann starts doing herself, right there on my virginal bed for Christ's sake. I tell her to stop, but she just closes her eyes and puts on that smile of hers, rubs her face into the pillow. I tell her again to cut it out, to knock it off, and then it occurs to me she's not really doing it. It's all like the hair and the beauty mark and the mirror stuff.

"You're faking it," I say.

She murmurs something into the pillow. Sometimes-Why has jumped back onto the bed and is walking on her back.

"Practicing for the cameras."

She bites her hair. The bed makes little tiny moans with her movement. She's got her other hand up inside her sweater.

"So this is essence?"

"*Jesus.*"

"Phony hair. Phony mole. Phony sex. This is your idea of essence?"

And without a word of warning I yank the wig off her head. She lets out a little cry but doesn't stop what she's doing. Her own hair is pinned tight to her scalp.

"I'm leaving," I say, and against the simultaneous sounds of the Dwelling House bell ringing the supper hour and the lower reaches of Medusa's *voluptatem*—real or otherwise—I grab my jacket and head out the door. But instead of climbing into the car I just stand sort of dead in the dooryard, looking out over the village fields. It's dusk and the air is drizzling with ghosts, two centuries of Shaker men and women, the kerosene light spilling on the grass, the lowing cattle, the baaing sheep: all of which, I know, are the dust motes of my imagination and my obsession, but Gentle Reader, honestly, they're out there all the same. I cross the grassy ruts of the abandoned wagon track that sweeps around the Hired Men's Quarters and sit on one of my derelict stone walls. Up on the hill I can see the warm light of the dining hall. Somewhere inside, Sabbathday is serving Eldress Rachel or is being served herself. Somewhere inside is twelve-year-old Lara plotting escape. Somewhere inside is the reason, or part of the reason, or the illusion of a reason why I started all this.

Behind me I hear the door of the Hired Men's Quarters open. I don't turn around, hoping she'll just go, she'll just get in the car and go. But at the same time I'm thinking this I realize I've still got her wig. The haze of her perfume comes up behind me. When she sits down I don't look at her, keep my eyes on the warm light up the hill, but all the same I can see her feet, her fetching shoes, her diamonded stockings, the taut drag of her short skirt over her thighs. She sits quietly for a time, and then starts with her hair, pulling out the bobby pins and throwing them one by one out into the grass. When they're all out, she drags her fingers through the snarls.

"Here," I say, handing her the wig without turning to her. She takes it from me but doesn't put it on.

"Is that better?" she asks.

I still don't look at her. Up at the Dwelling House a body moves between me and the light, across the window and then back. It moves slowly so I think it must not be her.

"Is that better?" Sally asks again and this time I look. She's got her hair out normal, long and unpageboyish, but at least sans snakes. Also she looks hurt and sorry as if for her, too, the world is too much. I gaze away, back out over the field.

"Better," I say.

We sit a full five minutes in silence. Whatever was left of the sun is gone down behind Spirit Mountain, leaving the sky a Disney purple. There are stars and imagined jets. The Big Dipper wheels faintly overhead; the TV towers blink; out in the field the ghosts turn and wonder at us; the spheres shiver and it's as if the world itself is an *argumentum ad misericordium* if we only had the wisdom and the humanity to hear it.

I want to say something, speak something, tell Sally the hurt and the regret and the sorrow that's in me, but I can't. Why I can't, I both know and don't know. Up on the hill the dining-room light goes out. After another minute Sally lays her hand on mine. Perhaps Eldress has her own spotting scope and is even now watching us.

"Don't you miss Eve?" Sally asks finally.

"Yes, I do."

"You used to need her so much."

It's true, Mother Ann. Four Christmases ago, on a mid-night walk an anguished Venner evicted a plaster Jesus from the Saint Mary's crèche and laid an eleven-month-old Eve in His place, not the blasphemy of a metaphysical jokester but the expression of a love and gratitude that was so great it could only find its analog in the Messiah.

"She wonders why you're not around," Sally whispers.

"She wonders why *you're* not around," I answer.

"Don't," she says and I don't. It's getting darker. In the east there's the snowy turnpike of the Milky Way, and up on Lovers' Lookout there are one, two, three cars parked with their parking lights on.

"If you could just have her some nights," she says. "Melanie would probably keep her indefinitely, but if you could just have her at the house weekends or a couple of days in the week. Drop her off at daycare or pick her up. Take her out for a pizza. Could you do that for her?"

I imagine Eve living in the Hired Men's Quarters with me. I imagine her in a Shakeressless Dwelling House, her on the second floor, me on the third. I imagine the world just the two of us, the masculine/feminine principles reduced to father and daughter, and the world chaste because, after all, I am not a monster. "You mean could I do that for you?" I say finally.

"V . . ." she pleads.

I stare off into my resentment.

"Maybe I could get up on weekends," she says. "If you could pick me up at the airport. What do you think?"

"I never intended not to be with her. I never intended not

to see her. It's just that I can't have her out here with me. And I can't live at the house."

"But you could stay at the house a couple of nights a week, couldn't you? Couldn't you stay at the house a couple of nights a week?"

"Yes."

"And I could do the weekends."

"All right," I say.

"All right?"

She's still holding my hand.

CHAPTER NINE

VENNER'S
PURGATORIO

Re: Jesus's eviction.

It was the Christmas after Sally began to go weird on me. She was off playing some ski lodge up in Vermont or maybe the White Mountains. It was late in the month, cold, and I just couldn't stand it anymore. I got Eve out of her crib, slipped her sleeping into her snowsuit and with her strapped to my heart went outdoors. I don't know where I thought I was going to go, maybe to my office, maybe to Dunkin' Donuts, but toward town at any rate, toward humanity, cutting across the frozen lawns on Undermountain Road until the sidewalks started. On Main Street the stoplights were all blinking yellow. I went down one side of the empty street and up the other, looking at the jewelry in the shop windows, the fluorescent display of Surf 'n' Ski skin lotion, a six-inch Santa ogling a Bulova wristwatch, all the time with the bird-flutter of Eve's heartbeat against my chest, a gray pearl of breath attached to her tiny mouth. I was confused because I had never fallen out of love before, never been fallen out of love with either, and I could see her going, never mind the Virgin Mary or MTV or Tower of Power, I could see Sally going on me and I didn't have the wisdom or the experience or the basic sadness of soul to realize it might pass, that it might be merely the first of many undulations in the map of our marriage. (Might it still be that? Can you imagine me and Medusa married again? My head and half my body cropped out of some paparazzo photo of her in *People?*) I was stuffed up with pain, the dizziness of unlove and other stuff I don't need to say, because, I mean, at this late date of human development, who hasn't been through this? What happened was we turned down a side street and God bless me I was kind of crying, and I kept placing my hand on Eve, on her forehead, which was the only part of her—I mean of her flesh, the real her—the only part I could touch without suffocating her. Because I was nuts about her. I couldn't believe that out of the slag of my loins, out of the heat-sink of lovemaking could come this beating aorta with hands to feel and eyes to see. She'd been born two days before Christmas, and the recovery-room nurse had been dressed up as Santa Claus, and when she crossed to me bearing the gift of Eve (seven pounds six ounces, twenty-one inches long, all nines on the Ballard Score), Venner nearly fainted. There were Crayola pictures of lambs and cows and shepherds on the walls, three wise men in the corner disguised as expectant fathers themselves, a buzzing fluorescent heaven overhead, and through the ceiling speakers—it's true! I swear—Handel's *Messiah*. It was weird and gave Venner the thought that God has a sense of humor after all.

The long and the short of it is this: at the crèche on the frozen lawn outside St. Mary's, at two o'clock in the morning, a tear-blurry Venner got down on his knees and, first tossing aside a plaster baby Jesus (who rolled to a stop against the papier-mâché hoofs of a drunk donkey), laid his personal messiah on the cold hay and prayed.

CHAPTER TEN

In Which Eve Tries to Sort the Good from the Bad

When I go to pick up Eve at daycare the mothers are there. I'm jealous of them, of the virtuosity of their baby-balancing hips, their smug ovaries, the magic act of their insides. It used to be worse. When Sally and I first separated she packed up Eve on the sly and moved in with her sister, and for months while my lawyer tried to convince the court to retrieve my daughter ("Whatever you do, don't take her back by force. Don't park outside the house in an unmarked car or something. Prove yourself the responsible party"), I wandered town and campus in a state of such disinheritance, throwing such looks of grief and jealousy at the ripe insides of the coeds passing me on the sidewalks that my department chair took me aside and explained certain subtleties of professorial deportment that seemed, he said, to have escaped my notice. For a solid six months, while Sally and I went through the worst of it, I was like Plato's Aristophanes, searching for my missing half. Toy stores, playgrounds, rain-faded hopscotch squares: they were like acts of violence to me. In the supermarket, wheeling my empty carriage through the leafy produce, I'd fix on some average Americaness just ahead of me—three-year-old riding the front of the cart like a hood ornament, baby in the boot—and follow her up and down the aisles, in and out of the grace and horror of shrink-wrapped America, past the olives and the Oreos and the shelves of Kotex, teary-eyed the whole time and imagining a life with her in which my inconsolable seed fell into her loamy womb and babies exploded out of her like popcorn.

Because this, after all, is the great cheat of being a man. You feel it particularly when a judge is about to kidnap your only child. I know my conduct since does not bear me out. I have been preoccupied and neglectful and not the responsible party, but that very irresponsibility is the proof of the pain. Is there such a big difference between my loss of Eve and Ann Lee's four dead babies? Okay, okay, but only a difference of degree. Either will drive the wounded soul into the antiseptic air of New Eden, whether a literal New Eden or the love-voided New Edens of promiscuity and prostitution and the Playmate of the Month. If Venner could be a eunuch or a hermaphrodite or a pervert, he would, but he can't, so it's the germless atmosphere of unlove for him. And in spite of the fact that for the past hour he's been hanging out across the street from the Auntie Dante DayCare Center, watching the four-year-olds frolicking in the playground, he still means it.

• • •

When finally I show myself there are mothers every which way. I duck and dodge, dive into the Reading Room, the Big Block Room, then head down into the Lower Circles, where it turns out Eve has been painting Halloween pictures (skeletons mostly). It takes a minute to clean her up. She wants to know where Mommy is, where Aunt Melanie is, and out in the car when I tell her we're going home, do I mean Mommy's home or Aunt Melanie's or what?

"Home," I tell her. "We're going home."

"The church?"

"No, home. Your house."

But she knows there's something wrong with that. "You don't live in the church anymore?"

"No."

"Did God kick you out?"

This, because the ongoing attempt on Auntie Dante's part to explain the unexplainable to my daughter has left her with the conviction that God lives in churches.

"No, God didn't kick me out."

"Who did then?"

"Nobody."

"Mommy?"

"No, not Mommy, nobody."

She's sure I'm lying but has the grace not to push the point. On Undermountain Road she watches the houses go by one by one and then cries out "Hey!" and squirms in her seat so she can see out the rear window. "What's going on?"

What's going on is your father cannot bring himself to visit the scene of the crime.

"Changed my mind," I say. "Going for a drive."

She keeps sight of the house for as long as she can and then turns back around and looks out the windshield like maybe there's something to see. "Why?"

"Why not?"

It's the middle of October and the streets are enwitched with the props of suburban Satanism: ghouls, ghosts, grinning jack-o'-lanterns. In the tract housing on the west side of town, we come across an elaborate tableau, a cobwebbed casket with waking skeleton, spotlit trio of black cats atop a tombstone. Eve gets all excited at the sight of it and wants me to stop, but I have control of her body just now, if not her soul, and hit the gas.

"Hey!"

Back out on Undermountain Road I find myself driving toward New Eden. It's not where I want to go—Eve being illegal there—but moral magnetic north is a force with which the dull iron of Venner's soul can seldom contend. He follows his headlights. But when the blind north side of the Dwelling House comes within his halogen grasp, and then the windowed facade, he keeps going, out past the Hired Men's Quarters, the decrepit orchard behind, the fallow fields, and finally onto the gravel road that runs up the side and along the face of Spirit Mountain.

"Now what?" Eve asks.

"Going to look at the lights."

"What lights?"

"The town lights. From up on the mountain."

"Why?"

"Because they're pretty, and I'm not ready to go home yet, and because I used to bring you up here when you were a baby."

"Oh," she says.

I *did* use to bring her up here when she was a baby, the two of us parked at the overlook with the other lovers. Back then I had dreams of myself as a family man, patriarchal Venner with a happy half dozen heirs, three of each brand, lowering his obese body into a wicker chair on the summer porch while they played about his feet, climbed up his legs, his arms, squealing with love and hiding their toys in the cornucopia of his rabbi's beard. For about half a year there I tried to convince Sally to have another baby, to do it right away, to translate us into the American family paradigm, but she was already growing her snakes, already inventing herself as one of a million electronic spirits of the American sky, and a baby—any baby, even the one we had—possessed too high a specific gravity for the flight she intended.

At the overlook I ease the car past the other vehicles and park as far away from humanity as I can, though in this case that's only thirty feet. I shut the headlights off and leave the motor running. Below us the town lights twinkle like Walt's been at it again. For Eve's benefit I start to sing "When You Wish Upon a Star" but she tells me to shut up. Those are the words she uses, "Shut up," and I am too dispossessed of my fatherhood to try scolding her. She's twisted around in her seat looking not out the windshield at the town but out the passenger window at the next car over.

"What are they doing?" she wants to know.

"Looking at the lights."

"No, they're not."

"Yes, they are. You too."

She rolls down the window to get a better look. I turn the heater on. "They're kissing," she says after a minute. "What are they kissing for?"

What *are* they kissing for? You, Reader. Or you, Mother Ann. Class?

"They're not kissing."

"Yes they *are!*"

I try to distract her by asking what she wants to be for Halloween, but it's no soap. She watches them with the intensity of a peepshow pervert. I tell her to roll the window back up it's cold, but she isn't listening. I try to see past her, past the green-lit whirlpool of her hair—Sally's hair, Sabbathday's right—to make sure there's nothing more untoward than smooching going on in the other car. "I need a pizza," I end up saying, turning the headlights on and putting the car in reverse. Eve whirls back around in her seat.

"Helen of Troy," she says.

"What?"

"I want to be Helen of Troy. For Halloween."

She means, of course—Venner hopes—Helen of Troy the hamster.

"How *is* Helen of Troy?" I ask.

She gives me a funny look, the dash lights painting her face. "She's dead."

"She's dead? She died? When?"

"I don't know," she answers, testy. "A long time ago."

Just after Marilyn Monroe and Miss America? I wonder. And then I have the horrible feeling that it's the real Helen of Troy she's talking about, that in addition to God and the Holy Ghost, she's been learning about Greek sluts.

"What do you want to be her for?" I ask but get no answer. "Because she's beautiful?" I try, fearing the worst. She shrugs. She's watching the black trees fling themselves into our headlights.

"Because she's dead," she says finally.

In the end we spend the night together in the Hired Men's Quarters, father and daughter in a single bed, *c.* 1920, her head on half a pillow, soul in the circle of my arm. I dream of Arcadian landscapes, marble columns in the greeny distance, a musical rill off to the side, shepherds with bent crooks, shepherdesses with hay in their hair, and pregnant sheep in every fold. I also dream that I am dreaming Eve's dreams, or rather that I am the stage manager of her dreams. Lots of flowers and rainbows and no boys, please.

When we wake for the first time it's to the six o'clock knell of the Dwelling House bell.

The second time it's to Sister Sabbathday walking in on us with a load of linen in her arms.

"Daddy?" says a confused Eve.

She just stands there looking at us. I am speechless myself, though I have enough presence of mind to let the covers fall from my labor-enhanced shoulders. But it's Eve who's got her eye, Eve wearing one of my dress shirts for a nightgown and sitting up so the shoulders slip down to her elbows.

"Your bicycle," Sabbathday says finally, looking at me. "I thought you were gone. I thought— I'm sorry."

And she turns around and disappears out the door.

"My car," I find myself saying, "it's parked out front. Big as life." At which Eve peers at me like I've lost it.

"It's not *your* car," she says. "It's *Mommy's* car."

Reader, it *is* Mommy's car, isn't it? And Sister Sabbathday knows it, doesn't she? She thought she'd deliver an innocent load of linen—bicycle not being there ready as an excuse—and catch us *flagrante delicto.* I can't figure it—no knock?—any other way.

I go over it in my mind the rest of the morning, driving Eve to daycare, eating doughnuts in my office, lecturing on the Transfiguration. And what I end up wondering is whether she did it as a kind of teasing dare, or out of an instinct for blackmail, or because her envirgined mind is so hungry to know how the world outside New Eden constructs itself that she'd risk embarrassment and exposure to learn something.

I cut my afternoon office hours short, pick up Eve and, just as the sun is doing the death archetype in the western sky, show up at New Eden. I park the car as conspicuously as I can and out on the grounds let Eve have the run of the place, show her the pickets that need painting, the walls I'm working on. We do a high wire from boulder to boulder, roam among the frostbitten flowers in the herb garden, gambol one minute, cavort the next, all to evidence her existence and the *a posteriori* fact of sexual congress. In the vegetable garden there's the smell of fecundity and decay, autumnal decomposition, general corruption. It isn't long before Eve finds the few blackened tomatoes still on the vine, the punky squash under their leaves. From time to time I look up at the golden windows of the Sisters' Weaving Shop, ditto the jaundiced ones of the Goods Shop. There's a pair of tourists inside with Rachel, paying for something at the cash register. When they leave, the lights go out, and in a few minutes Rachel locks up and walks her eighty-nine-year-old body to the Dwelling House. She doesn't seem to notice the scarecrow lurking in the garden, ditto the scarecrow's daughter.

"Hold these," Eve says, handing me four rotten tomatoes and a cucumber the size of a gherkin. She plunges into the squash patch.

When Sabbathday comes out of the Weaving Shop she too does not see us, and my extemporaneous strategy of presenting Eve as evidence of carnal nights seems suddenly pretty dumb. In the deep distance the sun has had it with me and drops all in a lump behind the western suburbs. I call Eve, tell her to come on it's getting dark, but she is down on her hands and knees, so taken with the putrescent treasure of the garden that I have to try to persuade her that her hands are freezing, that her father's hands are freezing, that it's late and

time for dinner and tonight we really are going to spend the
night at her house and yes I'm going to sleep in Mommy's bed.
I finally lift her by the armpits while she scrambles to hold on
to her spoils. This all takes such easy-does-it fatherly concentration that I don't notice Sabbathday coming out of the
Dwelling House and starting across the lawn toward us, a
basket on each arm.

"Hello," she says and at the sound of her voice, I nearly
drop my child.

"Hello," I answer, setting Eve down on her feet. But it
isn't me she's greeting.

"Did I scare you this morning?" she asks Eve. She's
stopped in the herb garden, maybe thirty feet away.

"What?" Eve says.

"This morning when I walked in on you while you were
sleeping. Did I scare you?"

"Oh."

"I didn't realize you were there. Your father's bicycle was
gone so I thought no one was home. I was going to change the
bed."

I can see Eve trying to put things together, but the decomposing cornucopia in the cradle of her arms becomes too
much for her. A tomato tumbles earthward. "Are these
yours?" she asks.

"Are what mine?"

"These."

"What are they?"

She considers a moment. "Vegetables," she says, and then
uncertainly, "and fruit."

"Did you pick them?"

"Yes."

"Then they're yours."

"Daddy!" she exclaims, turning to me.

"Daddy," I think I hear sarcastic Sabbathday murmur as
she turns and bends over some stalky herb.

So just what is this, Mother Ann? I mean this maternal

act? Is she trying to get me in my imagination, nail the hope in my heart? Is that it?

"There's a bad frost coming tonight," she says from down on her knees. She puts her two baskets down and takes out a pair of pruning shears.

And why the sudden solicitude, the sweetness of disposition, which let's face it has been in noticeably short supply in your final convert?

"Dill," she says in answer to Eve, who has climbed over the stone wall that separates the two gardens and is down on her hands and knees beside Sabbathday. "You use it for pickling things and also if you were alive in the seventeenth century to keep witches away."

"Witches!" says a wide-eyed Eve. She turns and looks at me for corroboration. I come and stand at the wall. "How does it keep witches away?" she asks.

"They don't like the smell."

"It smells?" And she takes hold of a stalk of the stuff and bends it to her nose. Whatever it is she smells, or whether the odor unsettles her about the quality of her own witchhood, her face clouds and she stands up.

"You hang it in your doorway and then everyone knows your house is a Christian house and you don't welcome witches or the Devil."

"What's the Devil?" Eve wants to know.

"A bad man. A man who fought with God."

"God made everything," she declares.

"That's right."

"He lives in my Dad's church."

"Does he?"

"But he kicked my Dad out."

And at that, Sabbathday peers at me, the first time she's acknowledged my presence.

"He's a hard landlord," I say.

She turns back to her herbs, picking over a plant that has already been frostbitten and then cutting it off at the stem

and throwing it aside. "You want to do some?" she asks Eve.
"Do what?"

"Cut some?" And she hands her the pruning shears. "You
can do the basil, what's left of it anyway. Just snip it off at the
ground, about an inch up. That much—" she gestures, realizing my four-year-old doesn't know what an inch is—"and
put it in this basket." She watches her until she's got the hang
of it, stands up and brushes the debris from the knees of her
dress, and then crosses to me. We stand silent, turned from
one another, watching Eve for maybe two full minutes. When
finally she speaks she doesn't look at me, or even turn toward
me.

"You have to tell me what you were doing in my room
that night."

Here it comes. I page through a fat dictionary of explanations but none of them is a suitable excuse for breaking and
entering, never mind what must seem like the madness of my
intention. Does she know about the note or not?

"Tell me," she says when I don't answer.

"I don't know," I say.

"Was it a failure of nerve?"

"What?"

Does melodramatic Sabbathday still think I was there to
rape her? Mother Ann, turn down the Technicolor.

"Was it a failure of nerve?" she repeats.

"Sister, please," I say. "Don't get carried away."

And at that she turns to me. "Don't talk to me like that."

"Like what?"

"Like that. That tone."

What tone? I wonder.

"I'm trying to speak to you," she says with visible strain.
"I'm trying—" and she breaks off.

What's going on here? For a second I feel a kind of brainy
vertigo, and then I catch a sudden glimpse of a potential
Sabbathday, a Sabbathday trying to reach me, trying to get
me to own up to my attraction to her, to admit having in-

tended violence toward her, because that would mean a man wanted her. I feel giddy at the thought. Is it possible that Sabbathday Wells wants me to want her?

"I'm sorry," I say and then that's it, I can't think of anything else. She gazes nervously away, and I realize with new force that I'm speaking to a twenty-three-year-old woman with the sexual experience of a thirteen-year-old, a woman bereft of the training of even one boyfriend, of the protocol of high school dances, kisses behind the YMCA.

"I was there to look at you."

She turns back and I can't tell what it is, alarm, suspicion, surprise at having the outside world corroborate your thoughts, but she laughs a sort of half-laugh, not a laugh of derision or even of humor but more of relief, as if something long looked for and feared miscarried was at last in sight.

"What did you expect to see?" she asks in a quiet voice.

"You," I say, "just you." And then, "It wasn't the first time." We gaze at one another, both of us a bit spooked, and then turn back to watching Eve.

"How do you get in?" she asks after a moment. She keeps her voice even and low. "Rachel locks the doors every night."

"Through the sluiceway," I say. "Up through the laundry."

She smiles as if that's a riddle solved. "I'd been checking the windows."

There's a quality of surrender about the way she's speaking, as if she's admitting that the ruse of our present relationship simply can't go on. But what she thinks our present relationship is, or what it ought to be, I haven't a clue.

"I was just there to see you," I say again, stumped but sensing a compliment in the semi-perversion.

"Why do you want to see me?" she asks, accenting "see" with a queer little laugh, as if she's aware of the humor not to mention profanity of a Shaker woman fishing for compliments.

"Because," I temporize. Why *do* I want to see her?

"Because why?"

"Because . . ." And O! Reader and/or Mother Ann! I say it. I really do. "Because I'm in love with you."

And that does it. Whatever thin ice Sister Sabbathday Wells has been testing breaks under her and she gets a good dunking in the ice water of her particular reality.

"That's ridiculous," she says and she turns and crosses back into the herb garden, where Eve is pulling up weeds by the roots.

"Of course it's ridiculous," I say. "It's always ridiculous."

"I wouldn't know."

I can't tell whether she's angry or embarrassed or what. And I don't know whether to push it or back off. I watch her in the twilight, and I think number one, how beautiful she really is and number two, how I am not in fact in love with her.

"I thought you said you were a Shaker," she says. "*Brother Venner*," she mimics.

"I am."

"A Shaker brother who's in love."

"Why not?"

"It's a stupid contradiction, that's why not. You ought to make up your mind one way or the other. Either you're here to prove to us that you're worthy of living among us or you're here to try to—" and she doesn't quite know what to call it— "to try to get me."

"I didn't say I was trying to *get* you," I answer. And for an instant various impossible worlds collide in my head. And then I get hit with a gift. "I said I was in *love* with you, not that I was going to try to *get* you."

She blanches with the thought that one state might not include the other. "What?"

"I said I was in love with you, not that I was—"

"Oh, forget it!" she says and she starts sorting Eve's basket, keeping the herbs and throwing out the weeds.

"Hey!" says Eve, picking up the expelled weeds and stuffing them back. I assume the professorial demeanor.

"There's nothing contradictory about a Shaker man in love with a woman. There's nothing even particularly surprising. The allure of the flesh etcetera."

"Oh, shut up."

Eve whirls around at that. "Daddy!" she says, expecting me to scold Sabbathday.

"But whatever feeling I have for you, I certainly don't intend to act on it."

"Breaking and entering isn't acting?"

"That was before. This is now. I intend to be a brother to you. I intend to control the urgings of my—" I almost say "fleshly appetites" but that would be laying it on a bit thick—"of my body and even consider it, consider *you*, your very existence, a test of my will and my election."

I've strayed into the Calvinist lexicon with that last but hey, I'm thinking on my feet and anyway she doesn't seem to notice, simply eyes me with something that circles around anger and malice and ridicule.

"We'll see how long that lasts," she says and she picks up her two baskets. "Those are weeds, sweetie, we just want the basil. See?"

Eve looks at the good and the bad on the ground trying to differentiate between the two. "Oh," she says. Sabbathday searches in the dark vegetation for her pruning shears, finds them and stands up.

"I don't know what you're thinking," she says straight at me. "I don't know what you think love is if you can love someone you don't even know. I mean just because you've been spying on me from the bushes and watching me sleep at night doesn't mean you know me. Does it?"

"I know you."

"You don't know anything about me."

"I know for years you've dreamed of letting new Shakers into New Eden and at the same time dreamed of leaving New Eden yourself. I know your mother named you after Julie Christie in *Dr. Zhivago* and you wonder what life as Lara would be like. I know you're jealous of the women tourists who come and look your weaving over. I know you wonder about their perfume and their high heels. I know you get migraine headaches. I know the kids in the seventh grade used to steal your lunchbag."

She stares at me like I'm Satan himself. "Who have you been talking to?" she asks in a strangled voice. "Who's been talking about me?"

"Nobody," I say.

"Who?" she cries. I turn and pick up Eve's orphaned vegetables.

"We have to go now, honey."

Eve looks up from where she's been stuffing weeds into her pockets. "Why?"

"It's late and it's cold. Aren't you hungry?"

I can feel Sabbathday watching me, her mind whirring with explanations: a vengeful Rachel, a senile Chastity, a be-husbanded Val. I bend over Eve and tug her jacket zipper up to her chin.

"We'll play the Goofy game on Mommy's computer."

"Okay," she says and she drops the weeds still in her hands and starts uphill toward the road.

"Say good-bye," I tell her.

"Good-bye," she says without turning around. I make an apologetic smile to a stunned Sabbathday and then start across the black grass after Eve.

"My diaries!" she cries suddenly. "You've been reading my diaries!"

I turn and stare at her in the dark. Is the jig up?

"What diaries?"

"God!"

"What diaries? What are you talking about?"

"You come into my room while I'm sleeping and read my diaries! My God!"

Put that way, Venner admits it seems a liberty. But it was only one diary, okay two, and only at the provocation of a desperate soul, and I haven't gone back, have I, for volumes two through nineteen?

"Come on!" Eve cries from halfway up to the car.

"How could you?" Sabbathday calls out.

"I didn't," I call back.

"How *could* you?"

"*Time* magazine," I say. "*National Geographic*. The PBS special. There's a lot of ways to find out about you, Sister." She drops her baskets and takes a step toward me. "Come here," she says. I shake my head no. "Come here."

"No," I say. She takes another step. I can't tell if she means to kiss me or coldcock me. "I've got to go," I say and start backing up. A tomato flings itself earthward in a suicidal panic.

"Your nerves are failing you, Mr. Venner."

"No."

"Yes," she says, and then just as I reach the car, her voice heavy with sarcasm: "*Brother* Venner."

CHAPTER ELEVEN

CHERUBIM POSTED
AT THE EASTERN
GATE

We pause a moment to adjust our wings.

Oh, Reader, you impossible nag! I know what you're thinking. You're thinking Venner talks a good game but when push comes to shove, when the virgin of his dreams begins to undress herself, he ducks behind the leafy verbiage of the nearest metaphor. Okay, okay, but consider that a genuine Sabbathday seems never to have established itself as one of my Alternatives and that the faint and tremble of the virgin in the garden took me by surprise. Consider, too, that what we're talking about here is a real human heart pumping blood to real human extremities—also, consider that she may be simply testing her allure, like a teenager, that sure she wants me to want *her*, but doesn't in the great scheme of things want *me* in return—in short that the potential here ranges from authentic hurt to slapstick indignity and that, though there are no doubt those among you who cannot understand why

Venner doesn't pack a condom and head up the hill right now, get going, caution doesn't seem unwarranted, does it?

All of which causes me to hide out in the Hired Men's Quarters most of the weekend. I fear not only a returning Sabbathday but also Rachel rerun and Medusa redux. For the first time since the beginning of the summer I miss Sunday Meeting. There are the usual cars out front, the usual tourists, the usual half-assed seekers from out of state. Toward noon Medusa stops by, toting a cassette deck in one hand, a Dunkin' Donutted Eve in the other. I let them knock and don't answer. Half an hour after that, it's Sabbathday coming across the pasture. I let her knock too, but she is either more sneaky than Medusa or she has had the HMQ under surveillance because she starts talking to me through the wooden door, telling me to open up, why wasn't I in Meeting, am I all right, and so forth. Her voice is kind and concerned and, let's face it, real. It's all I can do to keep from shouting love and/or obscenity through the locked door, but I manage to keep quiet and after a couple of minutes she goes away.

When it gets dark I sneak out for a pizza, maybe also a beer or two, keeping to the fields and the orchard trees until I'm out of sight of the Dwelling House and can climb up onto the road. At the Leaning Tower of Pizza there's a good-looking divorcee type with two kids in the booth across the way who keeps looking at handsome Venner. He smiles once and she smiles back. He gets up to get a third beer and on the way back, let's say, sits down with her and after the usual chitchat encourages her to tell him all about her sad self, a heartrending story which leads to his accompanying her back to her modest home, where, after the kids are in bed, they go through a whole grab bag of the more unusual sexual acts until Venner can't take it anymore and finds himself back at the pizzeria, studying the games on his place mat ("Help Giovanni Rescue Beatrice Before the Tower Tips!") with such oblivion that he only comes up for air after the divorcee's restless kids have gotten her to get up and go.

Riding back out Undermountain Road with a fifth of Wild Turkey in hand and the intention of getting potted back at the HMQ, I stop off at Sally's, sneak up to the bedroom window and peer in, then circle around to the living-room windows and then to the study, where I find her seated at her synthesizer, thick glasses on, wig off, snakes undone, writing some riff that may or may not contain the frequencies of her dubious soul. I listen as she plays it over and over, then as she tries to mate a melody to it, the same dogged expression on her face that she used to have when she was trying to disentangle the Virgin Mary from some Mesopotamian earth goddess. In the end I go sit under Eve's window, open the bourbon and let it cauterize my insides. I recite *Hop on Pop* by memory, sing *sotto voce* a nineteenth-century whaling song I used to lull her to sleep with, try to time my breathing to her sleeping suspiration, or what I imagine is her sleeping suspiration, murmuring "Life" with each inhalation ("Death" with each exhalation). By the time I get back on my bicycle I'm freezing and not a little drunk.

Pedaling, I compose a variety of apostrophes, to the moon, to the night, to Mother Ann, dying Sister Antoinette, to fertile-looking Amanda Green who wears tight sweaters and short skirts and sits in the front row of my New Testament class, to twenty decades of Shaker men who were buffaloed into doing without the comfort and joy of woman and child, to the pastures of New Eden, the tiny paned windows, the white picket fences, and I'm still apostrophizing this and that—the gravel, the grass, the light, which seems to have turned itself on in my absence—when I stumble into the HMQ and find, you guessed it, Sister Sabbathday sitting on my bed.

"Sister?"

She stands up as if she's been caught out in something, though she couldn't have helped hearing me coming. In the process Sometimes-Why gets dumped from her lap.

"You weren't in Meeting today," she says.

"That's right."

"I came to check on you. I thought you might be ill."

"Not ill," I say. "Just drunk."

She eyes the bottle in my hand. I lift it and, like the cowardly lout in a B movie who's sure to get shot by the end of the film, take an obnoxious swig.

"What is it?" she asks.

"Just the woes of the celibate."

"I mean the bottle. What is it?"

I turn the geeky-looking turkey toward her. "Bourbon. One hundred and one proof. I'd offer you some but it's against the Millennial Laws."

"Just my being here is against the Millennial Laws," she says and reaches for one of my plastic cups on the nightstand. I shake my head no, but she holds it out to me like a dare. And like a dare, I fill it for her. She gazes at the wicked liquid a moment and then drinks, and in this B movie (the Projectionist has mixed reels) the ingenue chokes and her eyes fill up with the requisite teenage tears.

"Holy macaroni!" she says hoarsely. Holy macaroni? "Is that what it tastes like?"

"That's what it tastes like, Sister."

She takes another sip, tiny this time.

"I gather you never drank before."

"I had something in Coke once," she says. "When I was in high school. But—" and here I get the slyboots look. "But you know that, of course."

I, of course, don't know that, but I am too drunk and too bereft to set her straight on this or any other matter. I cross the room, lift Sometimes-Why by his rear legs and walk him like a wheelbarrow for a few feet (our one and only trick) and then fall onto my bed. Sabbathday sits in the one chair in the room.

"So, what are you doing here, Sister?" I ask after a minute, draping my arm over my eyes. She makes a kissing sound which causes me to look up in some wonder, but it's only an invitation for Sometimes-Why to jump back into her lap.

"I came to visit."

"To visit."

"And to see how you were."

I let the crook of my arm fall back over my eyes. "You're full of shit."

"And to fuck you."

I sit up and stare at her. She's still got the prim Shaker look, white cap, long dress, mantle hiding her breasts, but on her face is an expression of pride and challenge and, we might even say, of destruction.

"You don't mean that," I say.

"Why not?"

Why not indeed?

"I have all the necessary body parts."

"Sister . . ."

"I have feelings just like anyone else."

"Sister . . ."

"Stop calling me Sister," she says and grabs the bottle away from me. "I'm not your sister."

"What do you want me to call you? Lara?"

"Sabbathday," she says. "My name is Sabbathday."

I sigh and grimace and lie back down. "We're not spoiling for a fight by any chance, are we?"

"What's wrong with Sabbathday?" she wants to know.

"How about Snow White instead," I say. "My wife calls you Snow White."

"Your *ex*-wife, you mean, don't you?"

"My ex-wife."

"Or have you been lying about that too?"

"Too?" I say. "What 'too'?"

She pours herself more bourbon even though she hasn't finished what I gave her. "Like with my diary," she says, "that's what 'too.' "

"Sabbathday," I say and take the bottle back from her, "get it straight. You can't say 'holy macaroni' in one sentence and 'fuck' in the next."

She eyes me with something of Rachel's suspicion.

"Not if you desire unity of—" and I can't think of anything to say except "image" so I don't say anything at all.

"I'm not after unity of—" and she makes a face to punc-
tuate the blank.

"What *are* you after?"

She swirls the bourbon around in her glass. "I don't
know."

And again I catch something like the true Sabbathday,
conflicted, helpless, burdened with the impossibility of her—
are you listening, Sally?—her essence. I feel suddenly so
drunken sweet toward her I want to say something nice, something loving, but I can't think of anything so I just smile. It's
one of those smiles you can feel sort of die on your face, but for
whatever reason, Sabbathday doesn't notice and smiles back.

"Did you mean it?" she asks after a time.

"What?"

"When you said you were in love with me?"

What do Venner and I say? That yes half of us is in love
with you, and the other half is only in love with the idea of
you? Or no we are not in love with you, we are recovering
from postdivorce stress syndrome and we merely picked you
for the object of our affections because you don't really exist,
do you?

"I meant it."

She gazes into her lap with pleasure and—damn my
soul—gratitude. "I don't really see how. You don't know me."

"I know you."

Now she's honest-to-God blushing. I mean the red cheeks
and everything, the whole nine yards of obsolete femininity.
What has she written in that goddamn diary anyway?

"What did it feel like?" she asks, still self-conscious.
"Reading it, I mean. What did it feel like?"

"It was . . ."

"What?" she says.

"It was like . . . looking into someone's soul."

Lenient Reader, consider: Venner is balancing the melodrama of the moment with the imperative of fast thinking with the residue of a Protestant conscience. Also he is trying to recall just how awful is the circle reserved for liars and cheats and the greasy of heart.

"I used to think sometimes that Rachel was reading it. I even wrote things for her to read. I mean slanted things toward her, told her things in disguise. But I never thought . . ." and she drifts off into that oblique smile, still gazing into her lap, and I realize that she actually wants me to have read it, that the illicitness of it touches her in some exciting way. Or worse, that the intimacy of the thing is so new and un-Shakerlike that she has mistaken the fermentation of her own longing for the headiness of love. For a second I am poised on the point of coming clean, telling her that she's misunderstood me, misunderstood the whole situation, but I am unnerved by the thought that maybe she hasn't, that she knows more about matters of the heart than I do. Is it possible that Sabbathday—confronted with a Venner intent upon the moral hieroglyphs of stone walls, paying her the compliment of sabotaging cabbies, breaking and entering, thrice incarcerated for his love—that Sabbathday is capable of falling for our ignoble self?

"And I hardly know anything about you," she's saying. "You know so much about me and I don't know anything about you. You haven't got a diary I can read, have you?"

"Just a doctoral dissertation."

"I mean I don't know how old you are or anything."

"Thirty-five."

"Or what people call you. They don't call you Mr. Venner, do they?" This last with an imitation of Eldress.

"Just Venner."

"No first name?"

"John."

"John," she says like she's more comfortable with that.

"But no one's called me John since my Little League team which had three Johns on it."

"You played Little League?"

"The Rexall Rabbits. Second base."

And I grin some sort of All-American grin. She's leaning forward, elbows on her knees, both hands around her cup so that her nose is just above the rim.

"Kiss me," she says out of nowhere.

"What?"

"Kiss me."

I stare at various hallucinations and don't move a muscle.

"I've never been kissed before. I want you to kiss me."

O Venner, you fornicator! You would-be defiler of Little Debbie Snack Cakes and Monica the Madonna! What a shock it is to find yourself capable of good! Because, reason it as you will, Reader, I can't do it. Even with her face turned to me, virginal mouth, delicate lash, unpolluted skin, I cannot lean over and put the hoofprint of my lips on the shimmer of her soul.

"I can't," I say finally. She opens her eyes.

"Why?"

"I don't know. I just can't."

"I'm not asking anything more. I'm not asking—" and she doesn't finish. "I just want to know. I want to know what it's like."

Sabbathday, you see before you a man less guilty of the glory of your violation than you think—just two volumes, that's all.

"I can't."

"You said you loved me."

"I did . . ."

"I thought the usual next step was kissing."

"There are all kinds of love, Sister."

"And your love," she says, "it doesn't include kissing?"

Oh, brother! What Venner's love can include! But he can't bring himself to start down that particular path. Instead he repeats with a touch of cowardly enigma, "There are all kinds of love."

"And *your* love," she says again, but this time with such a
look of are-you-putting-me-on mockery that there's no need
to finish.

"*Amor dei intellectualis*," I manage.

"What?"

"*Amor dei intellectualis*. Spinoza's 'love of God.' "

She gets exasperated-looking. "You're telling me that the
love you feel for me is the love you feel for God?"

I nod. "Something like that."

"Don't be ridiculous."

"It's not impossible, Sister."

"It's love of woman you feel. Don't kid yourself."

"Some people love the image of Christ on the cross."

"Love of woman. *Amor dei womanis*."

"And some people love a statue of the Virgin Mary or a
Saint Christopher's medal or a photo of Elvis or—" and I'm
on the verge of reciting a reasonable list of holy illusions
when there's a knock at the door. It's Sally, I think, and I am
suddenly taken with the thought of introducing her to a Sabbathday who is drunk and urging debauchery in my bedroom.

"It's my ex-wife," I say, crossing the room and going down
the short hallway. "It won't take a minute." But when I open
the door, instead of Sally it's Eldress Rachel, Rachel dressed
in a car coat out of the nineteen-forties and with a big red
Ray-o-Vac flashlight in her hand.

"I'm looking for Sister Sabbathday," she says without
apology or excuse. "Is she visiting you?"

"Visiting me?" I say before I have a chance to realize she's
probably seen her through the window. "No."

"You haven't seen her?"

"No."

"She's not in her room and she's not in the Weaving
Shop." She says this like there's only one other place she
could be.

"Haven't seen her," I answer, but even as I say it I hear
Sabbathday behind me, coming down the hall. I wonder if

I'm supposed to block her from sight or what, but in the end step out of the way.

"It's Eldress," I say stupidly.

"Must be past my bedtime," Sabbathday remarks and glides out the door. Rachel turns and follows her without giving me another look. I watch them from the precipice of various physical and metaphysical thresholds.

"It's *amor feminae,*" I call out, as if I've changed my mind. But she keeps on, up the hill.

"I hope you can get a heater for that steeple of yours, Mr. Venner," Rachel calls back.

CHAPTER TWELVE

DOING WHAT THEY DO OUTSIDE THE GARDEN

"And was the archangel in attendance?"

By which my ex-wife means not Sabbathday but the archangel Michael, flaming sword in hand, pointing Venner toward the disconsolate east, *cf.* various Renaissance paintings and *Paradise Lost.*

Because I got expelled. Just like that, bingo! kicked out of New Eden for indiscretions not even of my own devising. The whole thing was terrible and swift, involving Venner the next morning going out in his work clothes, then toward midmorning an incoherent summons from Sister Chastity, and Eldress seated at her table in the Elders' Room, no bookkeeping in front of her this time, just the menace of right thinking and the holy trinity of her trifocals splitting Venner into his component parts.

The charges were many. And though I made some effort to defend myself, whined the Adamic whine, the truth is I was feeling guilty and, you know, the responsible party. I tried to get her to tell me exactly what I had done wrong, but she waved me away, and when I persisted, let loose with a string of violations, among them lying, using alcohol, being a hypocrite, accepting clandestine visits from my wife.

"My *ex*-wife," I corrected.

"Worse."

It was a humiliating interview. At one point when I tried to do the insinuating bit, I mean tried to threaten her with a Sabbathday who was confused and unhappy, a Sabbathday who had been asking for it—which she had been, after all, hadn't she?—she heaved a big sigh and to Venner's surprise unpinned her cap, laid it beside her on the table and began rubbing her face and head as if just waking up.

"Listen to me, Mr. Venner," she said. "You're thirty-five years old. You've been married. You've been divorced. You've had a child. You've had, I suppose, carnal knowledge of numerous women . . ."

I began to say I beg your pardon, but she put up a hand to ward off the injured-party stuff.

"For all her intelligence and willpower, in many ways Sister Sabbathday is a child. The experience she has received in New Eden does not fit her to life in the world. She has no knowledge of—" and she grimaced at the thought of everything Sabbathday had no knowledge of. "The pressures on her are many and subtle, even insidious. Whether you took advantage of her by active intention or by passive opportunism is irrelevant to me. She is no match for you. It is up to me, as Eldress, to protect her."

And she picked her cap back up, pinning it to the memory of some hank of hair. Venner sat dumb and, maybe, human.

"In spite of her actions, I believe with all my heart that Sister Sabbathday is a Shaker, that she wants to be a Shaker, that she believes in the Shaker way. If you have ideas of luring her away, ideas of turning her head by telling her that you are in love with her and so forth, I don't think that is a wise, or even kind, course of action. Do you?" And she waited, as if for some evidence of common decency. "She tells me that you know about the time she ran away?"

I didn't answer.

"I can guess why she told you. I can also imagine the manner in which she told you, but the truth is the experience frightened her deeply. What happened to her I don't know, perhaps nothing out of the ordinary, but when she called us from New York City she was scared and crying. We had to ask an acquaintance of ours, a member of the Friends of the Shakers, to go and get her."

And she waited for some reaction, some admission from me, but I was busy watching Sabbathday pausing before the shops on Fifth Avenue.

"So you see you are not the first time she's toyed with the world's people. I have no doubt that had her toying reached a certain point she would have been just as scared, and just as quick to come home. But in any case I don't want that to happen." And like the Pope declaring an audience at an end, she got up. "If you don't have your car and need to call a taxi to carry your things, I'll be in the Goods Shop."

"Let me see her," I said suddenly, rising too. "Let me explain to her."

"No."

"Let me at least come out now and then. To work on the walls."

"No."

"I promise I won't talk to her ever again."

She walked around the end of the table and started out the door.

"Eldress!"

"Honor our wishes, Mr. Venner. You have no choice."

"I *do* have a choice," I said, following her out into the hallway and mentally pummeling myself at the same time. "I can see her all I want. With or without your permission."

She started up the stairway to the second floor.

"It won't be trespassing if I'm here by invitation."
She stopped on the landing. "Mr. Venner, this is the Sisters' stairway."
"I can bring her into the world. She's ready."
She gazed down at my feet standing where no man had stood for a hundred and fifty years. "You're probably right," she said. "If you think that would be good for her." And shockingly, she reached out and touched me, touched the side of my face. "Her soul is in your hands."

• • •

"I mean was there the flaming sword and the archangel and everything?"
It's nearly 1 A.M. We're lying on Sally's bed, Sometimes-Why in between us for a bundling board. He keeps trying to get up to get away and I keep pushing him back down. Otherwise I am paralyzed on the precipice of apostasy.
"I mean it's not everyone who gets to get kicked out of the Garden of Eden at this late date of the world's development. How does it feel?"
It feels rotten. Also, like the purpose of one's life has evaporated.
"V?" she says.
"Please. No more. It's late."
"Will you tell me at least why you keep manhandling Why-why?"
"No," I say; then: "He's our bundling board."
"Our what?"
But I don't have it in me to remind her of the Puritans and the nighttime separation of courting couples. Sally turns over on her side, toward me. She's wearing only a nightgown while Venner, Shaker or no Shaker, is still fully dressed.
"So that's the drift of things?" she intuits. "You're using Why-why to keep me at a distance?"
"Something like that."
"Why, sweetie?"
Because, Eldress, Venner is in need of a bed. His steeple is

too cold (it's early November after all), and the crummy motel he's been staying at is forty dollars a night and that adds up. As yet his advertisement for a vacant manger has gone unanswered.

"Maybe some music," Sally says and sits up in bed and aims the remote control at her cassette deck. In it is the final cut of "Essential Ecstasy," pro arrangement, saucy cymbals, risqué lyrics: a hit even to Venner's antique ears. In the jade light of the stereo system I can see the left side of Sally's face, the maddening lips, the high cheekbone that drove me wild back in "Mariology and the Cult of the Virgin. She's got her hair cut, back to the pageboy of my love, though she says it's not for me but for when she goes on tour, because of the wig. She'll be gone in three months, coincident with the release of "Essential Ecstasy," opening for some heavy-metal band (Nazi Detergent I think she said) first in Boston, then Albany, Ann Arbor, Toronto and so on across the continent. Plans right now are for a film crew to meet her in a couple of cities, getting footage out of which a music video will be made. That his ex-wife has progressed in her quest for electronic essence while Venner has suffered a serious setback should be apparent to everyone in the auditorium.

"What I don't understand is why you didn't kiss her when you had the chance."

Venner doesn't either. Given the long line of preparation beginning with posted pornography, the Peeping Tom phase, "Simple Gifts" during his ex-wife's *voluptatem*, why the cold feet when the object of his pollution was finally at hand?

"Was it because you love her or because you don't love her?"

"Both," I say; then: "Neither."

The tape has moved on to "Doobie-doobie-doo-wah," the lyrics of which consist solely of fifties shoobie-shoobie syllables ("woo woo woo woo-*ooh*"): I kid you not, Reader, even petulant Venner can see Medusa as the innovative temptress of postmodern rock and roll.

"If you didn't kiss her because you *don't* love her, would

you say it was because of the residual existence of what used to be called normal human decency?"

Shoobie-shoobie-shoo-wah.

"And if you didn't kiss her because you *do* love her, was it because of your nobility of soul? I mean you didn't want to taint the very object of your love?"

Doobie-doobie-doo-wah.

"Is that why you won't kiss *me?* Because you don't want to pollute the object of your love?"

Venner doesn't know or even ask himself why, but he leans over and kisses her. The bundling board squirms and jumps out of the way.

"Oh!" she says when I'm done.

"What's the matter?"

"You kissed me."

"So what?"

"So, if you love me, does that mean you're *trying* to pollute me?"

"Give me a break."

"Or does it mean you *don't* love me, and you don't have the normal human decency not to take advantage of me?"

"Give me a break. I just got kicked out of the Garden of Eden."

"It's a unique distinction," she says. "And to celebrate, what do you say we do what they do outside the garden?"

I get up and go stand at the window. The world is lying under the cold silver of a heavy frost. Or maybe the artifice of streetlight. I happen to be looking westward, toward New Eden, and I imagine Sabbathday asleep in her room, the still house, the golden floorboards, imagine a magical me standing in her doorway, a few quiet steps, a hand reached out, a kiss on the sleeping lips, various archetypal images out of the brothers Grimm.

"When I'm famous," Sally says from back on the bed, "I wonder whether Elektra's PR will feel obliged to hide your existence, *à la* Cynthia Lennon. I mean so all the teenyboppers won't get discouraged."

I'm gliding across the golden floorboards again only this time Sabbathday wakes up, and when I smile and make to kiss her she pushes me off, and on her face is a look of disenchantment, of fear even, the quick loathing of the beauty for the beast. Somewhere in the next room Eldress Rachel and/or Walt Disney are laughing.

"V?"

I sigh and turn around and, with the diapason of human gift and vice stinging in my veins, not to mention Medusa's voice like a soundtrack to the scene, begin to undress. I take off my sweater, my shirt, my undershirt, my socks, my pants, my—oh, Reader, you know how this goes.

"Venner!"

I cross to the bed and stand there a moment. She's smiling at me—Medusa or Sally, I can't tell which—holding her arms out.

"Baby," she coos when I lie down beside her. "Welcome back."

• • •

Mother Ann:

I am a member of the world's people. With all things invisible I no longer concern myself: the black light of the soul, the dark chambers of the heart, the metaphysics of white picket fences. For the next few weeks I content myself with the pleasures of the flesh, eating and sleeping and evacuating waste. I take to watching MTV in the evenings while corporeal Eve plays on the floor. In the bluish glow of photons I begin to get what Medusa is after, the ruse of it all, the physical reality of arm and leg arcing in radio waves toward the heavens, the arc become parabola, the return to earth, the mimic reincarnation in two dimensions, the transcendent that doesn't transcend anything. In a fit of self-abasement I make orisons to Saint Clare of Assisi, who in the thirteenth century had a Technicolor vision of the Crucifixion on the walls of her impoverished cell and for that was later named patron saint of television. (Oh, skeptical Reader, look it up in *The Oxford Dictionary of Saints*.)

In the cellar I dig out my dissertation and set about cannibalizing it for articles that will look good on my *vita* come tenure time. I buy a fifth of Jack Daniel's for the chapel custodian, have a man-to-man with him about how getting divorced puts you behind the eight ball, doesn't it, women can do it to you, can't they, and let's forget about the mattress in the steeple, okay? In my office I slog through a pile of papers on the Gnostic gospels, in the Faculty Club smile at the chair of the Tenure Advisory Board, make a lunch date with the dean of the college to discuss funding for a symposium on American Religious Splinter Groups. I start wearing a tie.

On my *vita* my stay with the Shakers of New Eden appears under Recent Field Work.

I get the old roof rack put on the Peugeot and under the cover of darkness pull up to the rear door of the chapel. Up in the steeple I take a deep breath and start dismantling my photos of Sister Sabbathday, half of which have peeled off from the cold anyway, start loading into cartons my books and pamphlets and scholarly Xeroxes, filing away in a garbage bag the this and the that of my former obsession. When I start to yank the sheets off the mattress I notice in the half-light a piece of paper lying on the pillow, the handwriting of which has a dreamlike familiarity.

Where are you? I need to see you. Please.

For a moment Venner feels the aphrodisia of forbidden love—string section swelling, color by Panavision—but the reality of Reality moves quickly in, the moral burden of Eldress's warning, and though he wonders what movement of soul and/or body is occurring in Sister (Ms.?) Sabbathday Wells, wonders too at the poetic symmetry of Venner become the pursued, Sabbathday the pursuer, after a minute the missive ends up in the Gladbag along with the other vanities.

Home on the weekend, searching out a house to rent for her backup men, Medusa makes love to me in ways that make me wonder what the guy in the black Porsche knows that I don't know.

On Monday, in my morning mail at the college, I find a plain brown envelope and inside, a magazine that makes even venereal Venner blush. It's dated from two years ago. How she knows or whether it's just a lucky guess, I can't fathom but for several days I am haunted by an invisible Sabbathday, and then toward the middle of the week get the real thing: on campus her gray cape in the distance, hood up the first time, down the second, the last Shakeress watching me from the steps of the Student Union, from the garden in front of the library. She's sans spotting scope, but I get the point anyway. Once or twice I gesture to her but each time she moves away, slips into the student traffic, only to reappear across the quad from my office window. I wave her homeward and pull the shade. But Friday afternoon while I'm lecturing on Calvin in the chapel classroom, I catch sudden sight of her handwriting on the blackboard at the back of the room:

The best way to save your soul
is to save someone else's body.

I lose my place and have to pretend the antics of original sin have me as buffaloed as they do my students.

"Since when do Shakers read twentieth-century Jewish philosophers?" Medusa asks when I tell her about my persecution. She's just returned from the outskirts of town where she's rented a farmhouse with a heated barn. "And just who's saving whom anyway?"

"I'm not saving anybody," I say. "I've given over imagining vain things."

"I mean does she think the best way for you to save your soul is for you to save *her* body, *i.e.* lay her? Or does she mean the best way for her to save *her* soul is to save *your* body?"

Venner puts on the face of the innocent. "What's a soul?"

"And does she mean to save your body by Shakering it or laying it?"

"What's a body?"

"You want me to go have a word with her?"

"Please."

"Do the enraged wife bit?" And she makes to slap Sabbathday a good one.

• • •

When the band members arrive Medusa throws a party for them out at the farmhouse. I'm invited, and in the spirit of my recent renunciations, not to mention my new allegiance to all things physical, I go. I've got intentions in the direction of the female populace, also of keeping an eye out for black Porsches, also of getting drunk. The band members themselves have all got the look of pros, studio guys with the requisite cool. Out in the barn they've got their Stratocasters and their amps set up and though no one plays anything all the way through I hear the riffs and chord progressions of some of Medusa's songs. The Orchids are there, also most of the Gorgons, also Melanie and her husband, some of our old friends, the owner of The Missionary Position, a sextet of lounge lizards, all in all the inklings of an entourage.

I drink Wild Turkey and hang out in the animal stalls. There's dancing to a collection of old sixties hits, lots to eat and at various strategic locations women complete with all necessary equipment. I listen to the bassist play along with the Stones ("Sympathy for the Devil") and exchange crudities with an orange-haired punkess named Mike, who drifts my way and who ends up making the sign of the cross at me and sulking like John the Baptist in the hayloft. Toward midnight I'm engaged in an inspection of stalls, wondering which if any would qualify as a manger, when someone speaks behind me.

"It's the doctor of divinity."

I turn and, guess what? It's the drummer who can't drum, the one with the breasts. Jane, I think.

"Jane," I say.

"Ann."

"Ann. How are you?"

"Not drunk enough," she says.

I lean over the stall I'm in and pour half my Wild Turkey into her glass. "Drunk enough for what?"

She knocks the bourbon off in one go and hands me the empty glass. "For this, for that," she says. "Get some more and we'll find out what else."

Oh dear and/or boy! we think. On the way to the bar I pass Medusa, who asks what's up.

"Just following orders."

"Whose orders?"

"Yours. Those concerning Abandonment to the World of the Flesh. Now excuse me."

And I muscle my way past her. At the bar I get the bourbon, load up on canapés, say "Hi" to an Orchid and start back across the barn. When I find Jane she's leaning up against a cow stall, a different one, eying the Slingerland drum set Deusie's drummer got set up.

"What a raw deal."

"What?" I say handing her her drink and a ham hors d'oeuvre.

"*We* put those songs together," she says. "I mean we arranged them, tried them out, refined them. You know?"

"Sure."

"I even heard one of my licks on 'The Flesh and the Spirit.' "

"Sue."

"Ann," she says with a face.

"I mean sue. Sue her."

"For what?"

For breach of contract, I think. For mental cruelty, abandonment, shafting the Virgin Mary. "I don't know," I say.

"They're *her* songs."

I nod. She looks through the bodies to where Medusa's talking to a couple of skinheads. "She's going to be fucking famous. It's hard to believe."

Is it ever: my ex-wife invading the intestines of America in the form of radio waves, *People* magazine, the *National Enquirer* at the checkout line (ROCK STAR GIVES BIRTH TO BABY WITH TAIL—EX-HUSBAND COMMITTED).

"What used to be in here anyway?" Jane/Ann/Sue says, turning and peering into the stall. "Cows, pigs, horses?"

"Animals."

"Yeah, animals."

And she gazes with moody concentration at the century of pig urine staining the cement floor. After a minute, in the spirit of my new allegiance to the etcetera, I say, "Oink."

"Oink!" Sue replies. She smiles at me and wrinkles her nose in the *comme il faut* fashion of rabbits. (Sabbathday, save me!)

"Tell me something," she says.

"What?"

"Medusa always hinted you were weird."

"Weird?"

"In bed I mean."

"Not me," I say. "Missionary position only."

She picks a cracker crumb off her chest. "I could go for a little weirdness."

"No batteries or singing allowed."

"I mean the guy I'm with now thinks screwing is a close-order drill. If it's not in the manual of arms you don't do it."

"And only for purposes of propagation."

She smiles an are-you-kidding-or-what smile at me. The top two buttons of her sweater have come mysteriously undone. (If only undergraduate Venner had known "oink" was all that was necessary.)

"Tell me what you like," she says.

"Everything," I say.

"Really?"

"If it's got to do with the human body, everything. But nix on the human heart. Ditto the soul."

She wrinkles her nose again, cute. "I don't get it."

"Let's dance," I say and lead her out into the airy apse of the barn.

We hold our drinks in one hand and do the *faux*-coital thing under the fir rafters. Venner's not a bad dancer, I find, once the soul is no longer tied like a tin can to his tail. In between the toss of a hip and the heft of a hoof, I see Medusa, surrounded by various male attendants, watching us from down in the transept. We dance to "Save Me" and then the Animals and then when slow-pulsed "Surfer Girl" comes on, close in on one another and—O! Sabbathday!—there's the feel of her skin, the slide of her thigh, the Darwinian fit of the female to the male. I close my eyes like a tumescent teenager and dream of German trains penetrating Viennese tunnels.

"You're beautiful," I whisper into her neck.

"Oh!"

"You've got beautiful flesh."

She pulls back and looks at me like maybe I've insulted her. I kiss her.

"Lips," I say.

She closes her eyes and leans back into me. "Yes."

"Legs."

"Yes."

"Cheeks," I moan, "tongues, toenails, hoofs, ham hocks."

She draws back. "What is it with you?"

"Pledging allegiance," I say, and then I smile the winsome Venner smile and murmur something about being drunk.

"Me too," she says, smiling, and she does the feminine-head-on-masculine-shoulder routine. Venner wonders if she knows that he knows that she knows his *membrum virile* is on the move. "I've got some dope in the car," she says after a minute. The Beach Boys glide into rock-and-roll eternity on a major chord.

"Does it require a needle?" squeamish Venner wants to know.

"No."

"Then let's go."

And I take her by the hand and lead her through the bodies. Whether Medusa sees us leave or not I don't know and I don't care. We tramp through the rutted driveway onto the lawn. It's snowing, the first snow of the year: crisp air, white flakes, white world, the usual cleansing imagery. We climb into the car, no Porsche but a Chevy Chevette wouldn't you know it.

"It's marijuana," she says and takes a Gladbag out of the glove compartment. An illegal substance Venner has not partaken of since his years at the Divinity School. Jane turns the engine on to get the heater going and starts to roll a joint, during which activity sophomoric Venner does his level best to paw her.

"No," she says.

"Yes."

"Not in the car!"

"Archetypal American experience," I answer. "Sure?"

"Not here."

Which answer seems to promise somewhere. We sit and smoke and listen to the radio over the hum of the heater. A year from now when I'm doing this (with what new blossom? in what new orchard?) will it be to the beat of "Essential Ecstasy" scraped out of the midnight sky?

"Where are you living now?" Sue asks.

"Medusa's."

"Still?"

"Again," I say. "A recent rapprochement."

She gives me a look of inquisition. The matter seems to be where to go to break the Seventh Commandment. From inside the barn we can hear "Essential Ecstasy" for the umpteenth time.

"I can't stand it," Ann says and jacks up the volume on the radio.

"Me either."

"Shall we split?" she says, giving me the quizzing look

and putting the car in gear. Before I can say yes we spin on the wet grass and take off out the driveway. Venner's head is soggy with alcohol and marijuana and self-destruction.

"Home, Jeeves," he says.

"That's just what I was thinking," says Jeeves.

"What?"

"As long as she's not there," she says and gives me a wicked look. The thought that Venner is being used for the purposes of revenge dawns on him for the first time.

"Better idea," he says and points westward.

"What?"

" 'They are bound in prisons of hell and their torment appears like melted lead, poured through them in the same parts where they have taken their carnal pleasures.' "

"Yuck," says Ann. "What's that from?"

" 'The Marriage of the Flesh Is a Covenant with Death, and an Agreement with Hell,' " answers erudite Venner.

"You *are* weird."

He points down this road, down that road. The snowflakes eat one another in the bright headlights. The black trees whip past. As we go we find ourselves more and more under the red cycloptic eye atop Spirit Mountain. When we turn onto Undermountain Road the radio freaks out from a surplus of signal.

"Here?" Ann wonders when I gesture the car to a stop in front of New Eden. "The Shakers?"

"The United Society of Believers in Christ's Second Appearing," I correct, stepping out of the car. But just as I do, the world performs some sleight of hand in the gravity line and I end up on my hands and knees in the wet snow.

"Are you pissed or what?" laughs Ann from inside the car.

What I am, damn my soul, is struck (*even now, inhuman Reader, even now!*) by the serenity of New Eden: midnight snow making a virginal veil over pasture and pond, the four-square quadrinity of twelve-over-twelve windows, heaven-pointing gables, right ridgepoles, pristine vistas, this museum of American ideals. O New Eden, seat of my former hopes in the soul-aspiring line! You see before you etcetera. I hate you.

"Your feet," I say to Jane, who has gotten out of the car and is coming around to me.

"What about my feet?"

"You're mucking up the snow!" I shout. I am still on my knees. To move is to pollute.

"You *are* pissed," she says again. She leans her rear against the fender and looks to the left toward the Dwelling House, to the right toward the stone barn. There is not a trace of reverence or *mysterium* or even old-fashioned awe in her expression. Venner is among the barbarians.

"Why here?" she asks.

Venner *is* a barbarian. Vanity and dust, etcetera. Remember? We spit in the snow and pick ourselves up.

"The American experience," I say. "To regenerate oneself by fornicating on sacred ground. Also, radio waves pouring through our parts. Also—" and I take out the key to the Hired Men's Quarters and hold it out to her.

"How do you rate a key?" she wants to know. I put on my best doctor-of-divinity face and gesture for her to follow me.

"The Shakers," she says after a moment, trying to match her step to my footprints. "Aren't they celibate or something? I mean like they don't ever do it, right?"

They don't, that's right, they don't.

"Or is that the Mennonites?"

We make it through the slushy snow and stop on the stoop of my former habitation, my former home, my former salvation. I put the key to the padlock.

But Reader, guess what? That octogenarian freak has had the lock changed and my key won't fit. Can you believe it? Various Viennese leitmotifs flutter about castrated Venner. Not to mention errant Adam trying to sneak back under cover of darkness.

"She changed the lock."

"Who?" says confused Sue.

"Never mind," I say and start across the wet pasture toward the Dwelling House.

"I don't have the shoes for this!"

I keep going, why I don't know, but I do, through the nightmare of utopia, the ghost of former cowflops hidden under the fresh snow, now and then the detritus of stone walls that will never know the curative of my hands. From up along the road Ann whisper-shouts "Come on!" but I keep going, right up to the Dwelling House door, where something about the metaphysics of the moment, not to mention the familiar patina of the brass, makes me try my key in the door. And sure enough, the octogenarian cheapskate has merely had the locks switched. I open the door and peer into the dark passage of the lower hall. Various possibilities involving Sabbathday's white skin and a pillow held over Eldress's face are in the air. Behind me, Ann is coming down the tar walk.

"Okay, I get it," she whispers.

"You get what?"

She pushes past me and peers into the hall. When she speaks her voice is conspiratorial.

"You want to do it here because . . . you know, because no one's ever gotten laid here before. Right?"

I take the Fifth.

"Right?" she says. "I mean of all the women who have ever lived here—hundreds, right?—I'd be the first to get poked?"

"Please . . ."

She slips her hands inside my jacket. "What a kick!" And she lifts her face to me and kisses me, on the lips, twice. "Come on," she whispers and takes me by the hand.

And we do it (not *it*, slutty Reader, but it): we violate the sanctity of Shaker order by putting polluted foot on sublime pine. Venner is twisted up with gifts, pro and con. Ann is eager and excited and walking ahead of him down the dark hall.

"They keep it heated," she says, sounding surprised and speaking too loudly.

"Ssh," I say, coming up behind her.

"Is there a bed somewhere?"

"Sssh!"

"Don't be so jumpy. No one can hear us outside."

"Not outside," I say. "Inside."

She gets a charge out of this. "You mean they're here?" she whispers. "This building? This is where they sleep?"

I point upstairs.

"Oh, wow!" And she stares up through the ceiling. "They're like a hundred years old or something, right?"

All but one, dear heart.

"A hundred years old and they've never done it."

And she starts down the hall again, turns into the dining room, where there are four long tables and dozens of chairs, five-figure tin chandeliers hanging from the ceiling. She tests one of the tables for sturdiness and then turns around, pulling me into her. She smiles and bites my lip.

"Here," she whispers.

Reader, what do I do? Do I consent to fornicate upon the table where every morning of her life Sabbathday Wells takes sustenance? O! if Venner had the true killer spirit, he'd do it! He'd idolize and adulterate! Blaspheme and hereticize and enjoy every minute of it! But no matter what I tell myself, no matter what pollutant pep talk or unholy harangue, I am lackluster in my kisses, tepid in my touch, hesitant even to unlock the remaining buttons of Jane's sweater, which, after a certain stretch of time, causes Ann to pull back.

"What are you, chicken?"

For the second time, maybe third, Venner's been proffered the apple of his basest desires and he has been unable to eat of it. As Adams go, Venner is a piss-poor one.

"Medusa's," I say. "Let's do it at Medusa's."

"Both," she says. "Standing up here and lying in bed there. *Her* bed."

"Can't," I say.

"Why not?"

"Because she'll be coming home," I say. "It's got to be two o'clock by now."

She looks unconvinced.

"If we're going to besmirch the marriage bed," I say, deputizing the pollution imagery, "we have to besmirch it now."

This seems to get her. She tugs me by the collar and we set off down the hall again. Somewhere above, Sabbathday Wells is taking oxygen in and expelling carbon dioxide. So it is with all who live, *cf.* "the world's people," pg. 1 *et passim.* When we go out I have enough presence of mind to lock the door behind us.

On the drive to the house I experience winter thoughts about the pursuit of happiness and the fulfillment of our desires. Ann reaches over to stroke my thigh, says "Tsk-tsk" when her fingers stray far enough to discover my *membrum* is no longer *virile.* When we turn into the driveway and she gets eagerly out I consider pulling the too-drunk-to-do-it act, but as we go up the walk I realize it won't wash.

Inside, this is how it goes: First we debauch for a while on the living-room couch, and then we defile, and then we get up and go into the bedroom where we besmear and besmirch, paw and whimper and—O! Reader! How much do you have to be told about this anyway? You know how it goes. You've done it yourself, I dare say, haven't you? *Haven't you!* Consider this, *hypocrite lecteur:* according to Venner's fifth-grade teacher the number of human beings who have ever lived on this earth is in the neighborhood of five billion; multiply this by the average number of adult fornications per week (three, according to Dear Abby), and that by fifty-two and that by, oh, let's be conservative and say thirty years, and you have a figure of some 23.4 trillion times that humanity has copulated since the dinosaurs ceased to do it, so what's the big deal about Venner's adding one more? It's just a blip in the history of human depravity. So don't point accusing fingers at me, *mon semblable, mon frère.*

When it's over, after the heat-sink and the horror and the cries of love, after I'm through thinking about sties and stalls and just what moral algorithm has brought me to this pass, after the sheets have cooled and the bedroom air has begun to chill, I turn over and look up at what I have been dimly thinking is a shadow from the living-room light and see instead Medusa, maybe even Sally, arms locked across her chest, standing in the doorway. I can think of nothing to say except oink.

"You bastard."

Next to me, Ann *et al.* lifts herself up on her elbow.

"Oh, hi," she says. Medusa smiles the winsome Medusa smile.

"I hope you fuck better than you drum," she says.

"She does," Venner attests.

"Get out. Both of you."

And she spins around and goes out into the living room. Ann makes a "whoops" face. I get up and put my pants on, then my shirt for good measure, wondering the whole time whether this was in fact the right strategy to adopt. In the line of saving Sabbathday's soul, I mean.

"I don't deserve this," Medusa says when I come into the living room. She's sitting on the couch. I find my socks and shoes and start putting them on. "Just because you're back in the world of the flesh, what do you think, you think you can go around dicking anyone you want?"

I knew there was a catch.

"You think you don't have any responsibilities to the feelings of others?"

"Feelings?" I say. All part of the airy invisible.

"You think you can do this and I'm not going to mind?"

"Shoobie-shoobie-shoo-wah," I answer. She does the I-could-scream thing and takes off for the kitchen. Ann comes out of the bedroom, dressed, tugging at her bra.

"Is the coast clear?"

I nod, but just as I do, Medusa appears in the kitchen doorway.

"Suppose I'd come back with Eve?"

"Doobie-doobie-doo-wah," says heartless Venner.

She catches sight of Ann, makes a face and goes back into the kitchen.

"Where are my shoes?" whispers Ann.

We start looking for her shoes.

"Or I could have come home with friends," says Medusa, back in the doorway. "With Melanie and Jim. What would that have been like?" She looks at me like she expects an answer, and then at Ann on her hands and knees in front of the couch. "Will you *leave?*" she says.

"I'm looking for my shoes."

She goes back into the kitchen. I hear the phone being dialed.

"Here they are," says Ann, pulling her pumps from under the couch. She sits down and puts them on.

"This is Sally Shannon at eleven fourteen Undermountain Road," we hear from the kitchen. "My ex-husband and his bimbo are in my house and won't leave. Could you send someone?"

"I'm out of here," says Ann pulling her coat on. She heads for the door but pauses long enough to look back at me. "You were sweet," she says.

Reader, did you hear that? Venner was sweet.

"Bye," she says and opens the door.

And I'm left with profaned air and polluted furniture. After a minute Medusa is back in the kitchen doorway. She's eating potato chips.

"You had to bring her here?"

This is perhaps not the time to tell my ex-wife that all I did I did under the rubric of her own metaphysics. I just sit on the couch, a sated old goat.

"Before you go," she says, "tell me truthfully. Do you think I deserve this?"

"I'm not going anywhere," I say simply.

"Do you? Do you think I deserve this?"

"I've got no place to go."

"Do you?"

I sketch a few calculations in the air. "I know a woman named Sally Shannon who doesn't deserve it," I say. "But someone named Medusa—"

"What is it with you? What's the big deal?"

"Why not Medea?" I quote. *"Why not Circe?"*

"Yes?"

"The meaninglessness of the name prescribes a meaninglessness of allegiance."

She just stares at me.

"You're a Visual Image," I say. "Visual Images don't get their feelings hurt."

She crunches a potato chip in awe.

"Anyway, you're leaving, the last I heard."

She comes into the room, lifts my jacket off the back of a chair and drops it on my lap. "It's you who's leaving," she says. "I want you out of here."

And she grabs me by the hand and yanks me upright. I maintain perpendicularity for a moment and then sink back onto the couch. She kicks me, hard, in the shin.

"Ow!"

"Out. Or I really will call the police."

I stand up and put on my jacket. "I was merely trying to live a life of pure physicality. I was shooting for essential oinkness. Oinkitude. I thought it was what you wanted."

She pushes me toward the door.

"Listen. If we define oinkitude as a state of pure flesh, then do I take it that you prefer me with a smidgen of soul after all?"

"I prefer you gone."

"Gone? Utterly without oinkitude, you mean? Pure soul?"

"Pure gone," she says and opens the door.

"It's snowing," I say, once again on thresholds both physical and metaphysical. "And there are no mangers in town. I've already checked."

"Out," Medusa says and pushes me onto the porch.

"*O little town of—*"

Behind me the door closes with an apocalyptic bark. I stop singing. The snow and the dark and the cold whisper all around.

Mother Ann, it's Venner in the wilderness again.

• • •

Out on Undermountain Road the orange snow plows patrol like prehistoric monsters, headlights burning, hazard lights flashing. They aim for me, whether on purpose or out of cosmic unconcern who knows, but more than once I am nearly buried in the accumulated detritus of a falling heaven. Halfway on my way into town a police car roars past on its way out so that I begin to think maybe Medusa called the cops after all, but a few minutes later an ambulance follows. It disappears into the whorl of its own headlights. I trudge into town.

The first hour I spend at Dunkin' Donuts drinking coffee and eating crullers. The second hour it's the all-night laundromat, devoid of humans and quiet except for the monotonous sound of an empty dryer tumbling emptiness. I open the dryer door and try to make it stop, but it won't. Toward five in the morning a woman comes in, scabby with insomnia. She dumps her dirty clothes into a washer, and then turns around and wonders who the homeless fellow doing his invisible laundry is. The dryer goes around and around, and if Venner were given to such metaphors he'd remark upon the cleansing of the soul's garments. Instead it's back out into the storm with him.

The problem with having a body is you have to put it somewhere. So the little Lord Jesus discovered when he found himself incarnated (*vide* "Away in a Manger"). The steeple is out, the HMQ is out, Sally's of course is out. There's always the chapel office, but Venner is not ready to give up the lapidary of his loneliness this poetic wintry night. He braves snowdrift and plowjob, stands in front of Video Voluptuary Inc. watching the *virgo genetrix* of "Mr. Ed." There's simply no one around. No one on the sidewalks, on the streets, no cars, not even the insomniac when I pass the laundromat again. Somewhere over the building tops I can hear the roar of a bucket loader digging out a parking lot, but no matter which side street I turn down, the sound is always distant, away, unhuman.

When I come upon the crèche at St. Mary's there's the

familiarity of one's private meanings at least. The big difference from the year I messiahed Eve is they've got music piped in now, a loop of tinny Christmas carols intermittently heard through the boughs of holly. Intermittently, I say, because of the storm-intrusion of radio frequencies commandeering the playback circuits and what sounds like Nazi Detergent's latest hit coming out of the mouths of putti and cherubim. Instead of "Away in a Manger" I mean. I go away feeling bereft. And the more I walk the more bereft I get. When I swing back onto Undermountain Road the snow looks purple. Up ahead, in the snowy distance there's Venner's ex-wife's house, lights still on. He turns up the drift-barricaded walk, rings the doorbell, and when his ex-Sally opens the door—nightgown blown aside by the melodramatic wind—he falls on his knees begging forgiveness, and is escorted to his once and future marriage bed where acts of tenderness are committed amidst tears of joy and forgiveness and swelling violas and, in Hollywood cursive, at the bottom of your screen, the fade-in FINIS. Why the snow is purple may have something to do with the fact that it's nearing dawn and the sun is considering giving Venner one more chance.

We keep walking, westward, toward you-know-where.

Because if knowledge is what she wants why not bust into New Eden, hop up the stairs and give it to her? Right now, I mean it. Baptize her into the world's people, into the fury and the mire. We could do it and get it over with and then there'd be nothing to shadow our soul with, nothing to offer hope or delusion or any other rhapsody of moral mirages.

We inhale life and exhale poison. Finis. Run credits.

An inventory of Venner's current physical state would include wet socks, runny nose, cold toes. He wouldn't be surprised to learn that he has a fever, that telltale of too much life. He needs shelter, a bed, warmth, some chamomile tea. Is this too much to ask? [SOUNDTRACK: WEEPY VIOLINS] In the distance the sublimity of New Eden begins to take shape out of the storm.

The fact is there are beds inside. And how the thought of

clean linen, warm blanket, a celibate mattress, appeals to wet, cold and sick Venner! Could he not simply throw himself upon their mercy, such as it is? Eldress, I have honest to God no place else to go. Sabbathday, yes, no, maybe, but right now I have a communicable disease. Chastity, it's me, Brother Venner, or John if you will, or Michael, or William, or whatever ghostly male your pixilated memory conjures before you. Leave me alone and let me sleep. Leave me alone and let me work out the chill in my soul on my own, the fever in my veins, the purgatory in my loins. This is a night that started out with John Venner integrating himself back into the world, and progressed to the unforgivable hurting of his ex-Sally. Now he's sick and cold and alone. He deserves it, but move over anyway, Mother Ann.

I put the key in the lock and yes the door opens. The downstairs hall is empty, quiet, but strangely, the light is on. Is someone up already? Or ill? Or simply suffering the sleep habits of the aged? I walk quietly down the hall, check into the Elders' Room to see if maybe there's an emergency meeting *re* Sister Lara having run off to Tijuana, but the room is empty. Near the Sisters' staircase I find a pair of slippers lying where they've been kicked off, and curiously, one rubber boot. I don't get it. They weren't there four hours ago. Okay, maybe this is the self-destruction routine—criminal trespass, breaking and entering—but something's up and Venner to the rescue is not a bad stratagem. I start up the stairs.

In Sabbathday's room there's a nightgown lying puddled on the floor and the bed is unmade, but Sabbathday herself is nowhere to be seen. I'm about to climb into the empty bed, with prepared morning remarks for Eldress about her not having lost a daughter but gained a son, when all at once I remember the ambulance I saw earlier, and I'm suddenly certain it's happened, Sister Antoinette has done the way-of-all-flesh archetype. I hurry down the hall and look. But no, she's in her bed, crumpled and misshapen under the sheets, but alive. I go one door more, see with surprise and relief Chastity sitting up in bed, pillow behind her back, gazing out the window at the purple snow. I back off in case she turns her head, and just as I do, realize it's Eldress's bed that's empty, the covers twisted and speaking some 3 A.M. convulsion. I get the existential fingertips along my spine.

What I do is I go down to the cellar, to the kitchen, where there's a phone, and I call Mercy Hospital asking for information about a patient brought into the emergency room that night, Rachel Brady, I say, one of the Shakeresses out at New Eden. I'm asked to hold please. I hear muffled voices, and then a half-minute of piped-in music, one of the local stations, Nazi Detergent again I think, though that may just be the hysteria of the moment. When the receptionist comes back on she tells me she's been instructed by friends of the family not to answer any questions from the news media, that a statement will be released in the morning.

"I'm not from the news media," I tell her. "I'm a friend of the family."

This time it's the opening chords of "Surfer Girl" for Christ's sake.

"I'm sorry," she says back on the line after a minute. "But I can't give you any information. A statement will be released in the morning."

"Is Sabbathday Wells there?" I ask. "Is that who you're talking to?"

Do you love me?
Do you, Surfer G—

"A statement will be released in the morning," the receptionist repeats. And then, like she's not used to this sort of thing: "Please."

Upstairs I throw my clothes on the floor next to Sabbathday's nightgown, climb into her bed and pull the covers over my head. Eldress dead is a major-league flameout in Venner's cosmogony. It may also be cause for hope and the stupefaction of wishes granted. But right now with the elements acting up outside the window, it's fear and trembling and the worms at heaven's gate. I can't even work up the appropriate euphoria over lying in Sabbathday's bed. This is the real thing, Mother Ann, the horror of the flesh that kept you up those nights, your four dead babies, your wasting body, the extremity of your semi-suicide. As to the soul, lifting through the air like Peter Pan, I mean come on. If it even manages to overcome its own specific gravity and launch, it gets barbecued by radio waves before it reaches cloud level. Your babies rotted in the ground, Mother Ann. Eldress is already beginning to putrefy. And Venner's heart, though currently stout and strong, is beating, like a crepe-muffled drum, a funeral march to the grave.

Okay, okay, okay, but right now, admit it: whatever his heart is doing, Venner's toes are getting toasty, his skin comfy in between Sabbathday's clean sheets. Oh, this is the tyranny of the flesh! Didn't we feel it earlier with Ann, Jane and/or Sue's bodily person? And now the shameless organ (not *that* organ, smutty Reader) is getting warm and dry and the usual tactile pleasure of 100 percent cotton and the heavy wool of winter blankets. Good night, Mother Ann. Venner plans on dreaming the dreams of the living, of luxuriating in the deep egotism of the alive: oh, let's say, dreams of pink oxygen and sparkling water, of trees budding, of Sally nursing Eve, of the Shaker Fountain Stone, buried long ago up on Spirit Mountain, rising Lazarus-like out of the earth to live again, dreams of a radiant Little Debbie Snack Cakes marrying a kind and handsome shipping magnate, segueing to visions of white-bridaled Monica the Madonna achieving multiple orgasms while the seraphim sing, and ending with birdsong and the morning sunshine and a haggard angel coming into the room, hair falling out from under her cap, wearing a nineteenth-century cape and a single twentieth-century boot.

CHAPTER THIRTEEN

THE PERSISTENCE
OF HUMAN VISION

At the burial there are TV trucks with satellite dishes on their roofs, Eyewitness News types in thousand-dollar suits, minicams, microphones, sun guns. Present too are members of the Friends of the Shakers from all over New England, a contingent of local pastors and priests, the morbid out for the day, the simply curious keeping a discreet distance and, in a circle around the grave: ninety-two-year-old Eldress Berea from Canterbury, scholarly Sister Mildred from Chosen Land, and also from Chosen Land the four male neo-Shakers, whose youthful presence Eldress Berea never acknowledges as far as watchful neo-Venner can tell.

It's Sabbathday—*Eldress* Sabbathday, I kid you not, Reader, *vide infra*—who emcees the service. She speaks of Rachel's singularity of purpose in the Shaker way, her integrity, her commitment to principle, the frequent gifts she shared with her Sisters, her uncompromising vision, etcetera, and then in the Shaker fashion, others who are moved by God to speak, speak, and this includes Sister Antoinette, seated at graveside in a ladder-back chair ($7000), and even Sister Chastity, who happily is leaning toward the lucid today, and even sober-garbed Brother Venner, who tells of Rachel's constant questioning of what it means to be Shaker and what it would take for the world to come 'round right, which is to say, to have a living Shaker community again, and so forth, for which gift I am glared at by Eldress Berea. We sing "Holy Fountain" and "Beautiful Angel Home," and all the time the minicams are trained on us, mostly on photogenic Sabbathday it seems to me, and the parabolic dishes on top of the vans point toward the sky at an urgent angle, as if beaming microwave messages to God.

Afterward, while the backhoe dumps Edenic dirt on Rachel's coffin, there's a reception in the dining room, during which Eldresses Berea and Sabbathday disappear into the Elders' Room for a closed-door consultation. What they're consulting about, who knows, perhaps Sabbathday's usurpation of the throne, perhaps her illegitimacy in the eyes of the Canterbury parent ministry, perhaps the matter of the Shaker Fountain Stone, buried in the late nineteenth century up on Spirit Mountain in a place only the Elders knew, and did that knowledge die with Eldress or was it passed on to the new Eldress? Or perhaps it's apologies for twenty years of giving the cold shoulder, a Sisterly embrace, leading to matters of administration, of the trust fund Berea controls and the monthly allowance allotted New Eden. Once or twice I stand outside the door to catch whatever words might leak out—maybe the coordinates for the Fountain Stone (an easy quarter million on the black market, if Venner could find the black market)—but neither Eldress Berea nor Eldress Sabbathday is possessed of a loud voice, and I find myself back in the dining room, ducking questions from the reporters, ditto the quizzing eyes of the neo-Brothers.

When I can't handle it anymore I sneak up to the decommissioned Brothers' quarters on the third floor, climb the stairway through the trapdoor into the bell tower and, taking up a position at one of the windows, start shooting tourists with my BB gun. It's been a weird three days, Reader. Transferred out of Sabbathday's room back to my bed in the HMQ, I found myself without even requesting it admitted into gathering order (the HMQ being unilaterally renamed the Gathering House by the new Eldress, who it seems did not want to be put to the trouble of fixing up the real Gathering House, empty since 1924), which means Venner has become a sort of Shaker j.g., on probation as it were, awaiting God's grace and the approbation of the Elders. The news was delivered by a standoffish Sabbathday who didn't even bother to ask about any Recent Carnal Experience which might be newly listed on my *vita*, or whether I in fact desired the promotion, or just what I was doing in her bed the night before. Nor did she explain how the decision came about, whether there was even a vote taken. She was brusque and businesslike and frankly I was suspicious of her. But she assigned me duties and tasks *re* Rachel's funeral, and since the HMQ looked better than 2 bdrm apt w/gar, I let myself be guided by the gift horse thing, gathered up my belongings from Sally's while Medusa was away and moved body if not soul back into the HMQ.

As to how she got herself elected Eldress, who knows, except the looniness of Chastity was a likely disqualification, and Antoinette is getting older and iller and more weary of all things human. Sabbathday as a backroom pol is a thought indeed, and maybe she was simply elected by default, but I'm skeptical. At any rate, she's acting the cool Eldress around me, as if she never sat in my bedroom and asked me to kiss her. As if the Sabbathday who shadowed me around campus those couple of weeks was a hallucination of mine. As if she had never needed to see Venner, please.

That evening, making four servings of *spaghetti alla puttanesca* down in the kitchen, I flip channels on the Shakers' Sony, trying to catch Rachel's funeral on each station. On Channel 5 there's a perfunctory adieu, on Channel 6, shots of the service with a voice-over, but on Channel 13 they go the whole hog, editing into the funeral some file footage of Eldress saying she would like to be remembered as a human being, not as a chair, mentioning the mystery of the Fountain Stone and whether the secret of its location went to the grave with her, and then showing twelve-year-old Sabbathday shooting baskets in the school gym, cutting to twenty-three-year-old Sabbathday speaking over the grave of Rachel, and afterward answering a reporter's questions with grace and charm and the ease of the media-wise. In the background, out of focus, trudging like a two-dimensional troll, are the dissected and reassembled atoms of Brother Venner's physical self.

"Television, Class," lectures Sometimes-Why, "relies on a physiological oddity called 'the persistence of human vision.' The human eye continues to see light for one-tenth of a second after it is no longer there, hence, a rapid series of stills seems to you like life. In short, you see a television image after it's no longer there; you see a dead scene and think it's alive; you see—"

"The world chopped up into 211,000 pixels, which because of faulty vision—"

"Because of the *persistence* of human vision—"

Because of delusion and moral myopia, Sabbathday Wells has been pixeled and radiated and sent up into the ionosphere and what I want to know is: How many doggy-loined, hairy-backed, creepy-souled American males have now got my beautiful Shakeress burned on their retinas like an electronic Madonna? [SPLICE IN MEXICAN PEASANTS GAZING RAPTUROUSLY INTO THE DUSTY AIR]

It appears by the gaga look on Chastity's face that "Spaghetti the Way the Whores Make It" has not heretofore been a regular item on the New Eden menu.

• • •

The day after the funeral autocratic Eldress Sabbathday summons us to the Elders' Room for a business meeting. First order of business it turns out is a formal welcome of Brother Venner, recently admitted into gathering order, who has already proved himself a help to the Sisters, let us hope for a long and happy relationship and eventual admission into full family order. ("Very nice," says Sister Chastity.) Second order of business is the continuing antagonism of Eldress Berea, who controls the several-million-dollar trust fund the United Society of Believers in Christ's Second Appearing has built up over the years (with the sale of the Mount Lebanon land, the Hancock land, the Alfred, the Harvard, the Shirley land: adieu, adieu, adieu!), and who has never recognized the legitimacy of your Sister, either as a three-year-old or as a twenty-three-year-old, and is not about to do so now, nor can we assume she will recognize Brother Venner, the upshot of which is the monthly allowance given New Eden will be based on a head count that includes only Chastity and Antoinette, which in effect means the allowance starting next month will actually be reduced by one-third, Rachel's share.

"On the other hand," says Sabbathday, "our income has been increased by some—is it forty thousand a year, Brother Venner?"

"Before taxes," interjects Brother Venner.

"The Brothers and Sisters should be assured that I have thought at some length—"

She has thought at some length about the advisability, the moral appropriateness (given the potential for harm to his soul) of Brother Venner's continuing his job among the world's people and, drawing upon the precedent—including, incidentally, Rachel, who, when she was a young Sister, sold eggs once a week in Manchester—the precedent of uncovenanted members historically having held outside jobs, she has decided Brother Venner should continue in his for the time being. Should he be accepted into senior order at some point in the future, his continuing to work in the world would undergo reevaluation.

"Point of information," says Brother Venner, who's got the lingo down from faculty meetings.

"Later," says fascist Sabbathday.

The Sisters will remember being informed during one of

the business meetings back in the summer that they had been approached by a New York art gallery concerning a show of Shaker weaving—that is to say, not historical Shaker weaving, but *their* weaving, that is, *her* weaving, and that both she and Eldress Rachel had said that they would consider it, though Rachel had been somewhat skeptical of the opportunity. She would now like to report to the Sisters—and Brother—that over the past six months she has been in constant contact with the gallery, has done some behind-the-scenes inquiring, as well as some profit projections, and that it has just been confirmed, indeed contracted, that the show would go on (ha-ha), sometime in the spring, April it looked like. Details were still being worked out, but there was some hope that, given the proper publicity (the gallery retained a publicity agent), the village stood to make a considerable amount of money. She would be busy, very busy, over the next several months collecting and cataloging and otherwise preparing for the show. She hoped it would be a success and she wanted to reassure them that she would do everything in her power to keep the show from violating the Shaker way. Was that all right? If so, then the next order of business—

"Is the show to be only of your work?" asks Sister Antoinette out of nowhere. Sabbathday looks at her and for a moment some old antagonism hangs in the air.

"That's the gallery's idea," answers Sabbathday. "They feel there's something of a glut of historic Shakerism. They want a show that has a fresh angle. I mean, the work of live Shakers." And she consults some papers in front of her. "Now, the next order of business—"

"*I'm* still alive," mutters Antoinette.

The next order of business is the matter of transportation. The village needs a car and she would like to delegate responsibility for purchasing one to Brother Venner, who is versed in these matters, perhaps a station wagon, secondhand, with good tires, previously rustproofed, say, under fifty thousand miles, the down payment for said vehicle to come from Brother Venner's salary and the monthly payments to be covered similarly, unless the Sisters, excuse me, the *Brothers* and Sisters, approve of the next order of business.

"Very, *very* nice," says Chastity.

The Sisters will remember Eldress Rachel bringing before them the matter of a Boston cabinetmaker who wished to rent the Brothers' Workshop for his place of business, and failing that to rent it as a showroom for his Shaker chairs and tables, and failing that to show his work in the Goods Shop, the community to receive a 25 percent commission on all sales generated through exposure in the shop. Rachel had deemed it inappropriate to allow this cabinetmaker into New Eden since the Sisters could not be certain that his living habits would embrace the Shaker way, but marketing his chairs through the Goods Shop was left open and Sabbathday wanted to now recommend that the community enter into agreement with this cabinetmaker, at a slightly higher rate of commission—wasn't 50 percent a common cut in retail?— and if he balked at that they might settle for 40 percent but no lower. All commissions would have to be placed through the store; the cabinetmaker would not be allowed to distribute his business card for fear of potential customers' doing an end run around New Eden. The arrangement would likely generate profits in five figures for the village. And entail only bookkeeping work. Such income would allow the village to hire outside help, not just repairmen to replace the eaves and reshingle the roofs, but someone to come in and clean and do the evening cooking, which was simply getting to be too large a chore for the Sisters. Berea and Alice at Canterbury had a cook. It was not a question of backsliding or unfaithfulness to Shaker belief, but of recognizing that the elder Sisters could not help out as they once did. And as to the other matters, she knew they seemed radical, but were they really? The Shakers had always been financially astute, had they not? They had always been involved in commerce with the world's people. What she was trying to do was to put the village back on its feet, to make a go of being a Shaker in the physical as well as the spiritual world. And wouldn't it be something if someday she could write to Eldress Berea and tell her to take her monthly allowance and . . . you know . . . didn't we see? Did we empower her to enter into negotiations with this cabinetmaker? Perhaps on a trial basis?

• • •

The car I settle on is a green Toyota station wagon with a crumpled rear fender but only 38k on the odometer. I put a thousand dollars down and get a loan from my bank for the rest. When I register it, I register it in my name.

And in Boston I go prospecting for Shaker clothes, which is to say, geeky clothes, find them in a chichi punk store down in Kenmore Square: black pants, gray shirt, white socks, clodhopper shoes. I buy three of everything, except the shoes and a kind of porkpie hat I come across in a Newbury Street milliner's. It's a woman's hat, and I raise a few brows trying it on, but it's got the mid-nineteenth-century look, low crown, flat brim. I buy it in the largest size available, request the removal of a decorative ribbon, and outside head for a McDonald's men's room, where I disrobe myself of unchastity and, while a boom box on the floor of one of the stalls segues from the final measures of "Love Is Strange" to the opening riffs of "Essential Ecstasy" (*For all you orgasm freaks, a hot new release from New England knockout Medusa!*), don the vestments of the virginal.

Back at New Eden Sabbathday eyes my clothes and then, like a mule trader, the Toyota. She kicks the tires, gets inside and tries the windshield wipers, the headlights, the radio, and outside again opens the back door, closes it, looks the crooked fender over, and then nodding some sort of approval, tells me we'll start tomorrow.

"Start what tomorrow?" I ask.

"Driving lessons."

• • •

(Eldress Rachel, this is tattletale Venner communicating to you through the Ouija board of his discontent *re* the stratagems of upstart Sabbathday. But first, tell the audience: What's it like up there in the ionosphere, disrobed of your flesh, soul the size of a quark? Do you keep in touch with your body? Pass intelligence of this or that battalion of worms massing on the border? Or is it all the rare air of heaven, the earth an impossible blue arc below, and winged babies doing somersaults out of boredom?)

• • •

I catch her looking at me, during meals, at Meeting, from the window of the Weaving Shop. It's not exactly revenge and/or love in her eyes, but it's not *not* revenge (and/or love) either. When we're at a distance or there are other people around, some of the old provocation comes between us—a Lara eyelash, the ghost of a Vennereal grin—but when we're alone, setting the table or doing the sheet-folding minuet, we get stiff and grammatical, say "Thank you" and "Please" a lot and have good posture. What she's up to, whether this nouveau Shaker purity is for real or not, the resident *faux* Shaker can't figure. But it all makes him so anxious he wants to scream obscenities at the clean pillowcases.

Instead he sits with patience and restraint while the last Shakeress makes crazy eights in the K Mart parking lot, narrowly avoiding the parking standards and on occasion, during the transcendence of first gear, laying down some rubber.

Something's happening inside Venner. What it is I can't say exactly, but he no longer seems able to view Sister Sabbathday merely as the sum of her underwear, which is to say, as the manufacture of his wounded imagination. I watch her doing her chores, eating her dinner in silence, catch her from time to time looking at herself in the dusky reflection of the windows and I am eaten up with something beyond mere desire for the female form. What it is I can't say exactly, perhaps the ghost of some preterit emotion that once played in the human heart, but I feel confused. Is it love? Or is it simply that God has been doing the Marquis de Sade thing and I don't see it? Creating beauty for the pleasure of its despoiling, and I don't possess the requisite depravity to imitate Him in this particular?

"Let's not get carried away," Sometimes-Why says. "It may no longer be the wet dreams of our steeple—the reality of Reality, etcetera—but love is love, and Sabbathday Wells, whatever the oddities of her upbringing, whatever the circuit overload of her underwear, seems a woman deserving of love, *n'est-ce pas?*"

• • •

Peut-être, says skeptical Venner, and to find out for sure he decides to do what he's been dodging since the drunken discovery of Sabbathday's serialized self: he waits until metaphoric midnight (really, early afternoon, when the nouveau Eldress enters the Goods Shop not to reappear until 5 P.M.), then invades the Dwelling House, clandestinely climbing the stairway to the second floor and, penetrating the *lacuna* (L., meaning *hole, hollow, crack*, from which is taken the English vulgarism for the female—oh, Reader, never mind: a long-ago playful pun of a Mariologist I used to know) penetrating the *lacuna*, I mean the doorway, of Sabbathday's room, he snatches the most recent volume of her diary and sneaks up to the third floor, then up through the trapdoor into the bell tower and there, sitting under the halo of the bell's rim, with the snowy fields of New Eden spreading below him—BB gun for comfort—he opens to the first page of Sabbathday's intimate self.

We pick up the action in midsummer, when a local man appears at New Eden one morning to rebuild the stone walls, which have been left to sorrowful neglect. We may assume the previous volume ended with some description of his manly form against the fecund verdure, his hair sun-streaked with blond, his handsome face, etcetera. *This* volume presents us with a Sabbathday watching the whole episode, cops and all, with Rapunzel-like amusement, not the anger of violation as in the taxi, but the aloof curiosity of the safely entowered. She refers to me variously as he, him, that guy, the Professor, the Peeping Tom, the Local Voyeur and, pen dripping with sarcasm, Brother Venner. And yet it turns out that it is she who suggests to Rachel that if this man wants to rebuild their walls for free, well, why not? She who plants in Rachel's mind the idea of gaining a bargain-basement facto- tum for the price of the HMQ. The Local Voyeur can't quite figure the tone of her discourse (in fact, Professor Venner the grader of undergraduate essays feels the urge to write in the margins: "Consistency?" "Irony?"), reads with wonder as Sis- ter Sabbathday migrates from contempt to concern to girlish effulgence, to the fringes of paperback romance. By the time we get to Eve and me in the garden at twilight (the Reader will remember a confession of love, a spilled cucumber, the confusion of weeds with herbs), her pen is comfortably call- ing me John and I can barely recognize myself inside the vegetation of her imaginings.

And then—the advent of it nearly freezes Venner's soul— she begins to address herself to "you." I don't get it at first, and then I realize we are post-garden now, that she is writing with the knowledge that I have been reading her diary, and instead of quitting or hiding herself under some loose floor- board, she is speaking to me ("... *but you know of course that I am bound to an impossible existence ...*"), to a Prince John who comes into her room at midnight and reads her secret self while she sleeps with the moonlight washing across her hair. She is so sincere, so teen-magaziney in places, so fresh and frightened, so . . . O Mother Ann! Did you really think you could isolate the human heart from the sewers and orchards of the world, or even from its own mute throbbing? The death of the Shakers is the triumph of desire. What I read here—let me translate for you—what I read here is Sister Sabbathday's longing for human touch, maybe Venner's touch, maybe not, but the yearning to make communion between her valved heart and the auricles of the world. You, Ann Lee, with your rules against touching, against shaking hands, against kiss- ing; your white paint, your white picket fences; the great stratagem of redeeming the earth by plowing its crust in par-

allel rows, marking it off with right-angled walls: it has all
ended here, with your final convert crying for contact, for
some hand to test her reality, to feel her and be felt. She says
it herself (future archivists: on November 2, just after she has
caused the expulsion of her particular Adam): *"It was like I
wanted you to kiss me so that I would know I was living, because so much of my life—you see, don't you—exists in my head
and I can't act out the things that go on there because there are
rules—oh, the rules!—only with you it's different, because you
see me, I know you do, you make me real."*

Back in the HMQ I hide my head under a pillow and
consider the possibility of life with Sabbathday Venner, a
house in town, a garden, pink flamingos on the front lawn,
His-and-Her towels in the upstairs bathroom, K-Y Jelly in
the discreet nightstand. Is it so goddamn impossible? After
all, nuns quit being brides of Christ every day, priests un-
frock themselves with joy and terror and relief. Do you
imagine Sabbathday—never mind Venner as immoral im-
presario—do you imagine Sabbathday will still be living in
her single room when she's thirty-three, forty-three, fifty-
three? Still the last Shakeress when the twenty-first century
marks its midpoint? The metamorphosis from American
Idealism to the reality of Reality will take place sooner or
later, whether there's a Venner holding up cue cards in the
wings or not. Why not be the one to reap the rewards of
apostasy, be the first to enjoy the incarnation of Sabbathday
Wells in heels and lipstick?

"Changing our tune, what?" says Sometimes-Why from
the windowsill, where he has been gazing at the physical
charms of Sabbathday's sheep.

Which tune is that? I ask from under the pillow.

"The ode to celibacy, the quashing of our carnal past, the
metaphysics of white picket fences. Remember?"

Vaguely, says Venner.

But just so there'll be no mistake about the evidence of
my carnal past, at the end of term I go get Eve out of daycare,
slip into Sally's house on the sly and pack her clothes and her

toys and her Wonder Woman toothbrush, and move her out to
the HMQ with me. Permanently, I mean. Let Sister Sabbathday take notice. Let Medusa set the police on me ("Reasonable visitation is defined to mean visitation by husband on
alternating weekends, alternating holidays . . ."), let her take
me to court, what a case I could make against a Gorgon! I call
Melanie to tell her, call her from the phone in the Goods Shop
while Sabbathday pretends to be busy with some bookkeeping. I tell her to tell Medusa. She tells me to tell Medusa
myself, tells me about laws against abduction in the state of
New Hampshire. Abduction from whom? I say. From the custodial parent, she says. I tell her I didn't abduct her from the
custodial parent, I abducted her from the custodial aunt by
way of the custodial daycare. When I hang up, Sabbathday
looks up and inquires did she overhear correctly, that I've
moved my daughter out to New Eden, to the Hired Men's—
that is, to the Gathering House, for good?

"Yes," I answer. "For good."

"Perhaps you should have inquired of your Eldress first,"
my Eldress says. I make a who-are-you-kidding face.

"*Is* it okay? Eldress?"

She gazes out the window at Eve making snow angels in
the pasture, and then drops her eyes back to her ledger. "Yes."

• • •

And so now there's Eve in the back seat when Sabbathday
and I go out in the Toyota. We're an odd but not impossible
family. Sabbathday guides us through the loops and switch-
backs of tract housing (she has graduated from the K Mart
parking lot), while Eve squirms under her seat belt and asks
where we're *going*. I sit quiet and serene, from time to time
coaching Sabbathday in the rules of the road or the fragility
of human life vis-à-vis the oncoming truck, but mostly I daydream about improbable combinations of essence and existence, including, but not limited to, Sabbathday pregnant with
twins. During one particular circumnavigation of town, we
end up driving past the farmhouse Medusa has rented and

I'm worried Eve will catch sight of her mother, or the Peugeot parked in the drive, but she's too busy asking for the umpteenth time how Sabbathday can be her *sister* and I answer for the umpteenth time that she's *not* her sister, we just *call* her sister, or Eldress, either one.

Back at New Eden I take her with me on my chores, into the barn to fork out hay for Sabbathday's sheep, let her snoop through the old stalls, climb on the ancient hayricks. At dinner she sits at the Sisters' table, contemplating her solitary father at the Brothers' table while Sister Sabbathday cuts her veal for her. Ditto at Sunday Meeting, where it's the "forth-and-back" Sabbathday helps her with. If the Reader is wondering what Medusa thinks of all this, the answer is we don't know, we haven't returned the phone calls she has placed to the Goods Shop. With each message delivered, secretarial Sabbathday eyes me with pointed amusement but doesn't ask what's up. Even when the messages change from the merely arch to the nearly homicidal.

"You'll keep me informed, won't you," she says, "of any intercourse out of the ordinary you have with the world's people?"

During another drive-by there's a TV van parked in the farmhouse yard, Eyewitness News logo on the side panel, satellite dish up top, electronic guts viewed through the open door. That night, while I'm making a chef's salad in the kitchen, there's a story about Medusa on the Shakers' Sony, Medusa the complete Gorgon, ensnaked, becostumed, framed by the camera in such a way that the soon-to-be-famous cleavage shows to good effect. Sabbathday comes in just in time to catch Medusa doing the "Essential Ecstasy" thing, voice-over concerning the world of fame and fortune awaiting this local girl. She watches until the closing chord brings back the blow-dried anchor.

"Your wife," Sabbathday says with equanimity.

"My ex-wife."

"Pretty," says Sabbathday.

"Poisonous," says Venner.

• • •

When the local girl finally shows up it's the day before Eve's birthday, three days before Christmas. She's wearing normal clothes, normal hair. When I answer the door of the HMQ, I turn first to stone, then salt.

"Where is she?"

We haven't talked or seen one another since the night of the party, and obstinate Venner considers playing dumb and interpreting the "she" referred to as (in maddening sequence): Ann/Jane/Sue, dead Eldress Rachel, alive Sister Sabbathday, and finally with a telling smirk that puts her in *her* place, boy!—oh, you mean *Eve*, your daughter!

"Where's who?"

She brushes past me, walks down the short hall into my room, across the way into Eve's. "Kidnapping," she says, coming back.

"Trespassing," I say, meeting her. She's wearing a parka I bought for her three Christmases ago.

"I could have the police after you. No joke. You've violated our divorce agreement. My lawyer says that's contempt of court. Not to mention abduction. Now where is she?"

"You've called your lawyer?"

"He called me. He saw me on TV and wants a date. Now where *is* she?"

"She's with Sabbathday," I answer. "In the Weaving Shop."

She pushes past and heads out the door. I grab my jacket and follow, wondering if she's really mad or just, you know, mad. She heads across the snowy field in the direction of the Dwelling House, then veers off toward the Goods Shop, and then stops and turns around to me.

"Where the hell's the Weaving Shop?"

I point to a clapboard building. She turns and crunches uphill through the snow. I crunch after her, wondering should Brother Venner go back to court, would the Shakers be liable for his lawyer's fees? (Come to think of it, are the Shakers liable for his current child support? Just how covenanted are we?) Up on the stoop of the Weaving Shop, Medusa is knocking on the wooden door. I reach the granite steps just in time to hear Sabbathday call, "Come in."

"Look, Mommy," says Eve from inside the yarn dolly. I reach the door just as she's holding up a handful of yarn. "Green!" she screams.

"Hi, sweetie," says Medusa, and then to Sabbathday, suddenly girl-friendly: "Hello. We've never met. I'm Sally Shannon."

Sabbathday nods from her seat at the loom, where for the past few weeks she's been turning out Shaker masterpieces for wealthy Sodomites. She smiles and doesn't say anything. Medusa crosses to Eve and gives her a hug. Some mother-daughter stuff goes on during which Sabbathday turns a quizzical look at Brother Venner standing in the doorway. With a musical upsy-daisy, Medusa swings Eve out of the yarn dolly.

"We have to talk," she says to me. I pause a moment for reflection, or at least to look like I'm reflecting, and then address myself to my Eldress.

"Permission to have intercourse with one of the world's people."

My Eldress gazes briefly at Eve spread-legged on her mother's hip, and I can't quite figure her look, whether she's miffed or amused or what. "Permission granted," she says and sends her shuttle through the loom. Medusa starts toward the door.

"In my presence, of course," says Sabbathday.

"Excuse me?" Medusa answers, putting Eve on her feet.

"Whatever Brother Venner says to you or you say to him must be reported to his Eldress anyway, so . . ." And she smiles the Sabbathday smile. Medusa does a slow take.

"I thought they kicked you out of here," she says to me, and then to Sabbathday, "I thought you discovered he was unfit for sainthood and kicked him out of here."

"The previous Eldress asked him to leave," Sabbathday answers. "The current Eldress has reversed the decision."

"The current Eldress?" Medusa repeats. She looks me over from sober head to temperate toe. "So that's why you're dressed like that."

"I am no longer a member of the world's people," I answer with solemnity.

She grimaces. "You were a member of the world's people a few weeks ago, I remember," she says and then turns to Sabbathday. "He was a member of the world's people a few weeks ago."

Sabbathday shrugs.

"You know how I know?" says Medusa, a tone of revenge creeping into her voice. "I know because I came home late one night and guess what was in bed with him."

"Untrue," says Venner, feeling some metaphysical toehold loosening.

"Go ahead. Guess."

We're slipping. We had hoped to endure eternity in one of the higher circles—a glimpse of blue sky overhead, white clouds, at night the starry vault—but we're slipping, sliding downward from circle to circle, past the adulterers and the onanists and the Sodomites.

"He's screwing this bimbo I know with imperfect rhythm. I mean the bimbo has imperfect rhythm, not that that's how he's screwing her."

Reader: adieu, adieu, adieu.

"I mean are you sure you want that sort of novitiate out here? I mean—" this with a look of distaste—"*him?*"

The last Shakeress stops her weaving. She regards first me, then Medusa. "The world," she says, "as I understand it, is given to that sort of thing."

Medusa gazes at her with a touch of awe. Eve has climbed back into the yarn dolly. "Are you putting me on?"

"What Brother Venner did while a member of the world's people is a matter between him and Christ. We accept him as he is. As long as he comports himself in line with Shaker doctrine while a member of New Eden."

Reader, it's blissful Beatrice to the rescue.

"Has he told you about Little Debbie Snack Cakes yet?"

"He has confessed all his earlier sins to me. It's a requirement for those who seek covenant with the United Society of Believers in Christ's Second Appearing."

It is, of course, a bogus Beatrice, Sabbathday doing the Shaker maiden thing to get the ex-wife's goat, but a bogus Beatrice is better than no Beatrice at all.

"Are you putting me on?" Medusa says again and she takes a step toward Sabbathday. "Do you know who this guy is? Do you know what he wants? All he wants is to do you in your white underwear. Do you know that?"

Sabbathday doesn't answer.

"Ask him. Go ahead. Ask him about the spotting scope and the photos of you and the pornography in your mailbox."

"I know all about that."

"Then ask him whether he wants to do you in your white underwear or not."

She puts the shuttle through the loom once again, and then stops and looks at me. "Do you?" she says.

Venner lets out a squeak, then gazes with as much dignity as he can muster from ex-wife to Eldress back to ex-wife.

"Love," he says finally, "love between a Shaker man and a Shaker woman is only to be expected. It's part of our trial, and part of our victory when we withstand it."

"Who said anything about love?"

"We might even add," ignoring the ex-wife and shading into Professor Venner, "that there's a kind of conservation of matter at work: love lost in one form—" here a meaning look at Medusa—"is apt to be found in another."

"Give me a break," she says, and then to Sabbathday, "If you think this guy is capable of being a Shaker—" and here a knowing shake of the head—"I'd count the silverware if I were you. Also, the chairs, the tables—"

"Excuse me," interrupts Eldress Sabbathday.

"—your underwear—"

"Excuse me, but did you have a reason for coming here this morning?"

There follows a queer sort of standoff between the two. Venner wonders if—like the Goody Two-Shoes ingenue in a B movie—he's being fought over. In the yarn dolly Eve is playing dead beneath a turf of green wool.

"If you think," Medusa says finally, "I'm going to let my daughter get indoctrinated into this half-assed religion you've got another think coming."

"I'm dead," says Eve.

Sabbathday goes back to weaving. "No one's indoctrinating anyone."

"I'm dead and buried."

"I don't want her out here. I don't want her going to your crazy meetings. I don't want her around you."

"I'm dead and buried just like . . . like . . . Daddy, what's her name?"

"That's between you and her father," says Sabbathday.

"No, it's between her father and New Hampshire District Court." And she turns to me. "I want you to follow the letter of our divorce agreement. Do you understand? That means I don't want you anywhere near Eve twelve days out of fourteen. I want her in daycare during the day. The rest of the time while I'm away Melanie will look after her. I mean it," she says. "If you don't think I'd be awarded full custody after my lawyer finishes with you and your steeple and your breaking and entering just keep it up. Eve," she calls and Eve buries herself deeper in the wool. "Eve."

"I'm dead."

"Come on, sweetie. We're leaving."

"I can't move. I'm dead."

"Move it or you *will* be dead," says Sally and Eve dives out of the dolly and runs in mock terror for the door.

"Christmas," I manage to say. "Every other holiday. You had her for Thanksgiving."

"Forget it." And she zips her parka up.

"It's my turn."

"So take me to court," she says and follows Eve out the door.

"Sally!"

"Forget it."

"Bye, Daddy," Eve calls from outside. I go to the door and watch them head down to the car, Eve running ahead and Sally on the march like a true ex-wife. Behind me, Sabbathday's loom sounds like the loom of the Fates.

• • •

For the rest of the day I go around kicking furniture and fence posts and, in the barn, Sabbathday's sheep. I get the keys out of the Dwelling House and let myself into the outbuildings—the Brothers' Workshop, the Machine Shop—and mope around the cast iron and the cobwebs. I don't know what I'm looking for, maybe the ghost of former belief, maybe a jury of my peers, maybe the engine of desire. From the bell tower atop the Dwelling House I watch the customers coming and going at the Goods Shop (Christmas means big retail at New Eden; CEO Sabbathday must be happy), even try shooting some of them with my BB gun, but this time I just haven't got it in me. I stay up there the whole afternoon. My toes go numb, fingers too. In the gloom of gloamings I wonder if Little Debbie Snack Cakes would entertain a marriage proposal from her former professor. If not, how about Monica the Madonna? If not, are castrati still fetching a price in Italy? In the Forbidden City?

It's the tragedy of gravity, Class. No matter how strongly the soul makes its parabolic arc there is always the killing suck of the planet to haul it back. This is how it goes: the earth breaks its heart trying to fight loose from the sun, the moon from the earth and Venner from the delirium of various desires. (One of his deliriums is even now visible through the Goods Shop window.) I mean here I am, as far away from the earth as I can get without boarding an airplane, night falling, pieces of heaven beginning to float down in the form of icy hexagons—we have, in short, the available archetypes arranged so as to bolster essence to the detriment of existence—and what am I thinking of? I'm thinking of the grace of Sister

Sabbathday's shoulder framed in the incandescent window-pane, the lyre of her illegal hips, the sift of her hair falling from under her cap, the way she hurries about when five o'clock comes, puts on her cape, her boots, steps out into the cold, turns around and—such is the nature of our deliriums—waves to me.

How the hell she knows I'm up here is beyond me. She starts along the walk, gesturing for me to come down. I pull back from the verge of the opening, as if that's going to do any good. Three floors below I hear the heavy front door open and close, and then nothing long enough for me to think I'm off the hook. But then it's footsteps on the floor below, the folding stairway pulled down, and the trapdoor thrown back.

"What are you doing?"

She's got her head poked up through the floor.

"Go away."

"You must be freezing."

"Go away."

She climbs up the remaining steps and scoots over to me, draping her cape over her legs. It's dark, and there's only the drifting illumination from the streetlights below. We sit in silence, looking out over the rooftops, over the fields, toward the town and—for better or worse—humanity.

"So is that what marriage is like?" she asks after a minute has passed.

I don't answer.

"Or did I only catch the second act? I mean, you know, divorce."

And she pokes me in the ribs through my jacket and says, "Ha-ha," like a regular guy. Behind us, up on Lovers' Lookout, there are (let's see: one, two, three) three cars engaged in what we may assume are various stages of love and destruction.

"I've been watching you all afternoon," she says finally.

"I've been watching *you* all afternoon."

She leans over to check just how much I can see of the Goods Shop from the opening. In doing so she touches my

knee. Also present in this gesture are motifs of careless revelation, by which we mean her glossy hair casually placed just
under my eyes, the seductive insouciance of her slender shoulder, the enchanting smell of her perfume (if she wore perfume, which she doesn't), etcetera.

"So tell me," she says, leaning back, "is it true?"

"Is what true?"

"That you slept with someone a couple of weeks ago?"

Do we lie and go to hell or tell the truth and go to hell?

"It's true."

She makes a face like she's been wagering with herself all
afternoon. "So you'll sleep with—" and she pauses a moment
to get it right—"you'll sleep with a bimbo with imperfect
rhythm, but you won't sleep with me?"

"Please," I say.

"Please what?"

"Please, I'm not a well man. I have a headache. Or maybe
leukemia. Something anyway that's keeping me from being
myself."

"And just what or who *is* your self?"

She sounds like Venner three years ago interrogating
proto-Medusa.

"I am," I say with dignity, "John Venner, Doctor of Divinity, Assistant Professor of Religion, divorced father of the
messiah, unloved as far as I can tell by either my ex-wife or
my Eldress, a more-or-less legitimate Shaker, I mean a more-
or-less bogus Shaker, I mean—"

"You *are* in a mood."

"I just had the messiah stolen from me."

After which, there is nothing much to say. Outside, the
world does the pathetic fallacy thing; I mean: whispering
snow, sad lamplight, the dimming lights of the distant town.

"So who was she?"

"I don't want to talk about it."

"Who? Who was she?"

"A friend of Sally's," I say. "Of Medusa's, I mean. A former
drummer in her band."

"A drummer with imperfect rhythm?"

"And beautiful breasts."

"Oh, well: beautiful breasts," she repeats, and she spends a moment watching the snow fall. "Do you ever wonder about *my* breasts?"

Reader, here we go again.

"Do you ever wonder—you know—what I look like? As a woman, I mean."

Dum-di-dum, let's see now: We've got the tragedy of gravity . . .

"Or do you already know? I mean, what with your telescope. And your habit of breaking and entering."

And the comedy of clouds . . .

"Brother Venner, I'm talking to you."

"I'm listening," I say. "I'm taking notes. I have to report all such conversations to my Eldress."

She heaves a theatrical sigh and sits back on her heels. "Is this how it goes?" she asks. "I mean is this how it's supposed to happen?"

"What?"

"Sex," she says. "Seduction. Lovemaking. Is this how it's supposed to go?"

I don't answer.

"Because, you know, I haven't got any experience in this line. Other than a load of phony books and a few movies. So I need you to tell me. Is this how it's supposed to be? The man tells the woman that he loves her, and then for months does everything he can to cut the woman off?"

She sounds—doesn't she, Mother Ann?—like an ordinary woman in an ordinary world.

"I should never have said it."

"You should never have said it because you didn't mean it, or because you're too chicken to follow up on it?"

"Both," I say. "Neither."

"I mean I come home from bringing a dead body to the hospital and you're sleeping in my bed. How am I supposed to interpret that?"

Venner remembers the cold, the dark, various metaphysical mangers. "That was a bad night," he says.

"You're telling me."

"I was looking for comfort, warmth, human sympathy." She pulls her hands inside her cape sleeves and doesn't answer.

"That was the night I tried to pollute myself for your sake," I say.

"Excuse me?"

"I tried to pollute myself with the drummer so that I would be unworthy of you—"

"Oh, please!"

"—so that I'd be unworthy of you and it would be impossible for me to drag you down to the seventh circle—no, eighth—all right, *ninth* circle. I mean the fury and the mire thing. The world's people, etcetera."

"That is *so* lame."

It *is* pretty lame, isn't it, Reader? And yet, on some level or other, it's true, or mostly true, or a little bit true, though the Sabbathday I was trying to keep pure was not the Sabbathday currently before us, but rather the iconic Sabbathday: Sabbathday the Visual Image, the American Utopia, unplowed wilderness, the pureness of the soul given bodily form, *cf.* "Away in a Manger."

"So what do you want?" I say finally. "You want me to sleep with you? You want to have a practice run with the world outside New Eden by getting into bed with me? You want to check if the Shaker lifestyle is in fact the correct one for your personal needs?"

She gets distant-looking, as if she's equivocating behind the scenes, but when she speaks she says simply, "Yes."

"Terrific."

"What's so wrong with that?"

"And the heart, the emotions, the—shall we say?—natural feelings that tend to go with such activity, what are we to do with them? After the fact, I mean."

"Did you find yourself burdened with natural feelings for the drummer? After the fact, I mean."

"That's different."

"How's it different?"

"Because," I say.

"Because why?"

"Because I sort of *do* love you, I mean I don't *love* you, but I sometimes *think* I love you, or at least there's some part of me that considers the *possibility* of loving you as not entirely out of the question—"

"Boldly stated."

"—and that's likely to lead to more bruises in the general region of the heart."

"So you *do* want to do me in my white underwear."

Mother Ann, let's face it, Shakers aren't what they used to be.

"Listen," I say, "I am no longer in the business of doing women in their underwear, white or otherwise."

"That's not what I heard."

"Nor am I any longer in the business of estimating the beauty of women's breasts."

"Also not what I heard."

"I'm especially not in the business of *verifying* said beauty. Now, I have to get dinner ready."

I stand up. She lifts herself onto her knees. "Don't you want to kiss me?"

"No."

"Touch me?"

"No."

"Um . . . feel me up?"

"Sabbathday, for Christ's sake!"

"What?" she says. "What? Am I doing it wrong?"

I throw the trapdoor open.

"Am I? Am I doing it wrong? Tell me how to do it."

"Cut it out."

She scoots over and swings her legs across the hatchway

so I can't get down the stairs. "Let's go on a date," she says. "I mean a *date*. A real one. You take me out. Dinner. No, a *movie*. We'll sit in the back row."

"Get out of the way."

"And afterward we'll—I don't know—what should we do? Share a root beer float. Two straws."

"Move your legs."

"Really," she says. "I'll dress normal. Pants. I've got a pair. No one will recognize me."

"Sabbathday. This isn't funny."

"Friday night," she says. "Eight o'clock."

I take hold of her ankles and swivel her out of the way.

"Eight o'clock. I'll be waiting in the Elders' Room."

I start down the stairs.

"Just knock on the window. I'll be waiting."

CHAPTER FOURTEEN

THE MONSTROUS MYSTERIUM OF THE LOINS

On Christmas morning I awake to find a package of Little Debbie Snack Cakes stuffed in an old stocking tacked to the door of the Hired Men's Quarters. Whether this is a parry of Santa Claus's or Sabbathday's or a final repudiation on the part of Medusa I don't know and I don't care. I eat them for breakfast along with a quart of orange juice and turn to the business of the day.

Which happens to be the writing of a brief biography for my Eldress. She needs it to accompany the catalog for her show (which appears to be a bigger deal than I'd realized), and since (as she said the night before, passing in the hall) she's not accustomed to writing for the public eye whereas Brother Venner is, would he mind putting his professorial hand to a paragraph or two? She makes no mention of Friday night.

The professorial paw postulates the following:

Sister Sabbathday Wells is the youngest member of the United Society of Believers in Christ's Second Appearing (Shakers). She was born in 1968 and joined the community at New Eden, New Hampshire, in 1971. She was brought up and educated in the Society's beliefs, which include worship in the form of singing and dancing, honest workmanship and abstinence from sex as a means of purification. Her weaving, which was taught to her by Sister Antoinette Des Pres and follows traditional Shaker patterns and technique, is on one level the creation of simple household goods for utilitarian purpose, and on another level, a profound expression of belief, for it is central to Shaker doctrine that the occupation of the body in work is a form of worship. As such, a Shaker blanket is a prayer to God given physical form.

Sister Sabbathday continues to live and work at the New Eden Shaker village.

Or:

Eldress Sabbathday Wells is the Chief Executive Officer of the New Eden family of the United Society of Believers in Christ's Second Appearing (Shakers). Having been a team player for the first twenty years of her membership, she has recently moved to fill the power vacuum brought about by the death of Eldress Rachel Brady. At stake are millions of dollars in real estate, antiques, trademark rights, etcetera, as well as the Shaker trust fund currently controlled by Eldress Berea Compson of the Canterbury village. CEO Wells has recently incorporated herself as "Sabbathday, Ltd." The bullish gallery-goer may purchase shares of her at the front door.

Or:

Sister Sabbathday Wells is the alias of Lara Wells, a twenty-three-year-old whose character hovers somewhere between the Virgin Mary and the hot-to-trot girl next door. She grew up in the impossible atmosphere of Eden, longing since child-

hood for the view from Sodom. For twenty years she plotted the revelation of her true self. What her true self is her biographer doesn't know, but it seems to involve the beating of the human heart, perhaps as well paradigms of prodigality, a longing for the moral fall, the Adam and Eve thing. The gallery-goer will see in her weaving patterns the warp and weft of her soul, in her mirrored designs the echo of her divided self, say: Sabbathday, metaphysical binoculars aloft, searching the Lara-horizon for escape or engagement or I don't know oblivion maybe, but something, dear God, something.

After lunch when I show the three sheets to Sabbathday she takes one look at my handwriting and asks what's the matter don't I own a typewriter?

So it's off to my office where I am ambushed by discarded rainbows, snowflakes, reindeer lying on the floor, a piece of letterhead with EveEveEveEveEveEve printed on it. I roll a sheet of paper into my typewriter, but I get so blue over the archaeology of Eve's existence that I end up just sitting there while the four o'clock dusk comes down. In the chapel someone is tuning the harpsichord for tomorrow night's *Messiah*, the discordant octaves of salvation driving Venner to the window, where, instead of the blank sahara of the quad, there's some art major's snow sculpture of Betty and Veronica in bikinis (Betty's ponytail iced into a quizzical question mark and the whole scene sans Archie). What to make of this synchronized insult is beyond Venner, who's having enough trouble trying to decide whether an avuncular visit to Eve *re* the bicycle Santa brought would be allowed by her mother or not.

We decide to risk it, throw Sabbathday into our briefcase and head out in the Toyota. But when I near the house there's a load of cars out front—Melanie's for sure, maybe the band members', who knows who else's?—and I'm on the point of chucking the whole idea when I catch sight of Eve's red snowsuit in the side yard. I pull over, back up, and under cover of darkness, cross the road onto the lawn.

"Daddy, why?" she says like a four-year-old metaphysician when she catches sight of me scuffing across the snow. She's been digging with a plastic snow shovel.

"Why what, sweetie?" I say kneeling down to her. I give her a hug and whatever why had sprung to her mind—why are you here? why is the world the way it is? why don't you love me enough?—disappears and she holds out the snow shovel for my admiration. I pretend to look it over when in fact I'm looking her over: tiny teeth, cheeks a Hollywood pink, face Botticellied by her hood, silvery breath attesting to life, oxygen in the arteries, hope in the heart . . .

I take out a handkerchief and wipe her nose.

"Did Santa come?"

So she starts listing all the things Santa brought her, somewhere among which is my bicycle. Who coped with the Some Assembly Required I don't know, but it makes me feel strangely bereft, jealous even, to hear her talk about riding it around the furnace in the basement, training wheels and all, like in addition to various other thieveries I've now been robbed by Santa Claus of a thank-you and a kiss. I watch the movement of her face, her lips, the earnestness in her eyes, the squiggle of hair leaking out from under her hood, and I feel like— Oh, hell, listen, I don't want to bore you with the banality of Venner's broken heart; I mean, you know: the near tears, the operatic choke, the sorrow and the regret, all the usual. Just take Venner at his word. It hurts, goddamn it.

"I'll show it to you," she says when I prod her about the bike. I tell her no, I don't think I can go inside right now, but without batting an eye she says okay, we'll look in the window, and trots off toward the house. I follow her, cautiously, but it turns out she means one of the cellar windows. "There it is," she says, kneeling down. I peer in and sure enough it *is* there, iconic red and everything. We gaze in silent appreciation.

"What did Santa bring *you?*" she asks eventually.

"Me?" I say, standing up by way of stalling. It's a testament—is it not?—to the loneliness of Venner's life that Santa Claus didn't bring him anything. "Santa couldn't find me," I say finally, lifting her by the elbows.

"Why not?"

"I don't think he knew I'd moved."

She squints up at me, contemplating the trauma of this, and then says, "You should *tell* him."

"I will," I say. "Next year. I'll make sure I write—"

I brace myself to be turned into stone—the front door's opened—but it's not Medusa; it's some guy I don't recognize.

"Evie," he calls from the front stoop, and then when he catches sight of us—of me—starts across the snow. He looks me up and down like maybe I'm the neighborhood sex offender. "Can I help you?" he asks.

"Help me?" I repeat. I'm standing there like an idiot. "No."

"Well, then," he says, "can I ask what you're doing here?" He's got a ponytail for Christ's sake and I think maybe I recognize him from the barn after all.

"Just visiting."

"Friend of the family?" he says, and yes, we're moving into male confrontation here. The door opens again and this time it's Medusa.

"Spike?" she calls out. Spike? "Oh," she says when she catches sight of me. She starts down the path. "Eve?"

"She's all right," says Spike. "It's just this guy here."

"What guy?" she says, drawing up to us. "Go on inside, sweetie," she says to Eve.

"This guy."

"Him?" Medusa says and she gives me the once-over. "That's just my ex-husband."

And she turns and takes Spike by the arm so that they walk toward the house the picture of sexual harmony. Eve comes running back for her shovel.

"Bye, Daddy," she says and she drags the shovel across the ground up onto the stoop and into the house. By the miracle of special effects, snowflakes are sifting down through the trees. They turn to little pieces of black crepe when they land on Venner's head.

• • •

When Friday comes, I'm ready. But instead of doing it the Sabbathday way—eight o'clock knock on the Elders' window—I appear in the hall outside her room at 7:30. I've got a coat and tie on, the biographies folded away in an inside pocket and—no kidding, Reader—I'm carrying a bouquet of roses.

"What are you doing here?" says Sabbathday. She's been reading in bed—Sabbathday the Shaker odalisque—but at the sight of me she sits up.

"It's Friday night," I say from the doorway. "Don't we have a date?"

She checks out my tie, the roses. "You're early."

I tap my watch. "We have an eight o'clock curtain." And when she doesn't get it: "The *Messiah*. Eight o'clock at the college chapel." And I hum a few bars of "He Was Despised." She eyes me like she's trying to decide whether this is on the up and up or not.

"At the chapel?" she says. "*Your* chapel?"

Venner is in fine voice: " '. . . a man of sorrows and acquainted with grief. . . .' "

"All right," she says, swinging out of bed. "Wait downstairs. You know you're not supposed to be up here."

I lay the roses along one of the bookshelves just inside the room and turn to go.

"I'll have to check on the Sisters," she says. "And I don't have that sort of thing to wear."

"What sort of thing?"

"That," she says, indicating the formality of my attire. "I've just got pants."

"You mean," I intone, "that you don't have a complete Lara outfit for the evening?"

She makes a face. I scratch where the rabbinical beard would be were Venner a rabbi.

"Then go as Sabbathday," I say finally. "It's the *Messiah*, after all." And I head down the stairs.

By the time she's ready, I've got the car out front and warmed up. She's wearing her cape, one of her simple dresses and a pair of dressy black pumps I've never seen before. The big deal, though, is that she's not wearing her cap, a violation of Shaker purdah which she hides at first by keeping her cape hood up, but as we drive into town, reveals with a teen-defiant toss of her head. If the author hasn't before described Sister Sabbathday's forbidden hair, it's light brown, verging on blond at the temples, long and thick enough to be the object of desire.

At the chapel we find seats and sit looking down at our programs until the conductor comes out. Whether the world's people are eyeing Sabbathday or not I'm too self-conscious to tell. We listen to the overture and then to the sad state of the Old Testament world: highways in the desert, lots of crying in the wilderness. I can't tell if Sabbathday is familiar with any of this—I mean the music, not the text. There's no stereo out at New Eden. From time to time I steal a glance at her, the side of her face theater-extravagant in the ambient stage light, her illegal hair nesting rubies, eyes all attention. When the lyrics get lost in the coloratura writing, she gazes down at the libretto in her lap to see what's happening and then it's back up to the singers. The performance itself is sabotaged by college string players, local oboists, a chorus made up of dentists and former high school phenoms, but she doesn't seem to mind or even realize it. When once she catches me looking at her she smiles and puts her finger to her lips as if to silence any marriage proposals I might have been on the verge of making.

When the first part is over and the lights come up for intermission we sit a moment in silence. There are curious eyes on us now for certain but whether they belong to tattletales who know who Sabbathday is or to those who simply wonder who the hot honey Professor Venner's with I can't tell, but it's uncomfortable enough so that I ask Sabbathday if she'd like to get up and see my office. She nods and we rise and walk through the milling crowd.

First thing she spots is my lithograph of Ann Lee.

"Holy macaroni!" she says, crossing to it. "Where'd you get this?"

"An antique dealer."

She sniffs at the mildewy paper. "It's phony, you know."

"I know."

Because, Mother Ann, nobody knows what you looked like. All we've got is this etherealized you with blond hair, eyes the color of heaven, drawn by some anonymous hack and peddled in nineteenth-century shops along with portraits of Hiawatha and Harriet Beecher Stowe.

"I remember when I was little there was one hanging in the Elders' Room," Sabbathday says. "I used to look at it with—I don't know—reverence, I guess. As soon as Rachel became Eldress, bang, it was gone."

And she smiles at the memory. Down below us where the chorus and orchestra have retreated a bored bassoonist is negotiating the first measures of *The Rite of Spring*.

"All these books," muses Sabbathday. She drifts from bookcase to bookcase. I sit on my desk. "So this is your life. Books. Students. Music."

Lust. Perversion. Insanity.

"How wonderful it must be!"

I don't know whether it's Handel or the freedom of being on a date or what, but she's serious. She runs her fingers over the spines of the books.

"I used to think of going to college. Rachel wanted me to quit high school when I turned sixteen, but I stuck it out because I thought someday I'd need the degree."

"Did you ever apply?"

"Money," she says, grimacing. "Also you need three recommendations."

I imagine a seventeen-year-old Sabbathday lying on her bed with a cache of college catalogs: Wellesley, Bryn Mawr,

Vassar. (Shall we add plaid skirt and knee socks to our inventory of icons?)

"I'd write a recommendation for you."

"Too late," she says, turning back to the books. "Besides, I put myself through college at home. Two and a half years' worth anyway. This was when I was eighteen, nineteen. I'd get the college catalog in the fall and choose courses. Buy all the books and read them at home. I was even doing the distribution requirements and everything. I mean doing it right. Not just haphazardly taking courses. I was a history major."

And again she turns around to me.

"I took one of your courses in fact. The New England Reformation."

"Did you like it?"

She shrugs. "It was okay. French is what did me in. I needed language proficiency but there's no way—I discovered this—there's no way you can really learn a foreign language on your own. I tried to get Antoinette to help—she knows Canadian French, but—well, anyway, it didn't work out. So I dropped out. I'm a college dropout." And she grins at the idea.

Back in our seats we listen to the Passion of Christ—betrayal, insult, the world's people spitting, plucking out your hair—until the Hallelujah chorus comes around, which is when Sabbathday grabs hold of my forearm, tightly, as if the experience of being in the world—the *normalcy* of it—is almost too much for her. When we hit the "forevers and evers" I sneak a look at her and damn my soul! if she isn't getting teary, her brown eyes (or are they green?) glistening with emotion and stage light. What I can't figure is whether it's the music itself or the doctrine behind it or just the experience of it all—Handel, Christ, Venner—but when the applause starts she reaches around behind her as if she can't take it anymore, pulls her cape on and stands up.

"I'm sorry," she says when we reach the back of the nave. She won't meet my eyes, but in the safety of the rear of the

chapel, turns and joins in the applause. There's been no bow-
ing by the orchestra: doesn't Sister Sabbathday realize there's
a third part to the *Messiah*, an Apocalypse coming? When the
applause dies down and the audience begins to get to its feet,
she heads for the door. I don't bother to set her straight.

"I had no idea," she says when we're outside. "I just had
no idea."

"You had no idea what?"

She doesn't answer. Her eyes are dry but there's a glitter
of something—passion? revelation? decision?—in them.
When we get to the car she asks if she can drive.

"It'll be icy."

"Let me," she says and holds her hands out for the keys.

Where we're going I don't know, not back out Undermountain Road anyway. In the electric halo of the dash lights
she has a saintly sort of look, hood back up as if that particular heresy could no longer be countenanced. The thought
that Sabbathday Wells might truly—*truly*—believe in Christ
and redemption has never really crossed Venner's mind before. Does she feel herself ambushed by the unexpected reality—here, out among the world's people—of Christ *cum*
crown, compassion and tenpenny nails? And is that the cause
of the tears and the premature exit? If so, what are we doing
driving *away* from New Eden? Why doesn't she just dump
Venner in the nearest gutter and hie herself home?

"Where are we going?" I ask when she signals for a turn
that will head us out into the country.

"Hold on," she says, taking the corner faster than her
driving instructor would have advised. "You'll see."

We drive along the River Road, pass an old mill—stone
foundation, clapboard siding, busted windows—then begin
the climb up the backside of Spirit Mountain. The headlights
bring into brief existence the trunks of trees, antique fence
posts, stone walls lying under snow and history. We keep on
in a kind of competitive silence, each waiting for the other to
commit to some comment or question. After a while Sabbathday turns the radio on and punches buttons like an old pro,

discarding wavelengths until she gets the one she wants. It's a local rock station, and boosterism being what it is, I silently pray that Medusa will not suddenly bloom between us in the car. We make it through the Talking Heads and the Beatles and I'm in the process of twitting Venner for his paranoia when in the dreamy fadeout of "This Boy" there explodes the opening riff of "Essential Ecstasy." I swing around to Sabbathday like maybe she's in on some plot ("I'd like to request a song to be played precisely at—"), but she doesn't even appear to be aware that the female voice occupying the air between us is the same one that used to wish her date good night. She keeps her eyes on the road and I end up slouching in my seat, gazing slantwise out the passenger window at the dim lettering: "Objects In Mirror Are Closer Than They Appear."

It turns out our objective is the Inn at Spirit Mountain. How premeditated our arrival is I can't tell, but for what it's worth Sabbathday eases the Toyota off the road and into the parking lot without any appearance of surprise or impulse. She parks between two Mercedeses.

"Feel like a drink?" she says.

"What's going on?"

She shrugs. "Feel like a drink?"

We get out, spend a moment at the overlook marveling at the Lord's world and then start up the path. The Inn itself is a nineteenth-century farmhouse of the New England type, the outbuildings contiguous to the house for ease of winter transit: barn, coop, shed, stable, sty—all of which have been quaintly made over into sleeping rooms. The manner in which Sabbathday leads the way up the front steps and along the piazza to the lounge suggests that she has previously scoped out the joint. When or how—did she sneak off in the car one day?—or to what end, I don't know.

Inside, it's quiet and dark and, in the manner of chic country inns, decorated with flea-market bucksaws hanging on the walls and a T-auger or two. There are the usual lame candles on the tables, potted plants growing downward from the ceil-

ing like somebody's soul in Dante, and a cocktail waitress
who is young and cute and—wouldn't you know it?—one of
Venner's former students.

"Well, hi!" she says when she sees me. She looks at Sabbathday with, I think, astonishment, but makes no comment,
bless her soul. "What can I get for you?"

"The gentleman will have a bourbon on the rocks," Sabbathday pipes up like she's been studying 1930s Hollywood
for clues about proper social behavior, "and I'll have a gin
and tonic."

I gaze at her in silence and alarm.

"Was that all right?" she inquires, smiling, when the waitress is gone.

"You're going to drink?"

"Sure," she says, sitting back and clasping her hands before her. "Why not?"

Why not indeed! Mother Ann, if Venner admits that, some
years back, he once spent a night of passion in one of the
bedrooms of the Inn (I think it was the chicken coop), will you
forgive him? It was winter (just like it is now), and it was
lonely (just like it is now), and he was needful of human
contact.

"Tell me something," Sabbathday says. "Did your wife
dump you or did you dump her?"

"What?"

"She dumped *you*, right?"

She's got her hair out again and she's twisting part of it
around her finger like a naughty ingenue.

"Was it the fame?" she asks when I don't speak. "Did you
have trouble handling her fame?"

Saint Clare, what is it with people?

"Because," she says, but breaks off when our drinks arrive. (Question: What's the waitress's name and was she one
of those solicited by the Dean's office to write a letter evalu-
ating Professor Venner for tenure? If so, a big tip seems in
order.) "Because," Sabbathday continues, "I'm going to be
famous, too."

And she smiles this perky smile that is part mockery part challenge. Venner continues in aggressive silence.

"And I don't mean that soft-focus PBS stuff. I mean famous for myself. For what I do. So—" she sings. "If you have trouble handling fame—"

"What is it that you do? Rob banks?"

"My weaving," she says. "There's great interest in it, you know. In fact, there's a writer at the *New York Times* who wants to do a feature for the Sunday magazine. Color photos and everything. I got a call from the gallery's publicity agent about it. He's up in the White Mountains this weekend, skiing, and he wants to stop by on the way back to New York. He wants to meet me and maybe set up a preliminary get-together with this guy."

"Great."

"I mean," she continues, oblivious to Venner's sarcasm, "it's one thing to be famous because—am I supposed to drink this through this little straw or what?—because your mother dumped you with the Shakers and you didn't have any choice but to become the last of the Mohicans. And it's another thing to become famous because of who you are, what you do."

I don't say it but, in her case, is there a difference?

"Of course I recognize that the initial reason why the *New York Times* or the 'Today' show or somebody would want to interview me is because I *am* the last of the Shakers, but that doesn't invalidate the fact that I've begun to do something individual and special, does it?"

Yes, Venner thinks; "No," Venner says.

"I put a lot of work into learning how to weave. I mean really learning. I'm sure you don't know this, I mean I'm sure you don't care about this sort of thing, but other weavers when they see my stuff are really impressed. Not just the Shaker patterns but the technique." She stops, aware that she's on the verge of some vanity, and then smiles the smile the "Today" show cameras would love: "I have very even edges."

"Even edges," I manage to say. She chucks the little straw

and takes a good gulp of her drink. "Well, if you're going to be famous—" and I unfold from my coat pocket the three typed sheets of paper with the three biographies—"you'll need these."

"What?" she says, and then realizing what they are, picks them up one by one and reads them. "Good," she says, at the end of the first, "that's just what I need." She reads the second, the one about CEO Wells, grimaces a "very funny" sort of grimace, and then starts on the Lara one, the one about paradigms of prodigality and the view from Sodom and (did Venner get it right?) the beating of her human heart. When she's done she puts it down and gives me this intimate look like maybe she's been practicing in the car mirror.

"Call me Lara," she whispers.

I shake my head no.

"Say it," she says. "Say 'Lara.' "

"Sabbathday."

"No," she says. "Lara. Say 'Lara.' "

"Lara."

She smiles and—I don't know what—shivers almost, as if the word, the carnality of it, thrills her in some forbidden way. She reaches out and takes my hand, turns the palm over and, more practiced than you would think, traces a fingertip along Venner's lifeline. Certain physiological changes begin to occur in Venner's flesh, but his spirit, his heart . . . dear Reader, what do we do?

"I reserved a room," she says.

"What?"

She smiles a smile of—of what? There's no nerves or worry or guilt, just a kind of schoolgirl naughtiness. "I did," she says. "I called a few days ago. It was like a dare to myself. I did it."

I pull my hand away from her.

"I didn't know whether I would tell you or not. And if I did, whether . . . you know."

"Sabbathday . . ."

"Lara," she says.

And we gaze at one another in silence. What is she up to? Is this like the time she ran off to New York, the trying on of an alternate life for the profit of self-scrutiny, for kicks, for the exotica it piles on your plate? Or is it possible—no dare or trap or bluff about it—that the last Shakeress's veins have the same pulse of destruction in them as you, Reader, or I, or the unclothed Eve?

"I don't trust you," I find myself saying.

"You don't what?"

"Trust you."

She blanches and sits back in her chair, all innocence. "What do you mean you don't trust me?" she asks, but before I can answer the waitress comes. Without asking me if I want anything, Sabbathday orders us refills and then leans back across the table. "What do you mean you don't trust me?"

"I don't." She makes a face of exasperation but I wave her off. "I want you to tell me something," I say. "I want you to tell me about New York."

"You know all about it," she answers, and there's a color to her, a defiance.

"No, I don't."

"Yes, you do."

"Listen," I say, leaning toward her, whispering. "You've got this idea that I've memorized your life or something, that I've read every single one of your diaries, but I haven't. I haven't read the one—what were you? sixteen? seventeen?—I haven't read that one. I want you to tell me about it."

"Why?"

"Because," I say, and when she doesn't respond, "I want to know why you went. And why you came back."

She withdraws across the table again. Her face is set against me, but too, there's a darkness there that's more than just resentment. She waits for the waitress to come with our drinks, and then says quietly, with how much sincerity of heart and how much manipulation of the theater of the thing, I can't tell: "I went to look for my mother."

I must be making a face, because she says, "Look, I was

sixteen. My mother had abandoned me when I was three. It was natural enough."

"Did you find her?"

"No."

"What happened?"

She huddles over her glass and doesn't answer.

"What made you think she was in New York? Did you have an address? A phone number?"

"No."

"You figured you'd just ask around?"

She blows bubbles in her drink by way of answer, and then with a kind of abandon, "I had a letter. My mother had written a letter."

"To you?"

"To Eldress Anne. When I was six."

"And there was an address on it?"

"No. Just a postmark. Okay, okay!" she says. "It was incredibly stupid. But I thought I'd find her. I'd look up Sharon Wells in the Manhattan phone book and there her name would be."

"But it wasn't."

"No, it was. One Sharon Wells and two S. Wellses. I didn't call. Just showed up. I mean never mind about trying to figure out the subway and stuff. I showed up at West Seventy-eighth Street, rang the buzzer and this voice comes on the intercom. So there I am saying 'Sabbathday!' into this metal speakerphone, and a voice saying 'Who?' and me saying 'Lara!' this time and again she doesn't understand but she buzzes me up anyway. So I go inside and of course I have no idea what my mother looks like, so when this woman answers the door, it's like hello, are you my mother? Jesus!" she says at the memory of the thing. "She was short and had dark, frizzy sort of hair. And I don't think she was much over thirty."

"And the S. Wellses?"

"A college student and a black woman."

"I'm sorry," says Venner.

"You're not the only one," she says and stabs the straw

back into her drink. "So there I am in the middle of New York, no cap but otherwise dressed in my clothes, although it's New York so nobody really notices, and I've already stayed one night in this crummy hotel that's costing me eighty dollars a day—money I stole from the Goods Shop, no kidding—and wherever my mother is it's not New York, or if it is she's named Sharon Lefkowitz now and living on Park Avenue or something, I mean who knows?"

"I'm sorry," I say again.

"I was terrified. Once the idea of it, the *quest*, was gone, I got scared. I couldn't remember the name of the bus station I'd come in at—Port Authority, of course, but I honestly couldn't remember it—so I ended up at Grand Central with all these creeps, I mean, *creeps!* And there's no train except one to White River Junction on the way to Montreal."

I don't know if it's the Vennereal iconography that has come to surround Sabbathday with a host of American progenitors or what, but I've never quite thought of her as the orphan she really is. It makes me feel, I don't know, tender toward her.

"Did you tell Rachel?" I ask after a minute. "I mean that the reason you went was because of your mother?"

"No. She always thought I'd run away because of—" and here, a rueful smile—"because of some wickedness in me."

There's also the Disney iconography: Snow White, Sleeping Beauty and now Sabbathday coming to life by the hopes and the lies and the donkey ears of what it means to be human.

"Really," she says, "what sort of woman leaves her three-year-old baby and never comes to see her or anything? She knows where I am. I haven't moved." And she spreads her hands out like the inhumanity of it is incredible. "There was a time when I used to look at every youngish middle-aged woman who showed up at the village and wonder if this was her. I'd look at their hair and their eyes and their faces, the way they touched things in the Goods Shop, trying to find some grown-up version of myself."

"But it never happened."

"I don't know. Maybe it did. There was one year when I had ten or twelve different mothers picked out. I always thought they were looking at me special, like there was a secret sympathy between us. But then everybody looks at me special. So in the end, after New York, I just gave up. The hell with her, I thought." And then: "The hell with her."

I have this urge to kiss her. I have this urge to lean over and draw her face to me and kiss her lips. Venner has, you understand, kissed a girl or two, say, three—okay, a dozen—in his time, but he feels like a grade-schooler with a crush right now. The props are many. There's the romantic candlelight, the phony fire in the hearth, the glitter of glass behind the bar. There's even MTV on the tube, though the sound is turned off so all you get are Nazi rock singers and iconic body parts. Sabbathday herself is wearing the regalia of the fair-skinned blush, either from the gin or the high sentiment of the moment. Venner thinks he has previously communicated to the reader that there is a quality of, shall we say, beauty about the last Shakeress's physical self. It isn't lessened by imminent destruction.

"Kiss me," I say.

She looks first startled and then embarrassed and then, maybe, pleased. But she makes no move toward me.

"Kiss me," I say again, and I lean over the table and— Reader, get out your Polaroid—it happens. We touch lip to lip, softly, even politely.

"You love me," she says.

Venner is dazzled by the physics of Sabbathday's and/or Lara's eyes, by this we mean the manner in which the irises, beheld up close for the first time, seem to dissolve and change color. It may be due simply to the melodrama of the moment, in fact it probably *is* the melodrama of the moment, but out of just such imprecision of perception we fashion the apparition of our love. Other perceptual imprecisions currently include: the flush of her cheeks *(vide supra)*, the *faux* Maybelline lashes, the overexposure of the hair near her temples, the feel of her leg under the table.

"Don't," she says. "Not here."

Dear Dean, the waitress is mentally composing.

"Let's go," I say.

She stays seated. There's a look about her of approaching nerves.

"Let's go," I say again and reach for my wallet.

"I've never been loved before," she says suddenly.

I lay my wallet on the table and gaze at her. Is Venner being a fink? Is some soul-searching *re* love preceding lust in order here?

"I've never been loved *personally* before."

"Personally?"

"I've never had someone come to me, out of choice."

I wonder at her. "Do you mean that whatever love Rachel or Antoinette or Eldress Sarah had for you was—" and I want to say ideologically dictated but can't get it out.

"Yes," she says as if she knows what I mean.

"Sabbathday . . ." I murmur and lean toward her. We kiss again.

(One of the many vows Venner made during the kidnapping of his child and the iconization of his wife was that he would never fall in love again. Or at least, not seriously. Not without a full recognition of the comedy of the thing, the vanity, the traducements of self and soul, the masquerade of the temporal as the eternal, the finite as the infinite. None of this now stands him in good stead for an experience of genuine—genuine?—innocence.)

"Is that what it's like?" she says when we draw apart.

"What *is* it like?" I ask in return, smiling.

She smiles too but doesn't answer. I'm filming soft-core pornography in my mind.

"I'm a little nervous," she says.

"I know."

"A little drunk too."

"Yes."

On the TV there are rows of women dressed in black bustiers and SS boots.

"Did you really rent a room?" I ask after a minute.

"Yes."

"Under your name?"

She looks away and then smiles. "Under yours," she says and bites her lip. "I charged it to your credit card. Over the phone." And when I don't seem to get it, "They needed a credit card to hold the room. So I read off the numbers from a receipt I had."

This time it's "Lara" I say, and she flushes with pleasure. What will it be like? The undressing, the first touch, the press of flesh to flesh? (Reader, if you think, when the time comes, you're going to be privy to all that, think again.)

"Let's go," I say once more, and yes, this time she pushes her chair back and stands up. She's coloring wildly, and for a moment I think she's going to run from the room, but she stands there with a kind of high magnificence while I put a twenty on the table. I escort her through the tables, smiling past our waitress, through the ell and into the farmhouse, where I leave her sitting in a Queen Anne chair while I go on to the front desk.

Mother Ann, as you know, it has been part of Venner's hopes and dreams these last two years to have imagined a variety of venues for the waylaying of Sister Sabbathday's body, *e.g.* his steeple, the Weaving Shop, the moonlit fields of New Eden in summer, the coal-fired HMQ in winter, at midnight the illegal climb up the Sisters' stairway to a heavenly Sabbathday lying in wait between fresh-laundered sheets. There was to be the brush of lip to cheek, the graze of thigh to thigh, the shadow of our embracing bodies breaking across the Shaker-planed wood. But in all that I never once imagined we'd be doing the motel bit and I'm not too sure how I feel about it. Should Venner turn around right now (he's in the process of trying to remember the license plate on the Toyota) and leave? Take Sabbathday by the arm and say,

"We're better than this," and so forth? Such an action would cast him in the role of messiah (salvation, etcetera: he rather likes it), as opposed to snake (destruction of New Eden, etcetera: bad on the *curriculum vitae*. Ha-ha). It's not just cold feet we're experiencing, but an honest-to-goodness quiver in the conscience. Because even if the degradation of the last Shakeress is inevitable, does Venner have to be the instrument of that degradation? Won't he feel better, say, when he's fifty years old, for *not* having done it with Sabbathday Wells? (What a chill I suddenly feel! When Venner is fifty years old New Eden will be a museum of dead air and dead ideas and the passion he—oh! cut the *he!*—the passion *I* feel for the body and soul of Lara Wells—whatever happens tonight; even if it ends with His-and-Her towels and pink flamingos on the front lawn—will be dust. Dust!) But even that leaves us with a familiar dilemma: Do we *carpe* a *diem* that is doomed to dust, or abstract ourselves from love and lust by, let's say, living celibate in a steeple? I mean wasn't that the whole point in the first place? The whole point of the steeple and the one hundred Kodacolor icons? You were trying to love the impossible, weren't you, Venner? You were trying to keep passion pure by loving a woman sworn to chastity, and to keep it pure so that *you* would be kept pure along with it. What happened? How did you get infected with life again? How did the abstraction of John Venner, divorced doctor of divinity, get incarnated at Christmastime in the Inn at Spirit Mountain with Sister Sabbathday Wells (complete with beautiful skin, hair, face, hips, ankles, toes) waiting for him in a reproduction Queen Anne chair? (I step back and look around the corner to check on her; she waves nervously at me.) Saint Clare, this would not be a bad time for Venner to achieve Assumption. Just lift him in Super Slo-Mo from the crust of this earth into your heaven, no questions asked. But the truth is—damn your soul, Reader! I hear you rooting for the flesh—the truth is, like the sad spirits in the *Paradiso*, I'd miss my body if I didn't have it. (I'm done registering now, got the key and everything, but I'm stalling for time by pretending to read a flyer on the Mount Washington Cog Railway.) What to do? Suppose I go with her and fall in love? I mean *really* in love, not the graffiti of American celluloid, but the real thing. And suppose after that's happened she plumps for clean sheets after all? Then what? It won't be warm enough to move back into my steeple for another four months. And even if it were, could I? Isn't it the case, Class, that no matter what happens tonight your professor will never be able to return to the distant admiration of an unappled Sister Sabbathday? Like it or not, he has gotten himself incarnated in his particular manger: flesh and blood, a dash of divinity and the passion awaiting him.

"We're in the barn," I say coming back to Sabbathday and showing the key. She smiles nervously and stands up.

"Okay."

"Okay?" I say and when she nods, lead the way back into the ell, through the bar and into the barn. We take the stairs up to room fourteen, which turns out to be part of the old hayloft: rough floorboards, hand-hewn beams, a sort of cathedral ceiling. There's a bed and a rustic nightstand and a pie closet for a bureau. I stand off to the side while Sabbathday makes a wifely inspection. We both have our coats on still.

"Now what?" she says, turning to me from the other side of the bed. I shrug and start humming "Away in a Manger." She gives me a curious look and crosses to the window.

"It's starting to snow."

It's time for the usual second thoughts, *e.g.:* Are we sure this is a good idea? Consider the dangerous drive home. Consider the first through ninth circles. Consider that Venner the reluctant libertine is no longer in the habit of packing a prophylactic.

"John," she says suddenly. She's turned back around, facing me. "Are you all right?"

"Yes."

"Do you want to leave?"

Venner decides that he'd better start looking like the idea of getting laid is a pleasure not a punishment and starts around the foot of the bed toward her. Outside, the snow is wheeling in the halo of the parking-lot light. I draw up to an expectant Sabbathday and put my hands inside her cape, on her hips.

"Sister . . ."

I mean the word as a thing of intimacy, but her face charges suddenly with doubt, maybe even hurt, and I realize she hears something else in it, some reprimand or reproach. I don't know what to do so I kiss her, once, twice, and then—*oh damn it!*—lift my hand to her breast and actually yes Reader feel her up. She lets out a little gasp of surprise or pleasure or horror (difficult to tell which) and then kisses back at me with a kind of blundering passion. (Reader, I think it's time for you to go.) I slip my hands into the sleeves of her cape so that it falls backward off her and onto the floor. She unbuttons my jacket. Etcetera etcetera occurs until we're lying on the bed, still clothed but more or less free with one another's anatomy. The usual physiological changes are occurring—um, let's see—increased rate of breathing, flushed faces, erect erectile tissue, quickening pulse, vocalization and so forth (as if you don't know what I'm talking about Reader you Peeping Tom, you Paul Pry)! I start to unbutton her dress but she whispers "No" and then "The light" with a smile that is, no kidding, fragile and afraid and even a little heartbreaking. I get up, hit the wall switch and in the silvery luminescence that's left undo my tie and strip my shirt off. She stands up as well, slips out of her shoes, then pulls the covers back and, fully clothed still, gets between the sheets. I climb in beside her.

There's enough light in the room from the parking lot and the snow so that I can see her face. It's not quite the blue light of stage and screen but by it I kiss her on the eyes and (are we feeling love? are we feeling life?) touch her on the cheek with my fingertips.

"John," she whispers.

"My name's Venner."

"No," she says; then: "Oh!" (I'm back to unbuttoning her dress.) "I'm scared."

"It's all right," I say. (Liar! Liar!)
"You love me."
"I love you." (Pants on fire!)
"Oh!"
Stop reading, Reader.
"I've dreamed of this," she says.
"No."
"I have. I've dreamed of being kissed. I've dreamed of making love."
Reader, if you have any self-respect left . . .
"I've dreamed of—oh!" (We're touching her in certain regions forbidden to PG-13.) "I didn't know," she says, "I didn't know. . . ."
She's got her eyes closed, her back arched. Dear Lord, there's the undreamable availability of her body parts, the kissable sanctuary just under her chin, her illegal hair in a halo on the pillow, her neck, her throat, her darling ears. . . .
Saint Clare, save us. Get the movie conventions going. You know what I mean: the hazy focus, the orchestra crescendo and, just when our lovers are about to lose themselves, the camera panning across the room to the window where the passionate snowflakes hurl themselves with clumsy poetry against the windowpane.

CHAPTER FIFTEEN

CONFESSIONS OF A ONCE AND FUTURE VIRGIN

For the next several weeks Venner's soul is shod in meta-physical clown shoes, clodhopping about in dopey sweetness: O Reader, Mother Ann, Saint Clare! He's in love!

How the defenses of the last two hundred pages (do you remember Venner *cum* BB gun? Venner hefting stones to keep out the barbarians?) could prove so insubstantial in the presence of simple human emotion is beyond me. And yet, there it is! To my classes I've become a jolly fellow easy with the A's; to the volleyball players entering the Body-Rite Fitness Club, a harmless soul blowing kisses through his office window. I write memos full of incoherent camaraderie to the Tenure Advisory Board (even now determining my future), and out at New Eden throw my BB gun into the trash.

Folks, we're a new man.

Ann Lee, what do you think? Isn't it a better way of paying God back for the gift of life—I mean, to care for another soul, not your separate staircases? All those rules against love,

against touching! When Venner goes back to rebuilding the
walls of New Eden, he's going to build gateways in them (to
match the gates in his soul—come in, everybody: you and you
and you too, Reader)! Mother Ann, this is how your celibate
utopia has ended: your final converts are in love. In the morning when we come upon one another in the wide hall we
secretly embrace, feel the press of thigh to thigh, the beat of
our hearts. I take her cap off and unpin her just-pinned hair,
bring it around to my lips. On the floor above us or below us,
Sister Chastity interrogates the ghost of some dead Brother,
some rotted Sister. What Venner says is this: The human
heart will not be quarantined. At the breakfast table, when
Sabbathday brings me my bowl of cereal, she lets her fingertips retreat across the back of my hand. Antoinette asks for
the sugar. What Venner says is this: We each of us need the
nourishment of another soul. At midmorning in the Sisters'
Weaving Shop we make a bed of coverlets on the floor. Outside,
the tourists wonder when the Goods Shop is going to open. Inside, Venner says, I am a member of the world's people.

Or maybe it's Sabbathday who says it.

Eve can tell something's wrong right off. Perhaps it's the
goofy smile or the kiss I plant on ugly Auntie Dante or the fact
that when we get in the car I don't tell her to put her seat belt
on. (How can we be at risk? Saint Venner wonders as the
Toyota weaves across the center line on Undermountain
Road. A beat-up Peugeot passes him going the other way.) At
New Eden I show her her new room on the Sisters' floor, then
her father's new room on the Brethren's floor. (Yes, Reader,
Brother Venner has moved out of the Hired Men's Quarters,
the result both of the progress of his soul and the price of coal,
but mostly of the need for him to caretake the elderly Sisters
when the time comes for their Eldress to go to New York.) In
Antoinette's hearing I instruct Eve on which stairway is the
proper one for her to use when she wants to come up to see
me, but when we're alone tell her to go ahead and use either
one, her heart should not be valved so. At the breakfast table
she eats her oatmeal and chatters at Chastity, who chatters

back. We spend a happy Saturday making a yarn doll out of Sabbathday's scraps, a happy Sunday hiking up Spirit Mountain. On Monday morning I bring her back to Auntie Dante's, effecting the transfer without once having seen her mother.

In the midst of all this, Sometimes-Why has taken to being a barn cat.

"It's not a bad life," he says on one of my trips out to feed Sabbathday's sheep. He's sitting on a joist overhead, paws crossed in contemplation.

"What isn't?" I ask.

"The pastoral life. It takes some getting used to—I mean the rankness of it all, the dirt, dodging the sheep doo-doo—especially after having lived in a steeple, but so it is with all dreams that end in waking. And there *is* compensation. For instance, I am no longer troubled by the relative weights of the flesh and the spirit. Ditto the degree to which one is given to Satan, the other to—um—what was His name again? To round out the picture: I've got a calico cutie from the housing tract who drops by from time to time, Purina Sheep Chow turns out to be to my liking and I'm at peace with my bodily functions. Perhaps a close-up of me peeing would be in order here. And then: Music up. Run credits."

When finally I see Medusa it's by accident. She's in the Revco buying traveling supplies—a little plastic case for her toothbrush, a lint roller—and I'm buying, no kidding, a pack of condoms. We meet at the checkout counter. She's wearing tights and a very short skirt that flatters her rear end, also: no beauty mark. To deflect her attention from the condoms I inquire when she's leaving. Thursday, she says. And is everything ready? I ask. She looks from the condoms up to my face. What do you care? she wants to know.

"I don't," I answer, handing the cashier a ten and regretting having opted for a flaccid package of five instead of a tumescent twelve.

In the parking lot she comes calling after me but I head straight for the Toyota. I'm inside with the engine revving when she opens the passenger door and slides in. For a time we just sit in the cold car and stare at each other. The breath is coming out of her mouth like a cartoon balloon.

"So what's the story?" she says finally.

"The story?" I repeat.

"Yes, the story. What's the story?"

I put the heater on, run the windshield wipers to get the salt off. "The story is this," I say. "We're divorced. What that means is that we once loved one another but now we hate one another. The result of which is rather extreme modification of behavior, *e.g.* your kidnapping of my daughter. We have yet to employ pipe bombs in one another's mailbox, but that's only a matter of time, wouldn't you agree?"

"I don't hate you," she says.

"Then give me my daughter back."

"All right."

I gaze across at her. She's got her legs crossed perkily and whatever the anger was that sent her after me has somehow disappeared. "What's the catch?"

"No catch."

"There's got to be a catch."

"No catch," she says. And then she smiles that smile. "Okay, maybe one catch."

"I knew it."

"Just come live in the house while I'm away."

(Reader, it was a mere five parking spaces over that Venner first stripped Sabbathday of her spark-plug cables.)

"Impossible," I say.

"Why? It would be good for Eve. Reassuring. And aren't you tired of playing Protestant priest?"

"I am not playing Protestant priest. I'm a covenanted member of the United Society of Believers in Christ's Second Appearing."

"You are?"

"Yes."

"You really are?"

"Yes."

"Then who're the rubbers for?"

[LIGHTING: HALO AROUND VENNER'S HEAD]

"Still doing the drummer, are we?" And she picks up the Revco bag off the dash and dumps out the condoms.

"No."

"Who, then?"

The urge to tell her, to shout "Olly-olly-outs-in-free" at having been the first to touch the goal of essence, is nearly overwhelming.

" 'Ribbed for her pleasure,' " she reads. "For whose pleasure?"

"None of your business," I say and take the condoms out of her hand, put them back in their bag and toss them into the back seat.

"They've got to be for *some*one," she says. "Unless you've taken to porking sheep out there and don't want any genetic accidents."

Which comment places between us the sight of a herd of little lambs each with the head of Venner gamboling and frisking. Medusa raises the quizzical eyebrow and then hums a few measures of "Baa, Baa, Black Sheep."

"Well," she says after a minute, "I've got to go."

"Good-bye."

"I'm doing a phone interview this afternoon with someone from *Rolling Stone*."

"Okay. Good-bye."

But she doesn't move. "Listen," she says. "Let me try out my interview on you. I mean try out the stuff I want to tell them. Okay? I figured I'd start off with the Ph.D. business—"

I zap the heater fan up to as loud as it goes.

"—then go into how unhappy I was, how meaningless my life had become there on the cusp of the twenty-first century writing endlessly about whether the Virgin Mary had ever screwed after that first time with the Holy Ghost. And then maybe tell them about my conversion experience. I mean the time I was in Appliance City—did I ever tell you this?—with all the televisions on around me and how I had a vision of myself fifty times over on the TVs, dancing and singing some song I hadn't even written yet, or maybe I should say it was "Essential Ecstasy" coming to me out of the ether, divine inspiration and so forth."

"Spare me."

"It was like Saul on the road to Damascus I'll say. I went into that mall as Sally Shannon and came out Medusa. Is that too learned a reference for *Rolling Stone?*"

"I'm in love," I say suddenly.

"What?"

"I'm in love."

She turns in her seat toward me and I can't tell whether she thinks I mean her or what. "With whom?" she asks finally. "Turn that goddamn thing down. With whom?"

I turn the heater down. "With Sabbathday."

"No kidding."

"I mean for real. And she loves me back."

"She's told you that?"

"Yes," I say, or rather, lie. Because—Reader, I've been meaning to tell you this—she hasn't actually said it, not yet anyway, but that seems to me more a matter of tact than fact.

"And the condoms?" Medusa says.

I nod.

"Holy shit."

She seems genuinely astonished. It's a reaction Venner rather enjoys.

"She's a remarkable woman," he goes on to say.

"Less remarkable now than she was a month ago."

"Not at all. She's done some extraordinary things." And I tell her about Sabbathday's putting herself through college, about the weaving show and her going to New York, about the Chilton's repair manual for a 1968 Corvette that's in her room.

"Extraordinary," she says when I'm done. "But how do you know you're not just one more course in the curriculum?"

"Meaning?"

"Meaning how do you know that Sabbathday isn't just using Professor Venner as her instructor for Sex 101? To find out about that aspect of the world's people. And then to graduate to other things."

"Jealous?" says jealous Venner.

"Not likely," says Medusa. "But you haven't answered my question."

"I know because I have faith in her goodness."

"Oh, brother."

"Also, because I believe I can feel when love is there and when it isn't. I've got some experience in this line."

She gazes at me with resentment. The windows have fogged up from our breath. It's beginning to get dark, but she doesn't show any signs of getting out of my car, which leaves me wondering just what the heck she wants anyway.

"So," she says in a musing voice, "this afternoon, you think I should feature the Appliance City thing? I mean turn it into part of my personal mythology?"

I don't answer.

"It lends a certain aura of spiritual inevitability to the whole thing, don't you think? The first miracle and so forth. Like the Pope picked me to be a rock star."

I turn the heater on defrost and wipe the windshield. "We were talking about Sabbathday," I say.

"We've moved on," she answers and continues to sit. I turn in my seat so I'm facing her straight on.

"So what's going on here?" I ask. "What do you want? What did you follow me out here for?"

Still she looks at me with antagonism and provocation, as if there's some secret temptation inside her. Finally she says, simply, "I miss you."

Oh, boy.

"I do. I miss you. I don't know why, but I do."

And she turns away, looks ahead out the windshield in the miffed female manner. I try to balance on various sentimental fences.

"Do you mean," I say after a moment, in a quiet, precise voice, "do you mean to say that you miss me as a friend? Or as a husband?"

She considers a moment and then says, "Both."

"And when did you start feeling this way?"

"Oh, forget it!" she cries and tosses me a dirty look.

"And Butch," I say, pressing the advantage, "how does he fit into this?"

"His name is Spike."

"Okay, Spike. How does Spike fit—?"

"It's really Myron."

"Myron?"

"Spike is his stage name." And suddenly, without warning, she heaves this big sigh as if there's something about the whole business, about the unrealness of the world she's entered—Reader, pay attention now because this is the first glimpse I've caught of this—something that leaves her feeling incomplete just like everything else. "Look, forget it," she says. "I'm just feeling weird and I don't know, scared I guess. The early sales of the record aren't as good as I'd hoped. Forget it."

Do I cry crocodile tears or smile Vennereal smiles? Perhaps she simply wants comfort from me, a quaint sort of thing, but something Venner was used to giving when he was in the husband line. But he's no longer in the husband line so he simply sits in the driver's seat in a state of gentle cruelty. Sally keeps her face turned away, her package of Revco stuff squeezed between her knees.

"So Snow White's going to New York?" she says after a time.

"Yes."

"For how long?"

"I don't know. Maybe a week."

She makes a face like it's hard to believe, which, of course, it is. Then there's silence for one, maybe two, minutes during which one of the back doors opens and the ghost of our marriage slips into the car.

"Did you mean it about Eve?" I ask finally.

She nods.

"I can have her while you're gone?"

"Look," she says, "I'm not out to deprive you of your child. You just pissed me off, taking her like that. And that business with Ann."

"I'm sorry."

"I mean really, V!"

"I was just trying to make a point."

"What point?"

Quick, Reader, what point? "I was trying to suggest to you—at least, I think I was—that what one does matters, that there's a moral weight to things that the Medusan metaphysic doesn't—"

"Oh, not now," she says and claps her hands over her ears. It's a genuinely despairing gesture and I have the good taste to shut up. "Look, I've got to go," she says and starts pulling her things together. "I'll try to call Eve as often as I can. I've got your number out there. Take good care of her."

And she pushes the door open. I want to say one last thing, some good-bye or good luck or something to make her feel better, but it gets stuck in my throat and she's gone before I can get it unstuck. I watch her hurry between the cars until she disappears a few rows over. Whether the smell of her perfume lingers in the car Venner isn't saying.

• • •

Toward the end of January the word comes from Idols and Icons, Inc. that a black-and-white glossy of Sabbathday—"face or full figure, we leave it up to you"—is needed for the gallery brochure. So, in spite of their offer to pay for a studio shot, I get out my Nikon and—after a trip to Sally's basement where my steeple furnishings are still boxed and where I spend a bittersweet hour looking over former Sabbathdays—shoot the current Eldress of New Eden in a variety of poses. There's the last Shakeress at prayer, at work, as virginal shepherdess among her sheep (tough-looking cat in the background), in *Vogue*ish poses that the photographer knows are inappropriate but figures what the heck as long as he's got the chance. And then, outside, with God's washed-out heaven for a backdrop and time-outs to warm Sabbathday's nose, we shoot three rolls of close-ups, head-on shots, profile shots, shots of Sabbathday looking directly into the viewer's soul, looking out of frame into the imagined distance, into some visionary future. I note again, just as at Rachel's funeral, she's oddly at ease before a camera, with an instinct for how the lens sees her, what slight angle or inclination will flatter her. In the viewfinder the perfection of her looks unsettles me: she's so much the Beautiful Young Shakeress. I try to get her to do a few with her cap off, hair out, but she is adamant that we play it straight, which leaves Venner wondering just where on the continuum of novitiate to sophisticate Sabbathday sits *re* the manipulation of iconic imagery in this our postmodern America.

When the gallery's publicity agent stops off on his way back from skiing in the White Mountains (Reader, does this ring a bell? Is a certain pattern in Venner's recent life being repeated?), he sits in the Elders' Room saying "Nope—nope—nope—maybe—nope," running through Venner's photos with what appears to be disinterest but which is in fact a kind of camouflaged awe over the real Sabbathday sitting across from him. I'm standing in the doorway, not exactly invited to this meeting but not uninvited either, and I can tell his mind's going a mile a minute on the subject of what a plum telegenic Sabbathday would be for the tired national media, an honest-to-god virgin for Christ's sake and a knockout to boot! Half-way through my photos he's got her in *People* magazine and on "Hard Copy," answering questions on what it's like to be a Shaker in the modern world, on the virtues of sexual abstinence, on the allure of leaving the order (he's got the wrong terminology, of course, but who cares?), doing a book tour (*The Last Shakeress*, by Eldress Sabbathday Wells) in which the author confesses to sexual attraction to a boy in high school, running away to New York for love of a marine lieutenant (but scorning him at the last minute, lips still unkissed), and advises the single businesswoman on making it in a man's world. He chooses three photos out of the hundred-

and-something—"this one because it shows spirituality, this one because it's got the Shaker look to it, and this one because let's face it it's got, um, appeal, you know what I mean?"— and then lays out how in addition to his friend at the *Times* he knows someone with the Hearst papers and how did she feel about maybe having an article done on her, mentioning the show of course, but also with photos of her life up here, also how he's a personal friend of one of the screeners for the "Today" show, it was a long shot of course, but they were always looking for the special angle, if not them then he could try "Good Morning America," and of course Geraldo would go gaga over a virgin, that is, he meant, if she wanted that sort of exposure, if it wasn't against her beliefs and if she felt she could handle the interview format, because he realized she wasn't used to studio cameras or being at the center of . . .

"I can handle it."

"Good," he says and smiles like finally this—this!—is clay he can model. Out in the hallway Chastity shuffles past singing "A Companion to Old Stiff I Will Not Be." In the doorway, Brother Venner is not happy.

"Geraldo might be going a bit far," he manages to say.

"Well . . ." the publicity agent murmurs. He looks my Shakerly clothes up and down.

"There's such a thing as the Millennial Laws."

Sabbathday gives me her Eldress face. "The Millennial Laws do not prevent an Elder from attempting to spread the word," she says.

"The word?"

"I can think of no reason why the early Shakers would not have used television had it been available to them."

And for a moment we stare at one another in silent antagonism and then Sabbathday turns back to the publicity agent and tells him to go ahead, make preliminary inquiries, she would be glad to speak to anyone who was interested in what she was doing and who would respect her beliefs.

• • •

"Just which beliefs are those?" Venner asks the animal air half an hour later. He's out in the barn, shoveling sheep shit. In another half an hour he has to lecture on Thomas Aquinas. "I mean what does she think? Does she think she can hold to the outward show of Shakerhood and defile the essence of the thing with impunity?"

"Oh, shut up," Sometimes-Why says from along the railing of one of the sheep stalls.

"Does she think America's just waiting for a virginal evangelist to come along and show it where it's gone wrong and point out the true way?"

"Shut up and hold one of these sheep still for me." And he points to one with cute black legs like stockings.

Because honestly, it's been over a month now. Where's the emotional scene of regret? The teary remorse? The hysteria over what she's done? Venner would like to think he has an impact upon the virgins of the world goddamn it! But she seems so calm in her corruption, as if she'd planned it all out: thirteen-year-old Sabbathday allocating her life in strategic chunks, say, ten years of chastity to gain the world's confidence followed by a year of Augustinian debauchery so that the ensuing *Confessions of a Once and Future Virgin* will have the right mix of sin and salvation, not to mention sales potential, making Venner a mere accessory in the last Shakeress's personal pageant of loss and redemption. ("We pick up the action in Chapter Fourteen—" says Sometimes-Why. "Shut up," says Venner. "—some pages distant from the marine lieutenant, several chapters shy of repudiation, wherein Sister Sabbathday, oppressed by the responsibility of historical chastity—seven generations of virgins behind her, zero ahead—morally falters and, in a scene dependent perhaps a bit too much on movie imagery, fumbles her chastity into the hands of a local college professor [not a bad-intentioned man if somewhat reluctant to go whole hog in the flesh line], the ensuing scenes being full of the usual motifs of illicit passion, the director insisting on red interiors [we've moved on to the film version], clandestine bedrooms, absinthe on the boulevard, close-ups of the lovers gazing at one another with the sorrow of the damned, *cf.* Adam and Eve if you must.")

The fact is, clown shoes or no clown shoes, Venner has been wondering about the depth of Sabbathday's feeling for him. His ex-wife's lucky shot (*re* the ex-husband as just one more course in the curriculum) hit home, the more so since it's a thought he's had himself. The question is this: Is her silence, her backwardness in matters of love (not physical love, at which, Venner is happy/sad to report, she is increasingly expert, but rather the emotions, *e.g.* her inability to say the "L" word), the result of perverted relations, by which we mean twenty-three years during which the ordinary human feelings ("Ordinary what?") of, say, daughter for mother, friend for friend, girlfriend for boyfriend, were forbidden by the dictates of a woman who couldn't take the touch of skin on skin and hence are grossly malformed, even withered: the last Shakeress as a victim of emotional thalidomide? Or is she simply using me? Lara Wells with fully formed psychological biceps aware that this professor guy with an *idée fixe* is not for her, but the Hand of Fate etcetera. So okay she'll do him while she's got the chance, get the much-needed experience in the fallen-world line and, once regenerate, dress up his character for the teleplay.

"Can we spell 'paranoia'?" Sometimes-Why asks.

At any rate she has yet to mention His-and-Her towels. Ditto the pair of pink flamingos.

• • •

Out at the mall I stop in at Ricky's Record Reality to check the *Billboard* charts and find that "Essential Ecstasy" has made it up to thirty-two (from thirty-four last week): not exactly a runaway hit but not a flop either. I go to the CD bins and locate the M's and there she is, posed and enclosed in plastic, three copies, down from seven last week. So also like last week it's over to Appliance City, where I stand among the televisions like a troubled peasant before a shrine, close my eyes and concentrate. I'm waiting for my own conversion experience is what I'm doing—the flash of infused spirit, the certitude—but what I get instead is Fred and Wilma and the virtues of Spray 'n Wash on one's undergarments.

This is the sign our God sends us.

We are not among the Elect.

• • •

She receives mysterious phone calls. I don't know whether they're from the gallery or the publicity agent or the "Today" show or what, but when she gets them she informs me in her business voice that "it's New York calling" and I'm expected to leave and go kill time like the hayseed boyfriend who everybody knows is going to be left in the lurch by the end of the film. (Reader, *am* I going to be left in the lurch by the end of the film? Does everyone in the auditorium know except me?) I help her compile an invitation list when the gallery requests one, cribbing from the Friends of the Shakers mailing list, adding colleagues and whomever else I can think of. A few weeks later I receive an invitation myself:

IDOLS AND ICONS, INC.
presents

Simple Gifts: the Weaving of Eldress Sabbathday Wells

March 21–April 28
172 Spring Street

etcetera, and with it a photo of one of Sabbathday's designs and bio #1. We spend a weekend packing up the first load of coverlets and blankets and shawls and capes, and on Monday haul them down to Art Shippers Inc. in Boston. The current plan is for Sabbathday to spend a week in New York, four days helping the gallery set up the show, three days for the opening. This is an eventuality that does not sit well with your narrator, though he's trying not to appear worried or

CONFESSIONS OF A ONCE AND FUTURE VIRGIN

jealous. When questioned, Sabbathday answers that she feels perfectly able to handle herself in New York, no she isn't afraid of Moonies or slashers or the son of the Son of Sam, and thank you for the offer but the New Eden treasury couldn't afford a second hotel room. I suggest with, oh, just the right mixture of fiduciary responsibility and sexual charm that perhaps we could share a single, but she doesn't think that that would fit the image.

"The image?"

"Suppose Oprah were to find out," she says, laughing, "or 'Late Night with David Letterman.' "

Ha-ha, we say and then ask if there isn't an ironic color to her laugh.

Reader, there's an ironic color to her laugh, right?

• • •

When the March thaw comes, I take my now five-year-old daughter and march her up Spirit Mountain in search of the New Eden Fountain Stone, a quasi-fabulous obelisk something on the order of two feet by six feet whose message, chiseled on one granite face in Roman letters (if it's anything like the Canterbury stone, of which there is a photograph extant), uses the "L" word a total of fourteen times. That is, if it exists at all. (The stone, we mean, not the "L" word.) The chimerical quality of the Fountain Stone, Class, is chiefly due to its having been secretly buried toward the end of the nineteenth century (we refer not just to the New Eden stone but to its interred siblings at each of the other communities) to protect it and its message of universal love from the various vandals impatient for the twentieth century to begin. Venner has, natch, no hope of finding the blessed thing (what does he expect to see, a tumulus, a numina, the Virgin of Guadalupe a modest six inches off the ground?), but it's fifty-one degrees outdoors, Sabbathday is weaving away, Venner is already down three of those five condoms he purchased twelve pages back, and seeing as how love is in somewhat short supply around New Eden proper (though not sex; Mother Ann, consider the implications), a quest for the fountain of love somewhere in the environs seems not out of place.

We will list here the archetypal ingredients of the quest motif to have done with them straight off: the New England wilderness our wasteland, our chalice a Kool-Aid-filled canteen, various Sloughs of various Desponds, sweet Sir Eve with the requisite innocence for whatever gifts from above might be forthcoming. She keeps ahead of me, whacking at the undergrowth with a stick and pointing to this fallen trunk, that screen of scrub pine, certain the Fountain Stone is under/ behind each. Every five minutes she asks for a drink from the canteen, every ten can we go home now? The air has got that piney spring smell, like God's washed the world with disinfectant. The melting snow tinkles down the mountain in a myriad of rivulets; the chickadees flit from branch to branch. Jaded Venner, of course, is merely walking, climbing the mountain without a thought to where the Fountain Stone might actually be (though the idea that it's here *some*where— Spirit Mountain as a kind of New England reliquary—pricks his moral imagination), but his daughter is genuinely searching, wiping the slushy snow off the stone faces that present themselves, hoping for the telltale runes but finding only blank granite.

"Why don't we just *ask* someone?" she half pouts half shouts at me.

"There's nobody who knows," I answer and then, when she tosses me her give-me-a-break look, tell her how for a century the secret has been passed from Eldress to Eldress, and that if anyone knows now where the Fountain Stone is it would be Sister—that is, Eldress—Sabbathday, but she isn't saying. And that it's possible Eldress Rachel ("She's dead," interjects Eve) *before* she died didn't tell anyone because Eldress Rachel was not the type to think she was ever going to die and so the precautions taken ("The *what?*") were few indeed.

"Which leaves the matter of universal love somewhat up in the air."

"You're bugging me," says my daughter, mimicking guess which parent.

Anyway, what if, by the luck of grace or erosion, Ponce de Venner were to stumble upon the Fountain Stone complete with the "L" word fourteen times over? What good would it do him? (Saint Clare, you had your pyx to ward off the pagan armies: Tell me the thaumaturgic power resident in a slab of New England granite?) In short, what good is love universal or otherwise? I mean it. Maybe the Shakers knew what they were about after all: having done away with sexual love they gathered up what was left, dug a hole in the earth and threw it in. And that was that. Love got rid of just like the human appendix, embryonic gills, the dodo bird. [RUN CREDITS]

Reader, you're bugging me.

I mean here Venner is, *nel mezzo del cammin' di nostra vita* (lost and getting loster by the minute), looking for universal love, not for *his* benefit, understand, but for the world's, for yours, for his daughter's. It seems a noble thing to be doing in this our ignoble world, prospecting for love he means, no Virgil or Beatrice in sight, his daughter getting tired and needing to be carried, the afternoon wearing on, the Kool-Aid run out ("Daddy?"), and yet here he is continuing to search, to hope against hope, the sun fading in the west and casting on his mud-plodding feet a reddish tinge ("Daddy, I'm tired"), his face taking on the strain of—let's say—Christ climbing Calvary in any number of Renaissance paintings (your choice, though perhaps Fra Angelico's flatters us—us?—most), until finally oh shut up, until finally, Jesus! until finally *in a flash of understanding* ("The best way to save your soul is to save someone else's body") he upsy-daisies his daughter, kisses each of her red cheeks and starts down-mountain to where he promises a mug of hot chocolate and honestly he promises Oreo cookies await her on a shiny white plate.

(Damn our soul! Yours too, Mother Ann. And yours, Reader. And yours, and yours!)

• • •

That evening there's a phone call from the missing mother in Madison. I hide around the kitchen corner while Eve, holding the too-big receiver to her ear, tries to keep from sobbing.

• • •

"Did Rachel tell you?" I ask Sabbathday a few days later. We're in the Sisters' Weaving Shop measuring the second installment of blankets and stuff, and I've mentioned how Eve and I, just happening to go for a walk the other day, started up Spirit Mountain, playing a game of—oh, you know, find the Fountain Stone.

"Tell me what?" answers suspicious Sabbathday.

"You know. Where it is."

She calls out a measurement for me to record. Then: "Why would she tell me?"

"Because she was Eldress and she was supposed to tell whoever was next in line, yes?"

"Chastity was next in line."

"Oh, right."

"And then Antoinette."

I try the History of Western Civ angle, speak at some length about the duty she has to the world, how the Hancock stone, the Watervliet, the Mount Lebanon, the Alfred stone, all of them have been lost in the earth (we're talking forever here, barring some condo developer's bulldozer), and doesn't she owe it to the world to let at least one of the stones see the light of day, in some museum let's say, after all it's a piece of history, not to mention its symbolic importance, its inspirational value, etcetera (let's not lay it on too thick)—

"—I mean it's lost," I wind up. "If Eldress Sabbathday Wells doesn't break silence and give it to the world, it's gone for good."

"What's it to you?"

"I believe in love," I say with an innocent smile. "Don't you?"

She gazes at me with some mistrust and then goes back to her tape measure. "It's just a stone," she says.

• • •

The next time the phone call's from Denver. She seems touchy in word and tone when I ask how things are going, says she wants to talk to Eve, but Eve, I tell her, is in bed already. "Two-hour time difference, you know."

There's silence, and then I think I hear her crying into the receiver. I almost ask what's wrong, then decide it's not her but some electronic shadow on the line. I wish her luck, and we hang up.

• • •

It is *not*, of course, just a stone, it's Venner's heart (that troublesome organ). How to proceed? How to proceed? I find that I've begun watching her again, spying on her I mean, not quite with spotting scope but the same general idea, once even, at night, hiding in the penetralia of a weeping willow while in the electric gold of the Elders' Room she fixed the books and/or Venner's wagon. What's she up to? Reader, understand, that though I've not reported them in gory detail, there have been the usual caresses and cuddlements of the postcoital type, not infrequently accompanied by Venner's whispering nothings along the love-and-marriage horse-and-carriage lines. And though they bring a smile of, um, affection to Sabbathday's face, there's little in return (there's, in fact, nothing in return) so that we wonder whether it isn't Sabbathday's heart which is petrologic in character. In short, why won't she say she loves me for Pete's sake, even if it isn't true? Is she afraid of committing herself to a course of action that requires, well, action? Afraid that by voicing love in the emotional she exacerbates the sin in the physical? ("Okay, sure, Mother Ann and/or Saint Peter, I dropped my drawers for him, but I never said I *loved* him, did I?") How can she—unless we admit a soul so shadowed that even inky Venner shudders—how can she keep the actions of her body so divorced from the laws of her spirit?

(The answer may be that she can't. The implication of

which is that the laws of her spirit are not what they appear
to be. That animal you hear screaming, Reader, is, in fact, our
Venner.)

• • •

Out at the mall, "Essential Ecstasy" has slipped to thirty-
nine. Across the way at Appliance City it's still no soap for
Venner in the salvation line. That night when Medusa calls I
ask her how the video's coming but she says don't ask. So I
don't, but get told anyway that Elektra's decided it's too late
to do a video, MTV won't feature a song that's already begun
to fall on the charts and blah-blah-blah, but the next release—
they're thinking of putting out "The Flesh and the Spirit" in
a few months—will have the full support of the company
because she's proved herself and more blah-blah-blah or so
they say.

"Then why so glum?" I ask.

"Because I'm tired and confused and homesick and one of
the Nazi Soap Bubbles sucks dog dicks."

We remind our ex-wife of her ex-husband's aversion to
metaphors.

"It's no metaphor. He sucked a dog's dick. The drummer.
I saw him do it."

"Sally," I say.

"I'm miserable, baby, I really am. I'm tired of hamburg-
ers and heavy-metal groupies and I want to sleep in my own
bed."

Upstairs Venner sleeps in his own bed.

• • •

There's the detritus of winter everywhere, matted grass,
decomposing leaves, rot. I look each day for signs of life along
the Dwelling House foundation, the pale greens and toy yel-
lows of crocuses and daffodils, but there's nothing. It was just
a year ago that I was first settling into my steeple, destruction
behind me, hope ahead, Scotch-taping portraits of Sabbathday to my walls and praying for regeneration. What hap-

pened? How did I get lowered from that illusory essence to this illicit existence? Is it simply the American thing—I mean the pursued ideal become the sullied real—and would crybaby Venner please quit whining about it? Not for the first time I search Sabbathday's bedroom for her current diary. What I'm hoping to find is anybody's guess but Professor Venner for one would guess revelation, confession, a clue to what she's up to. But it seems that with the advent of sexual love the need for putting her life into contemplative order has ceased for Sabbathday. The old diaries sit on their shelf like historical documents. Reader, what do you think? Should I just wait until the show is over and she realizes that, though she might have purified the wives of investment bankers for an afternoon, the world is still the world? Wait for the dazzle of fame to wear off? For Sabbathday to be added to the ash heap of media darlings? Will she come crawling back to Brother Venner then?

The last few days before she goes she rehearses me in the necessities of running New Eden, Chastity's medication, Antoinette's diet, the ringing of the morning bell (unmissed since 1808), but on the necessities of Venner's heart she is silent. I make one last try to engage her in the question of just what the Christ it is we've been doing (though my terms are more circumspect), to get her to talk about the future, about the past, about "us," but she dodges me with the deft cruelty of someone who is not—I repeat, *not*—in love. I end up, once again, kicking sheep in the barn. The night before her departure I ask her point-blank if she's coming back. But she treats the question as absurd ("Of *course* I'm coming back. Don't be silly!"), leaving me with the impression that she's *not* coming back (though the end is no doubt more mundane than that). I spend the night drifting in and out of dreams in which Sabbathday appears sequentially as the Virgin Mary, Medusa, Donna Reed (or maybe June Lockhart, difficult to tell which) and finally (big apple with even bigger worm) as unclothed Eve. I wake with the sheets twisted around me like serpents.

In the morning we load her suitcases into the Toyota, say

good-bye to Chastity and Antoinette and head downtown to the bus station. It's spring break so the waiting room is crowded with students and the only place to sit is in a row of plastic bucket seats with tiny TVs attached. "Got a quarter?" Sabbathday asks once we're seated. I say, "Ha-ha" but evidently she's serious so I fish out a quarter and she puts it into the TV. Up comes "Oprah." She smiles at me and nods at the TV but of course I can't see it from my angle. All I get is the sound, something about "The Better Sex Video Series." Two of my students are trying not to look at me.

When the bus comes we stand up, lift a suitcase apiece and, still without saying a word, head outside into the mild March weather (where there are red robins in the trees for Sabbathday, black crows for Venner). On the flank of the bus there's painted a greenly smiling, airborne Peter Pan (Peter Pan Lines, Montpelier-Manchester-Boston-New York), which somehow adds insult to injury. After the suitcases are stowed, Sabbathday comes and stands with me a moment, like a lover ought to do, but there's no kiss, no surreptitious squeeze of my hand. When finally she says, "Good-bye, see you in a week," I nod and smile, stand there like a rube as she climbs through the door of the bus and disappears into the smoke-glassed interior.

Ten minutes later what you're viewing, Viewer, is a crane shot of the bus pulling away from the station, a sad Toyota following, first through town, then out past the mall, until finally when the bus rises up onto the interstate the Toyota limps off toward New Eden, dirty earth under its tires and metaphorical sunsets on all horizons.

CHAPTER SIXTEEN

VENNER'S PARADISO, SUCH AS IT IS

Ahem.

My name is John Venner. I'm the last Shaker. I live at the New Eden Shaker Village, where I'm in charge of things of the flesh, to wit: feeding the barn animals, washing the laundry, fixing the ball cock on the upstairs toilet. I'm a man who used to be without land, light or love; now, it's lots of land, a little light, love mostly theoretical. Still, we have progressed from the impoverished state of living in a steeple, have we not? And learned something along the way? *Damnum absque iniuria.* Or nearly no injury anyway, though the loss, the loss . . .

The day after Sabbathday leaves I rise at 6 A.M. to ring the morning bell, pull the heavy hemp as hundreds have pulled it before me. Oh, let's pretend there's the sound of salvation in that peal, the promise of new life, crocuses along the foundation, fecundity at the open window. I'm almost happy those first couple of days, doing my chores, going from maple to maple with tap and hammer and sap bucket in hand, Antoinette following me with her walker and instructing me on which trees take four buckets and which three, Eve running ahead to oak and elm. It wouldn't be such a bad life. The pastoral thing I mean: Venner keeping watch over his flock by night, New Eden the venue in which he crawls between heaven and earth, air deodorized with flora, earth kept covered with a carpet of grass, maybe some sheep shit allowed in the garden as fertilizer but boy! that's all, I mean it!

In the mail I learn that the president of the college regrets to inform me that the Tenure Advisory Board cannot recommend to his office, etcetera, the upshot of which is that after next year I no longer have a job. In the same mail I at long last receive a thirty-minute videotape from KKAT-TV6 Manchester, on which is recorded, in addition to the journalistic detritus of December 2, 1980, a twelve-year-old Sabbathday shooting baskets in the school gym, walking through the halls during class change, her simple dress in eloquent contrast to the hot-to-trot togs of her punky classmates (voice-over relating how this exceptional young lady manages to have the best of both worlds). And if that weren't bad enough, when the weekend comes and I decide to check up on the world's people by purchasing the Sunday *New York Times*, guess who's the magazine's centerfold? (You can go look it up on microfiche, Reader, I'll be damned if I'm going to tell you about her saved soul.)

She calls for the first time on Monday (five days after she left; she'd promised to call within a day or two), tells me how swimmingly the opening went, and then asks to speak to Antoinette and Chastity. I summon the Sisters and park myself around the corner. But there's nothing indicting in their side of the talk, just oohs and aahs and lots of reassurance that things are okay. When I'm called back to the phone it's to be told that she's decided to stay another week, to which I say "Oh?" in as meaning a voice as I can muster, which meaning she chooses to ignore, saying instead, "And guess what? I'm going to be on television."

Mother Ann, they're closing in.

"On 'Good Morning America.' Isn't that amazing? I was interviewed on Friday, *pre*-interviewed, I mean, and I guess I was interesting or unusual enough or something...."

"Or pretty enough."

She pauses a moment. "That, too. Who knows? But I'm going to be on for real this Thursday morning. They want me to wear my bonnet. I mean inside the studio. I told them no, I didn't think I could do that. What do you think?"

I want to tell her that I think she should pack her bags, hug her soul tight to herself and hurry home. But really what difference does it make now? What difference does it make whether the last Shakeress incarnates herself forty times over out at the mall? A million times across America? With or without bonnet? In the end I say simply, "Sure. Why not? Wear it. Each to its purpose."

There's silence on the line as if she's wondering at me. When she speaks her voice is changed, intimate, or at least attempting intimacy. "I'm looking forward to coming home," she says, and when I don't answer, adds, "I miss you."

"I miss you, too," I say.

"Look for me."

"Okay."

"Wish me luck."

"Okay."

Again, there's silence. Then: "Are you all right?"

"Sure," I say. "Good luck. Remember not to look into the camera."

And we hang up.

When term resumes I go to my office to try to catch up on my grading. There are stacks of papers on Antinomianism, on the flesh and the spirit in the poetry of Anne Bradstreet, on God's mistress Wisdom as revealed in the apocryphal book of Ben-Sira. I pick up the first one that comes to hand, but I can't bring myself to read it. Out on the quad Betty and Veronica have long ago melted away, but not to worry: in their place are real Bettys and real Veronicas throwing Frisbees, clad in spring shorts and spring shirts, long arms, lithe legs. (They bring to mind an old grading system of ex-Professor Venner's: A's for the ugly, C's for the beautiful, just his way of evening out the Lord's gifts.) I watch them with envy and spite and sadness. Ah, Venner was young once. Venner's still pretty young (thirty-five, I think), though *nascentes morimur* doesn't he know it. Still he's got a doctor of divinity from a classy divinity school, charm, intelligence, good looks (Would it be bad form to call on the president and ask him just *why* we were denied tenure?) and all that ought to be enough to make him a candidate for ordination, assuming he could find some sufficiently enfeebled Protestant sect that would have him. (Did the decision have something to do with rumors concerning our grading system?) Reverend Venner has a nice ring to it, don't you think? And when one considers that there are lots of Protestant wives out there in need of pastoral counseling (Our living in a steeple? Our chastity?), and that congregations frequently come with free houses, sometimes a car, one's prospects could be worse.

One's prospects couldn't be worse. Oh, Reader! All I wanted was to roll in the mud with a clean conscience, to live my doggy life without the intrusion of barks from above. Was that too much to ask? Little Debbie Snack Cakes, Monica the Madonna, I don't apologize for what I did. Ann, Jane and/or Sue: ditto. In the deliverance of such evil we are merely midwives for our maker. The Marquis de Sade thought human perfection was the ability to inflict suffering without a twinge of conscience, that such a being, in some proto-Darwinian sense, would ascend toward the likeness of its God. Venner can wield a guiltless BB gun, but a twelve-gauge is beyond him just now. Still—like an enlarged cranium, opposable thumbs, walking upright—it's something to strive for, isn't it?

On Thursday I watch "Good Morning America," waiting for sufficient revulsion, despair, a critical mass of destructive tendencies. There are news bits, weather bits, sports bits, reminders of what time it is, commercials, a visiting auto mechanic, a former call girl demonstrating tummy-flattening exercises for use during sex, and then after a commercial for Wonder Bread, the youngest Shaker sitting in an overstuffed chair, bonneted and smiling, one of her coverlets hanging like a tapestry behind her. She's self-possessed, personable, pretty. I get to listen to her speak about the history of the Shakers, about their beliefs, their work, how she learned to weave, how she balances traditional Shaker design with her creative vision, and when the interviewer asks about the future—will she remain a Shaker? will the Shakers continue? will there be new converts?—how she doesn't know what the future holds, but whatever happens she will always believe in the Shaker way, in purity of life and dedication to work. Thank you, Sister. Thank *you*. It's ten minutes after the hour.

It's the crack of doom.

When the phone rings, I expect a breathless Sabbathday, but get an irate Medusa instead.

"I can't believe it."

"What?"

"I'm sitting in this crummy motel room in Chapel Hill doing my nails, wondering what it's like to be concentrating on tummy-flattening exercises while this stranger is going up and down on you, when there she is, on fucking television for Christ's sake! Why didn't you tell me?"

"I didn't think you'd care."

"Why wouldn't I care?" she shouts into the phone. "That was *me*! That was *mine*! That was *my* piece of essence!"

I don't respond.

"Is that what America wants?"

"What?"

"Tell me. Is that what they want? They want some phony virgin in a fucking bonnet?"

"You should've named yourself Grace, or Faith, or Freegift," I tell her. "Freegift and the Shaker Maidens. Worn white clothes, white underwear, sung about chastity, charity, virginity. That would've got you on MTV."

"Very funny."

"It's true."

She swears into the phone. "As it is I'm just one more Nazi-underweared Madonna wannabe with nice legs."

"Nice breasts, too."

"Oh, shut up."

And she hangs up bang! just like that.

Upstairs I lie down on my bed to get up energy to face the world but end up falling asleep instead. I dream I'm living in my steeple again, gothic sky out the four windows, winged sheep flying past. There's birdsong, young voices from the quad below, the odor of lilacs. Magically, Sabbathday's there, only it's not quite Sabbathday because she's dressed in Medusa's underwear, beauty mark on her breast, hair ensnaked. She's singing "Simple Gifts" except somehow she's got the bass line from "Essential Ecstasy" under her. I'm looking for my BB gun but instead find a twelve-gauge leaning in the corner. Outside, the sheep are shitting in midair. When I turn back to Sabbathday she's gone a little out of focus so I reach to adjust the picture, think I've got hold of the horizontal, but it must be the vertical because when I turn it she rises off the floor. I try twisting the knob back the other way but she keeps going, up past the bells, into the open sky where there are seraphim and putti and golden light and those ultra-high Hollywood sopranos singing the celestial soundtrack. The falling sheep shit turns into snowflakes.

For the next few days I'm a basket case. I've got Mother Ann talking to me in one ear and the Marquis de Sade in the other. I can barely make it through my classes, barely keep a Brotherly face in the presence of Antoinette and Chastity. In the Jack-B-Nimble there's a "Help Wanted—Assistant Manager" sign (should I apply?), in Friday's horoscope a gloomy outlook for Virgos. On Saturday Sabbathday calls and this time it's David Letterman for Christ's sake. On Sunday Venner gets the urge to shake, I mean *shake*, in Meeting but something—good manners, an old habit of professorial dignity, Ann Lee appearing like a hallucination in the far corner—

keeps him in his seat. Outside the Meeting House, he gets waylaid by some Mercedes-driving Massachusetts wife who identifies herself as a Friend of the Shakers and who wants to know if it's true, has the Society admitted him as a full member, and at whom Venner has the nearly overwhelming urge to bark obscenities. And it doesn't stop there. It doesn't stop there. At night his dreams are filled with strange lights, strange shapes, voices, sounds, inhuman faces, after one of which he wakes with fear and trembling, bundles Eve out of bed and drops her off at Sally's sister's, then weaves into town, where somehow (it's Monday morning now) he ends up in front of Rob's Sporting Goods eyeing the high-powered rifles through the window. (Were he to purchase one, would the bell tower of New Eden achieve mythic status along the lines of the Book Depository, the University of Texas tower, and Venner himself make it onto TV like Oswald, the Son of Sam, the Hillside Strangler? Is that the only essence available to him? And should one grab whatever essence one can get?)

At The Missionary Position, waiting for it to be time to pick up Eve, I sit at the bar and drink shots of Wild Turkey. It's raining cats and dogs out. I can hear it against the windows. A couple of stools over there's this bar girl I think I recognize from the old days, fortyish, cigarette in hand, the usual perfume. She keeps looking at me. Finally I look back and she says, "So what's with the hat?" It's my porkpie hat she's referring to, purchased at a time when hope was hope, you may remember it, Reader. I don't answer her, just smile noncommittally and cross to the jukebox, where I stand scanning the titles a minute. I put a quarter in, punch D8 and go back to my stool.

"She used to sing here, you know," the B-girl says. I tell her I know. "This very song," she says, "I remember it."

Venner remembers it too. It has a kind of purity to his ears, I mean against the daytime darkness, the maroon Naugahyde. Perhaps this is the result of the soul decanted

into sound waves. Or perhaps it's simply the contrast between Sally's voice and Venner's polluted ears. (For a few
drinks, Monsieur le Marquis, would the B-girl let us do to her
the sorts of things you recommend for personal salvation, we
mean of course sadism, sodomy, strangulation in the midst of
the sexual act?) I look up at the empty stage, where Medusa
used to do her Medusan thing, the very stage where Venner
insists the eyes of the crowd brought her to orgasm (Sally
insists not), where she met the first of her many adulterous
admirers, where Venner the Luddite once accidentally pulled
the extension cord that powered the PA system and was booed
by a dance floor of drunks. Should he give in? Should he just
give in to the detritus of Western Civ? Take off his phony
Shaker hat and begin the downward slide: unemployment,
dipsomania, bar girls by the dozen? How distant life with
Mrs. Sabbathday Venner seems! The pink flamingos and the
His-and-Her towels. How distant, too, life with Sally Shannon and her forty-two prints of the Blessed Virgin. Shakeress,
Mariologist, Gorgon: Venner's lost them all. The alternatives
are not pretty.

Somewhere on my fourth bourbon the B-girl and I get up
to dance. She's put in a quarter and the flip side of "Essential
Ecstasy" is playing "Doobie-doobie-doo-wah," a close dance,
so that Venner feels the give of womanly breasts against his
chest. It's nice. Never mind the bartender and the half-dozen
smirking yokels, it feels nice to have someone in your arms,
the softness, the care, the breathing in and out. If this is Venner's place in the social hierarchy, then so be it. Even a night
manager at the Jack-B-Nimble can love and be loved, right?
We dance around the empty floor, our soles shuffling to
Medusa's double-tracked voice—"shoobie-shoobie-shoo-wah"
—a haze of perfume around us, and then the dance floor lights,
halos of blue and yellow courtesy the bartender. When the
song ends, there's a smatter of sarcastic applause. Venner the
fallen gentleman escorts his partner back to the bar, where,
smiling, he tells her she's a good dancer—really, a *good* dancer—and presses her hand good-bye.

Back at New Eden with Eve asking if we can go see if the grass is growing on Rachel's grave yet, I make up a bed for her in my room (to hell with the Orders Concerning the Separation of the Sexes), bring the TV up from the kitchen so she can watch "Sesame Street" and then carry all her clothes and toys and stuff up from the Sisters' floor. We lie down together and watch Big Bird explain how bird babies are made. I cradle her head in my arm, drape my hand across her heart. When six o'clock comes I ring the dinner bell, make peremptory bowls of cereal for Antoinette and Chastity, and in the dining room leave them eating in silence while I minister to what I claim is an ill Eve on the third floor. They don't seem to care or mind. We eat our own bowls of cereal, play a game of checkers, two of Old Maid, then change into our nightclothes and, lying in bed, read "Rapunzel." Sometime around nine o'clock she falls asleep.

I lie quiet for an hour or so, the TV sound muted but the light from the picture making phantoms on the ceiling, the rain drumming against the windowpane. And then I must drift off too, because I start having dreams of Nazi-underweared women with—cut!—start having dreams of sheep—cut!—start having dreams of Sabbathday making her film debut as Rapunzel, trapped in a witch's tower, gazing out upon the passing world, which world includes a Handsome Prince in a Jack-B-Nimble uniform who's dope enough to call out for her hair which of course comes tumbling down and etcetera until the next time we see him instead of elevated into the ether he's lying blinded in the brambles. There follows a short with subtitles and lots of body parts.

When I wake it's to the sound of someone pounding on the front door. The TV's still on, Jay Leno milling about with his guests, credits running. I extricate my arm from under Eve's head and get up, stand there for a moment expecting whoever it is to go away. But no, they keep knocking, so I hurry down two flights of stairs, slide on my socks along the hall floor and debate whether coldcocking a drunk townie would enhance or imperil my reputation as a Shaker. Not that it matters anymore.

"Who is it?" I say through the heavy door. There's another knock, impatient. "Who is it?"

"Open the fucking door. It's raining out here."

It's my ex-wife, Reader. Are we sure we want to welcome her back into the narrative?

"What do you want?" I ask, again through the door.

"I'm applying for membership. Open the damn door."

I slide back the iron bolt and swing the door open.

"Christ!" she says, stepping inside. "It was a lot warmer this morning in North Carolina."

She's wet and shivering, shorter than I remember (or have I gotten used to tallish Sabbathday?). She's wearing a tight skirt and a tight top, but otherwise the Medusan elements are kept to a minimum, no heels, no beauty mark that I can see and, best of all, no snakes.

"Where is she?" she asks, hugging herself. I point up through the ceiling.

"In my room. She's sleeping."

"She sleeps in your room now?" she says, and there's something about her voice that makes me realize she's talking about Sabbathday.

"*Eve* is. Sabbathday's still in New York."

"Oh," she says and then she looks more closely at me. "Is it just the light or do you look awful?"

Vanity being what it is, there are no mirrors at New Eden, but Venner supposes it's not just the light. "Times are tough," he answers.

"You're telling me," she says and pushes past. I follow.

Reader, it's my ex-wife. Her name is Sally. Her name is Medusa. I used to sleep with her, every night, the same bed and everything. In the morning we would both wake up, brush our teeth, get dressed, eat breakfast, greet the world. That's how it was. I remember.

"Can I wake her?"

We're upstairs, standing just inside my room. The TV

light makes a kind of blue numina around Eve, reflecting off the sheets. She's got her thumb in her mouth.

"She's sleeping," I say quietly. Sally nods and moves closer and for a minute we just stand and gaze down at her. On the TV, Jay Leno has suffered electronic extinction and David Letterman has grown in his place. But it's just the opening monologue so there's time still.

"I couldn't wait to see her," Sally says. "Has she been all right?"

I nod. But who knows? Mother run off with Nazis, father diddling the celibates: who knows what perversions have crept in unawares? We stand and, I'm not sure, but I think we're both thinking the same thought, looking at her, some whispering thought of the grace of that Christmas five years ago and now, our failure. So it is with all dreams, all perfections.

"I'm drenched!" Sally says finally, stepping backward and turning to me. "I've been in these clothes all day. Is there something I can change into?"

For a moment I think she means something female, like Brother Venner keeps different-sized negligees on hand for his woman visitors [MEDUSA CHANGES INTO SABBATHDAY'S DRESS. CAMERA IN. LOOK OF INNOCENCE REGAINED. MUSIC UP. RUN CREDITS], and then realize she just means a shirt or something of mine.

"Are you planning on staying?" I ask, handing her one of my gray shirts.

"I don't know. I don't know what I'm doing. My suitcases are still sitting in the rain on the front porch."

"Downstairs?"

"No, *my* front porch. I just left them there and got in the car and drove over here." And she shakes her head at the impulse. "Now turn around," she says. She's got her top undone. "Go on now, I mean it."

I turn my back and listen to the sounds of her undressing, the fall of fabric on the floor. When I look again she's standing there in her bare feet with my too-big shirt on, the tails hanging down to her knees.

"Some socks?" she says, wiggling her toes.

I throw her a pair of socks.

"Better," she says and she stands there, smiling the sad, shamed, resigned, comfortable smile Eve #1 must have smiled just after the apple business. (A quick calculation informs us that there are currently more world's people in the Dwelling House at New Eden than there are Shakers, three to two. It had to happen.)

"Your suitcases," I say after a moment. "Don't you think you should go get them? Get them out of the rain at least?"

"No."

"You can come back."

"No," she says. "Let it all rot. Let all that spandex and Victoria's Secret crap just rot in the fucking rain." And she goes and stands at the window, leans her forehead against the pane. "Forty days and forty nights."

The truth is, Sally Shannon looks pretty good to unemployed, evicted, defrocked Venner. The mere sight of her has evoked in him an old litany of lovers: the student in the BT 600s, Persephone in her Toyota, the Mariologist, the Orchid. If only a genuine Old Testament deluge were in the cards.

"Tell me," I say, coming up behind her. I want to put a husbandly arm around her waist, but I don't dare. "What went wrong?"

"I don't know," she sighs. I can see her reflection in the windowpane. Mine too. "But it wasn't what I thought it would be. They liked me well enough, for a heavy-metal audience. But somehow it seemed, I don't know, incomplete I guess. At least no one's seen my face in a water stain on a church ceiling or in a laundromat lint trap yet. Or if they have, the line of people with crutches and broken hearts is pretty short."

"You didn't really expect that."

She turns around and faces me. "Did you really expect to become a virgin again by moving out here?"

On the TV, below an 800 number it says, NO GODS PLEASE.

"I don't know what I expected," I tell her.

"You know," she says.

Now it says: NO CODS PLEASE. Outside the rain pit-pats a modern melancholia, runs in the eaves, drips down the windowpane. Sally and I are standing face to face like in the next frame we'll be kissing, passionately, inevitably, but when the next frame comes, and the next, we aren't. We don't. I back off and she plops backward onto Eve's bed.

"I'm hungry," she says.

"You want me to go down and get you something?"

"Call out for a pizza. That'll be a first."

On the TV Letterman's back on and talking into the camera. "Just a minute," I say and cross around the foot of the bed and turn the sound up.

"What?" Sally says, but even as she says it, Letterman is doing the Ed Sullivan shtick *("—appearing on our stage tonight, a genuine virgin—").* There's laughter and then he gets mock-chastised-looking and does the introduction for real. "Are you shitting me!" Sally cries, rising up onto her knees. Eve turns over, kicks her covers off, but doesn't wake. "Are you shitting me?" Sally whisper-shouts and she looks from the TV screen to me back to the TV.

And there she is, green gown and white bonnet, looking long-legged on the stage, and smiling at her standing host. There is, of course, applause from the audience, and the usual whistles and catcalls. The band is playing "Simple Gifts" to a rock beat.

"I'm sorry," Letterman says when they're seated and the audience has died down, *"that was tacky of me."*

The audience laughs.

"It's all right," Sabbathday says.

"No," Letterman answers, making a face like he knew he was going to blow this interview but like he knows too that the charm will lie in his blowing it, *"it was tacky."*

Sabbathday gives him her most fetching smile. *"I've come to expect a certain amount of tackiness from the world's people."*

The audience goes "Ooh! Ooh! Ooh!"

"I can't believe it," says Sally.

They start talking about the Shakers versus the Quakers

versus the Amish, Letterman polite now and a touch debo-
nair, Sabbathday flashing the brilliant teeth, the beautiful
eyes. Since Venner has given over imagining vain things, he
simply watches and listens in defeat. Beside him Sally is reciting a rosary of expletives.

"—*that she didn't want to be remembered as a chair. What
did she mean by that?*"

What do you think, Mother Ann? Saint Clare? Is Sabbathday the beginning of charismatic Shakerism, an application
to the FCC for a cable channel to follow? (Here's Eldress Sabbathday Wells making pleas for America's salvation, followed
by appeals for money, 800 number down where her breasts
ought to be.)

"—*because you have to understand that for the Shakers our
work is an expression of our faith. And yet the world's people
insist*—"

"*The world's what?*"

A big satellite dish out behind the barn, and the Hired
Men's Quarters turned into a TV control room, banks of rheo-
stats and meters getting out the word. And a white limo waiting out front.

"*And there are no male Shakers left?*"

"*There are several up in Maine at the Chosen Land village,
but none at Canterbury.*"

"*And at*—?"

"*New Eden? No, none at New Eden.*"

So okay, I can't help myself. I creep over to the TV to feel
the screen, the static leaping to my fingertips, the distance
between the thick glass and the image of Sabbathday behind.
This is a woman I once made love to, America, this the very
face, the very skin. And now she's in your living room or your
den or your bedroom. She's flying through the ionosphere at
the speed of light, simultaneously Appearing Now in—

"You're in the way," Sally says. I duckwalk back to the
bedside.

"—*so you really are—how shall I say this—a virgin?*"

"Yes."

"But you're, let's be honest, a beautiful woman."

"Thank you. So was our Mother Ann."

"Christ!" Sally says beside me. "The hypocrite! The Shaker slut!"

They go on to talk about her weaving, about the show, about the extraordinary price of Shaker artifacts, Letterman asking whether it wasn't Oprah Winfrey who recently bought a Shaker chest at auction for two hundred thousand. (It's true, Reader, I've been sparing you.) By the time the interview's done and Sabbathday's smiling in shy triumph first at Letterman and then out at the applauding audience and the withdrawing camera, Sally has quit her rosary and Venner is thinking how there's a historical progression in here somewhere, in the ascension from genuine virgin to apprentice pop icon. We sit in a kind of stupor, Sally muttering an occasional "Letterman, I mean, shit!," watching commercials until a pair of bimbos playing pool come on, their cleavage showing above the eight ball and a 900 number.

"I'm going to become a nun," Sally says finally and she falls backward on the bed so the springs move under Eve. Venner's thinking that $2.95 a minute is not so bad if you're quick about it. You keep things clean and distant and anonymous and all on your credit card. "A Carmelite. It's the obvious answer, don't you think?"

I exterminate the bimbos with remote control. "What I think," I say to Sally, "is you're suffering post-tour blues and that Medusa is lurking in you still, snakes ready to sprout at a moment's notice."

She lifts herself up on her elbow. "And Sabbathday?" she says nodding at the television. "What's her story? Is she coming back or what?"

"I don't know."

She rolls over on her stomach. "Maybe I'd take you back if you admitted that you made a big mistake," she says over her shoulder.

THE DIVINE COMEDY OF JOHN VENNER

"I made a big mistake."

"And that dumping me for Sabbathday was the biggest mistake of all."

"I thought it was you who dumped me."

"And that 'Essential Ecstasy' should have made it to number one."

"See?" I say. "They're starting."

She pulls at her wet hair as if to check for reptiles, and then with a pointed look sings a bar of "Tijuana Mama," a cha-cha from the old days, which makes me wonder who's doing the receding here and who the pursuing. Outside there's the distant rumble of thunder.

"I used to love you," I say out of nowhere.

" 'D'ya wanna, Tijuana?' " Sally sings. She rolls over, away from me.

"Body *and* soul," I say.

"Please," she says and pulls the pillow out from under Eve's head and puts it over her ears.

"I used to love you body and soul and what I want to know is just where do we currently find ourselves on the existence-essence continuum?"

She lifts the pillow off her head. "Who?" she asks. "You or me?"

"Either of us. You, for starters."

The pillow comes back down. "I've given over imagining vain things," she says, sounding like Venner a hundred pages ago.

"The giving over imagining vain things is in itself a vain thing," I say, and I reach out and touch her.

"Don't."

But I do. I risk it. I lie down next to her on the edge of the bed, spoon my body to hers. She pulls her head out from under the pillow.

"What do you think *you're* doing?"

I am, I realize, endangered by gravity on the backside, but my frontside's got just enough purchase on the white linen to make the risk worthwhile. I drape my arm across Sally onto Eve, who snorts and turns over but doesn't wake up.

"This is what I wanted," I say, closing my eyes. "This is what I wanted all along."

"What?" Sally asks.

"This."

"What *this*?"

"The abyss below but you and Eve carrying me to heaven."

"I'm not sure I'm ready for this," she says and lifts my arm off her. "And whatever happened to that snack you were going to get?"

"Just like those Renaissance paintings of the Assumption. Gravity suspended, bliss all around, and lots of chubby cherubs in the margins."

"I'm hungry."

"Venner's feet winged and just lifting him off the ground."

She pushes back with her rear so I tumble onto the floor. "Get me a sandwich and then maybe we'll discuss my taking you to heaven."

And she closes her eyes and snuggles deeper into Eve.

Outside the rain is falling downward, not upward.

I take, for once, the Brothers' staircase, past the Sisters' floor, down through all that historical air to the cellar, where I get out the Wonder bread and the Miracle Whip. And while I'm slapping together a couple of sandwiches, I try to lay out a definite course of action, which action begins with the responsibility of seeing Antoinette and Chastity taken care of, moves on to 2 bdrm apt w/gar (and perhaps DWM, 35, seeks SF for fun and family, prfrbly by immaculate cncptn), and peters out with thoughts of the chapel steeple and how—O how?—can we regain our very own Paradise? Because even if it was an illusion all along, Venner was never quite so alive, never quite so fully Venner, as when he believed in the possibility of Paradise. [FLASHBACK: EARLIER SCENE OF MAIN CHARACTER SITTING IN STEEPLE WINDOWSILL, GUN ACROSS LAP, NEW EDEN IN THE DREAMY DISTANCE] Which suggests that the cha-cha theory of love is perhaps applicable to a wider field, *i.e.* that it's the pursuit of Paradise that's purifying, the ripe fruit forever distending its bough, not the unpickable plums of heaven. If, by the magic of special effects, I had you here, Mother Ann—right now, tonight—I'd ask if that's why you chose such a quick exit. Once the idea of the United Society of Believers in Christ's Second Appearing began to lift off, did you check out because you knew the end would be disintegration and death, a couple of antique maidens and the last Shakeress's video virginity beamed across the land?

"Is that it?" I say out loud. I stare at the shadows in the cavernous room, at the cast-iron stoves and the stone floor worn smooth with two centuries of soles. "Were you smart enough to know that as soon as the dream began to come true it was all over?"

And I wait, as if for an answer. But there's only me and the usual ghosts. And the sound of the deluge outside.

"I'm talking to you," I say.

Over in the corner a shadow moves.

"I'm asking one-quarter of the heavenly quadrinity if she—"

"Don't get sarcastic," a voice interrupts.

I peer into the shadows.

"Who's there?"

"You're asking one-quarter of the heavenly quadrinity if she what?"

And stepping forth into the light, looking considerably more full-bodied than in the lithograph in my office, though she's got the same fair hair, fair skin, blue eyes, is—and why not, Reader? If they can do it in Hollywood, they can do it in heaven—is Mother Ann.

"Don't act so surprised," she says, and she draws up to the table, pulls back a chair and sits down. All the props are in place, the gown, the cap, the maidenly mantle. Professor Venner is aware that Ann Lee was in the habit of doing the Virgin of Guadalupe thing during the nineteenth century for certain blessed souls (*vide* the journals in the Hancock archives) but really, *here?* In the twentieth? And with *him?*

"Would you mind?" she says, pointing at the dish of left-over ham.

I put my hands over my eyes. "Don't try to pull a fast one on me," I say. "You're just another illusion. I know an illusion when I see one."

"Okay," she says, agreeable. "If you say so."

"Illusion and I have parted company."

"Okay."

"It wasn't always so . . ."

"Naturally . . ."

"But I've learned a thing or two."

"Fine. Pass the ham."

"Damn!" I cry and leap out of my chair so it bangs backward onto the floor. "Look here," I say, starting to pace. "You have a few things to answer for."

"*You* have a few things to answer for."

"Me? Like what?"

"Like porking my final convert."

"I didn't pork her," I say. "She porked me. And *I'm* your final convert if it comes to that."

"Some convert."

And we square off and stare at one another.

"Point of information," I say finally. I'm standing over her like a bouncer. "Are you or are you not the female Christ?"

She shrugs and reaches for the ham.

"I mean are you here courtesy of heaven? Or are you just restless in your grave?"

"How about some mustard?" she says, pointing at the refrigerator with a fork.

"I ask all this in light of the basic tenets of Christianity: resurrection, the afterlife, the *magnum mysterium*, etcetera."

She doesn't answer. Out the window, there's a raven sitting in a tree branch, wondering which way back to the ark.

"I take it then that you're *not* the female Christ?"

She shrugs a second time.

"*Are* you?"

"I'm as close as the world is going to get." And again her fork points at the refrigerator.

"And 'Hands to Work, Hearts to God'?" I ask, opening the refrigerator and holding a jar of Gulden's hostage.

"What about it?"

"And laundered and folded underwear?"

"Yes?"

"None of it's going to get us any closer to God, is it?"

She gazes at inquisitorial Venner and simply shakes her head, whether to the question or to the hopeless state of his soul I don't know, but it's such a sad gesture that I put the jar on the table and slide it over to her. Then I collapse back into my chair.

"Never mind me," I sigh. "I'm just a piece of disappointed humanity having a hallucination."

"Aren't we all," she says, digging into the mustard and spreading it on a piece of ham. "I expected to be sitting on the right hand of God by now. Or the left, at least. Instead it's aluminum bats from April to September."

"Aluminum bats?"

"My private purgatory."

And then I remember the legal stink over a baseball stadium's being built next to the graveyard at Watervliet where Ann Lee is buried, in the end one icon of Americana muscling out another.

"But everything you said, all that about seeing angels' wings and a redeemed humanity in America and how you had a vision of Adam and Eve copulating and became convinced that sexual relations between men and women were evil."

"I'll stand by that."

"But what does it *mean?*" I cry.

"What do you *mean* what does it mean?"

"How do I live my life? Do I copulate or not?"

"Who cares what you do? If you don't copulate, you'll find some other way to dirty your drawers. By the way, you should have seen how they were doing it." And she wrinkles her nose.

"Adam and Eve?"

She dismisses it with a wave of her knife. "I tried to create heaven on earth and you wouldn't believe—once I got my converts to quit dropping their drawers—you wouldn't believe the bickering and bitching. It's the one thing the world's people never quite caught on to. They were so enthralled by sturdy chairs and apples good all the way down to the bottom of the barrel that they never realized how petty and hateful and spiteful life in Paradise was. What I've learned—can we score for full orchestra here?—what I've learned in these two centuries, Professor Venner, is how doomed to our dreams we are, no matter how we draft Paradise, whether it's New Eden or America or the little commonwealth of marriage."

I'm sitting there imagining Adam and Eve doing it in a variety of positions. It's a postlapsarian subject the Renaissance painters seem never to have considered.

"I've at times thought," I say slowly, contemplating, "that Adam and Eve were just a dream in the mind of God until Eve ate that apple. That it was only then that we were precipitated out of the solution and fell to earth."

She's chewing on a piece of ham and can't answer, but she points at the falling rain outside as if for proof.

"In that respect," I say, "God, too, is disappointed in His dreams."

For a good minute we sit in silence. And I have an odd conviction that Adam had this same conversation with Eve somewhere east of Eden, the same realization of defeat, the same persecution in the sound of the rain falling on the earth.

"One last question," I say finally.

"Shoot."

"What are people *for?*"

And she smiles as if she knows the answer but isn't telling.

" 'Be ye therefore perfect,' " she quotes Christ.

"What?"

" 'Be ye therefore perfect.' "

"But I thought you just said—"

She shakes her head and, smiling at me, reaches out to touch me just like Eldress Rachel that day. But wouldn't you know it, the special-effects budget runs out or something and (with a rumble of thunder offstage) Venner finds himself alone in the cold kitchen. He sits a minute listening to the sound of his own breathing, the sound of the blood beating in his ears, the sound of the deluge outside, and then goes back to Sally's sandwich.

For your final exam, Class, tell Professor Venner: How long do we wait for the dove to return before we recognize that all we get is the raven in the rigging? Can you make a case that our salvation lies not in an antique grace but in the enduring of heavenly insult, *i.e.* in the raven's droppings and not the white dove's gliding across the golden waters? All Venner wanted was square morals and clean underwear, and if not that then at least the dust of his private destruction washed away, and if not *that* then how about applause for the highwire stunt of the human heart, yearning for that which is not and can never be: perfect love, imperishable civilization. But what I wonder now is whether it isn't the fury and the mire itself that saves us, the tragedy of gravity and not the comedy of clouds, each of us pulled earthward by the implacable limitations of human life, and yet still fighting to climb toward the light—Eve upstairs knocking out new cells by the dozen, Rachel a wormy smorgasbord of lips and lashes. Or is that just one more delusion, your professor trying to philosophize a FINIS, and still the dupe of his heart's desires?

Good night, Mother Ann. Good night, New Eden. Let me tuck you in this night, on the edge of your oblivion. Perhaps, after all, there's nothing for it but to continue to live, to keep alive within us the old paradigms of transcendence—the cleansing water, the refiner's fire—even though destruction floods the earth. Let's have MUSIC UP now, and while the credits run, a shot of Venner ascending toward the upstairs light, nourishment in hand for those he loves, and in the air over his head, flying babies with red cheeks and fat buttocks and, on the soundtrack, the great chorus of all those who dreamt a life of heaven on earth and woke to find they were only human.